As if the events of the last sixty seconds have just caught up to her, she's gasping for air. "You—you just—you . . . ," Swan stutters, unable to get the words out.

Yeah, I think, *I flew across the roof and saved you. Spit it out.* But I'm caught between the thrill of actually having saved someone's life (because OH MY GOD THAT WAS BADASS) and using my powers for good and the sheer terror that she knows who I am—sort of—and she knows that I can fly. Peter never gave me any rules. He wasn't really the kind of guy who gives the newbie a Superpowers Orientation for Beginners, but instinct and years of pop culture have taught me that the best thing I can do is keep my recently acquired talents to myself.

I don't have many options here. *Think fast, Faith.*

OTHER NOVELS BY JULIE MURPHY

Dumplin'

Puddin'

Pumpkin

Ramona Blue

Side Effects May Vary

Dear Sweet Pea

TAKING FLIGHT

JULIE MURPHY

BALZER + BRAY
An Imprint of HarperCollins*Publishers*

VALIANT

Balzer + Bray is an imprint of HarperCollins Publishers.

Faith: Taking Flight
Copyright © 2020 by Valiant Entertainment, LLC

Library of Congress Control Number: 2019956324
ISBN 978-0-06-289966-8 (pbk.)

Typography by Jenna Stempel-Lobell
21 22 23 24 25   PC/LSCH   10 9 8 7 6 5 4 3 2 1
❖
First paperback edition, 2021

To Kristin Treviño, a superhuman librarian
and friend among mortals

Mostly, my flying has been solo,
but the preparation for it wasn't.

—AMELIA EARHART

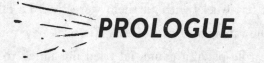 **PROLOGUE**

THREE MONTHS AGO

It was supposed to be an epic summer. It would be my last summer with Matt and Ches before our senior year and we had big plans—the kinds of plans that involved a whole lot of nothing. Like racing to eat snow cones before they melted down our arms and floating in Matt's neighborhood pool until our skin wrinkled and curling up together by night to watch every episode of *Battlestar Galactica* followed by a marathon of our favorite episodes of *The Grove* (selected by yours truly).

All of that changed the day Matt and Ches showed up at my house during our first full week of summer break and broke the news that Matt would be spending most of the summer with his grandmother in Georgia. Not only that, but Ches would be joining him.

"I won't go if you don't want me to," Ches had said to me apologetically.

But I couldn't blame her. Matt's grandma had a soft spot for Ches, who'd never even left the state of Minnesota. I was sad and felt left out, but I couldn't blame her. Matt felt bad too, but his grandmother's retirement community only allowed her to host two people at once.

The first few weeks without them were fine. I'd fallen deep down the rabbit hole of *Kingdom Keeper*, a new multiplayer online role-playing game. I'd tried but failed to get Matt and Ches into it, so that we could play from afar, but they were busy exploring Atlanta. At least they sent me selfies from their adventures at the aquarium and the Coca-Cola museum. Besides, there were plenty of other people to play with in *Kingdom Keeper*, and putting yourself out there is a heck of a lot easier when you're an avatar.

One night, a private message popped up on my screen from an orc who went by Sting.

STING: Hey, you're in the Midwest, right?

A few of us had organized into different regional groups with the hopes of doing some meet-ups. Sting knowing I was from the Midwest was the least alarming thing about him. (Trust me. You should have seen his victory dance. It involved thrusting. Lots of thrusting.)

YOUGOTTAHAVEFAITH: Yeah. The land of cheese and malls.

STING: Cool. A bunch of us are meeting up at Mall of America on Friday. You should go!

I wish I could say I took the time to consider all the reasons why meeting a stranger from the internet was a less-than-stellar idea, but I missed my best friends desperately. Besides, we were meeting at a mall. What could possibly go wrong?

YOUGOTTAHAVEFAITH: Count me in!

Grandma Lou dropped me off since she needed the car, and I headed straight to Nickelodeon Universe, where I was supposed to meet the whole group. Sting said he expected at least fifteen or twenty people. I loved Matt and Ches, but the idea that I could make my own friends separate from them excited me in a way that now riddles me with guilt. What if I'd just stayed home? But I was so lonely without them.

There was only one person waiting for me that day. Sting. A white guy with mussed brown hair and a square jaw. Jeans, a black T-shirt, and a black baseball cap. He was definitely too old to be in high school, but I could imagine him in college. Okay, well, maybe grad school.

"YouGottaHaveFaith?" he asked, a charming smile playing on his lips. "I thought it might be only me."

"No one else came?" I asked, my stomach plummeting. I was basically one second away from starring in an episode of *To Catch a Predator*.

He smirked, appearing suddenly boyish. "Just me and you. I guess that's what I get for trying to make new friends."

I could kick myself for how gullible I was, but that little

response set me at ease. "I know the feeling." Extending my hand, I added, "You can call me Faith."

He chuckled. "Pleased to make your acquaintance, Faith. It's Sting . . . from *Kingdom Keeper*. You can call me Peter."

Peter and I spent the whole day together, riding roller coasters, eating pretzels, and playing with all the different gadgets in the types of stores people rush to for Father's Day. At the end of the day, when it was nearly time for Grandma Lou to pick me up, Peter and I took one last turn at the pretzel place.

"I think you might be special, Faith," he said. "Have you ever felt like you were special?"

I snorted. "Uh, definitely not."

He shook his head, and I could swear he blushed a little. "No, I mean, don't you ever wonder if your whole life is a TV show and you're the star?"

I gulped down my orange soda, not sure how to respond, because, yes, of course, I'd had that very same thought, but how could I even admit to that? I'd sound nuts, plus this was quite possibly the cutest guy who'd ever given me the time of day. But there he was, putting himself out there. It only felt fair to do the same.

"I know exactly what you mean. Do you want to hear something really weird, though?"

He tore off a piece of the cinnamon sugar pretzel we were sharing. "Oh, yeah. Lay it on me. I'm the king of weird."

"So my parents died when I was a kid. Both of them. In the same car accident."

"Oh, Faith—"

"It's okay, it's okay. That's not what this is about. Well, it is. Kind of. Anyway, sometimes I wonder if them dying was part of some bigger thing. Every superhero and character I've ever loved had to go through some awful thing to achieve greatness. What if that was my awful thing?" I sighed, feeling guilty about how self-centered I knew I sounded. My parents didn't live and die just so I could be a superhero or something ridiculous like that. "Some days," I say, "that was the only way I could get past it all, pretending that their death was part of some bigger picture. But it wasn't. They're just dead. Gone. Forever. No higher—"

"Faith." He looked straight at me, unflinching. In a matter of moments, he'd become someone or something else completely. There was nothing boyish about him anymore. "What if I told you there was a way to find out? A way to get the answer to every question you'd ever asked? Maybe your parents' death was for a higher purpose."

"But—how could—"

"There's only one way to find out. I've been through some shit, Faith, okay? I'm not perfect." He zoned out for a second, concentrating on his hands before shaking his head. "Hell, I don't even know that I'm good, but sometimes the only way I can cope with it all is to know that everything I've done and everything that's happened to me has brought me to this point." He shook his head, and for the first time I felt like maybe I was getting a glimpse of the real Peter and not the guy who was trying to be on his best behavior or feeding me some line I'd want to hear.

After a moment, Peter looked me right in the eye. "I know I haven't given you a lot of reasons to trust me. As far as you know, I'm just some rando from the internet, but Faith, I need you to know that I've felt lost like you do and sometimes I still feel lost. What I'm offering isn't a magic pill. But I think there's something special about you, and I think you might have the kind of potential you can't even begin to imagine."

I felt like he was dancing around the real question here. "I don't quite understand what exactly it is you're saying."

He must have seen the skepticism on my face, because he added, "Your parents were great people, Faith. I believe that every moment in our lives serves a purpose, and maybe everything in your life has led you here to this moment. I don't know for sure, but I bet Jack and Caroline would agree."

"How do you—"

"We know everything about you, Faith. We've chosen you for a reason," he said with absolute certainty.

Part of me was unnerved by him knowing my parents' names, and the other part of me just wanted to know how.

"Just say it. Just tell me what exactly it is you're talking about."

He scooted to the edge of his chair, so that his voice could be the quietest whisper in the midst of the chaotic food court. "Superhuman abilities, Faith."

Everything around me silenced until there was nothing left in the entire mall except for me and Peter.

I felt like a bird that had just flown straight into a glass window. "Wait. Are you telling me superheroes are . . . real?"

Peter grimaced. "I wouldn't exactly call us superheroes. I don't think you could really use the word 'heroic' to describe the people I work for," he scoffed.

"Wait. Go back. You're saying superheroes are real and you think I might be one?"

He glanced from side to side and then finally shrugged. "Well, sort of. Yeah, I guess that's what I'm saying."

"Sign me the heck up." I didn't know if I could trust him or if I even should, but I knew one thing: I'd do anything for answers. The logical part of my brain told me this guy was a creep and that I should run, but I couldn't help but think back to every movie, television show, and comic book I'd ever loved. Peter could lead me to my Giles or Professor X or Gandalf or Nick Fury or Dumbledore.

"There's no guarantee, Faith, and there are possible side effects. You'd also have to find a way to leave home for the rest of the summer, but we've got a solid cover for you. We do think you have the potential to be someone very special. We think you could be a psiot."

"A psiot?" I asked. "What even is that?"

"Psiots are people gifted with superhuman abilities. We think your abilities are dormant inside of you. Potential waiting to be unlocked, and my organization has the keys."

"Just freaking say superheroes!" Despite his aversion to the superhero label, the flashing neon sign in my head read *SUPERHERO*. You, Faith Herbert, could be a superhero. Grandma Lou says I believe in too many things, but I can't help but think life is a little more fun that way. And if superheroes were real, then maybe my whole life had prepared me for this moment. Maybe the massive collection of comics my parents left behind was more than a reminder of what was. Maybe those comics—some of my most prized possessions—were meant to be the ultimate guidebook.

Peter sent me home with everything I would need. Permission slips, camp brochures, and emergency contact information for Grandma Lou. I'd only be gone for a few weeks, and he swore I'd be perfectly safe. He'd gone through the same program, he said. And look at him! He was fine! Normal even!

"So this is basically like superhero camp?" I asked.

"Sort of. Fewer canoes. Definitely no campfire songs." He dropped a hand on my shoulder. "See you on Monday, kid."

The next Monday, Grandma Lou dropped me off in the school parking lot, where a bus waited for me along with Peter, dark bags under his eyes and much less boyish than I remembered, in a Camp Pleasant Oaks Staff T-shirt. Grandma Lou stuffed some cash into my pockets and gave me a tight hug before sending me on my way.

"You're sure about this?" Peter asked quietly as I boarded the bus, his easy confidence from just days ago beginning to waver.

I nodded with absolute certainty.

As I sat on the bus, with a handful of other kids my age who I didn't recognize, eager nerves ate away at me. The small Asian girl who sat beside me, freckles spread across the bridge of her nose, leaned in and whispered, "Can you believe how lucky we are? I always knew there was something different about me. My name's Lucia, by the way."

I smiled, too nervous to remember my own name, let alone introduce myself.

After hours on the bus, we drove into the heart of Chicago. I'd never been to Chicago, and if my nerves weren't eating me up, I'd have taken in the sights a little bit more. As the sun set across the glistening skyline, the bus turned down into a parking garage and into a giant freight elevator that took us deep underground, and my stomach immediately sank as dread slowly crept over me. This wasn't the camp of burgeoning superheroes I'd expected.

As we plummeted down, a few kids around me screamed, and beside me Lucia began to cry. Whatever we'd each been sold, this wasn't it.

When the elevator finally stopped and the door to the bus opened, a tall blond white guy who looked like an evil Ken doll on steroids trotted up the steps. "Everybody off the bus," he barked. "Line up in a single file. Welcome to the Harbinger Foundation."

Peter sneered at the man. "Better keep a lid on all that charisma. The new recruits might actually start to like you, Edward."

Outside the bus, Peter leaned against a headlight, while the evil Ken doll, Edward, paced back and forth. "You're here thanks to the goodwill of Toyo Harada. Follow me to your rooms, where you'll find your uniforms. Please leave your personal belongings here, to be collected and tagged," said Edward.

I had hope that this could still be a good thing. Maybe these people were just really serious about what they were doing. And shouldn't they be?

Edward led us down a long cement corridor through a door that required his thumbprint to open and into a hallway of rooms made entirely of glass, leaving very little privacy, with Peter on our heels. One by one we were assigned rooms with a bed, sink, and toilet behind a small partition.

"Faith Herbert?" Edward called. "Until further notice,

you will be referred to as the number embroidered on your uniform."

I walked into my room and the glass door slid shut behind me. I pressed my palms against the glass, trying to push it back, but I was locked in.

As Peter walked past me, he kept his gaze focused on the ground.

"Peter," I said, but he didn't look up. "Peter, I need to talk to you." I knocked on the glass, trying to get his attention, but he was gone and the group was on to the next room. I told myself that the rooms were soundproof and he probably didn't hear me, but I had a feeling that wasn't true.

Waiting for me on my bed was a pair of white pants and a white shirt with a *6-973* stitched to the front. I wasn't Faith Herbert. I was 6-973. I created a million different reasons for why anyone would treat us all like this, but every show, movie, and comic I'd ever read told me everything I needed to know. I'd been assigned a number. I'd been labeled. I was an experiment.

PRESENT DAY

PRESENT
DAY

 **1**

I stand between Reese and Greta, our shoulders pressed together as we hold hands. Remnants of early morning fog linger around our feet as we stare down our new reality, a reality where Parker McLean is six feet under instead of standing here with us where she should be. I turn to Reese and search for the words in the bottomless pool of her blue eyes, but for once, she's just as lost as me.

Thunder claps above us and the sky cracks open, releasing a downpour on the cemetery. The Grove is forever changed. Nothing will be the same again.

Greta gasps. I open my umbrella and turn to offer her shelter. But the source of her shock paralyzes me.

"Parker," *Reese whispers.*

I open my mouth, but all that comes out are soapsuds.

"Faith!" shouts Dr. Bryner.

Dog-flavored soapsuds. *Yuck!*

Great. Daydreaming. *Again.* I make the mistake of

wiping my tongue with my hands before I realize that I'm just getting even more soap in my mouth. Amateur move.

"Darn it!" I pull up the collar of my T-shirt and use that to wipe the suds away before spitting into the utility sink. Ladylike, I know. Carley, the corgi mix who I'm prepping for the adoption drive tomorrow, dodges just in time. "Sorry," I moan.

"Faith!" Dr. Bryner calls again from the front desk in her singsong I-mean-business-but-in-a-polite-way voice. "You think you can squeeze in another grooming before heading home? Bumble really needs the extra love. And I have a feeling this could be the weekend she finds her forever home!"

I glance up at the clock. Grandma Lou is a stickler about Thursday dinners. It's casserole night.

Bumble, a scrappy pit mix who came to us with a face full of beestings, is practically a resident here at All Paws on Deck Shelter and Clinic. I think if she doesn't find a home this week, Dr. Bryner's wife, Kit, might just give in and let her come live with them.

"Yeah!" I yell back to her, as I rinse off Carley's belly. "I'll take care of Bumble."

I close my eyes for a moment, letting my imagination wander back to last night's season finale of *The Grove*. I knew it! I just knew Parker wasn't dead. First of all, she's too integral to the plot, and if they kill her off, surely it won't be for another season or two. And second of all, I knew Meredith

Souza, the actress who plays her, was just on hiatus after her very public breakup with *the* Dakota Ash, who plays Reese. I'm not one of those people who always has to be right about everything, but there's something extra satisfying about being right when you run one of the biggest Grover (yes, that is our fandom name) blogs around and your theories on Parker's mysterious disappearance have been on the record for months now. Talk about some serious Grover street cred. As if I needed any more!

I'm gloating, I know. But is it really gloating if your online persona is mostly anonymous and you're only internally smug?

"I think not," I mutter to no one but myself and my corgi companion.

Carley shakes the suds off in response and leaves me covered once again in dog-flavored soap. She even manages to splash the *ADOPT, DON'T SHOP* poster above the sink.

"Real nice," I tell her. But I can't hold back a laugh. The only thing cuter than a corgi butt is a soapy corgi butt. Well, actually, Dakota Ash is cuter than a soapy corgi butt. Okay, well, maybe Oscar Isaac, too. He is a literal cinnamon roll.

Katy Perry's voice echoes out from the pocket of my apron as she sings "Hot N Cold," interrupting the Star Wars slash fic rabbit hole my imagination had disappeared down. I run my hands down the front of my apron before answering the phone on speaker and dropping it back into my pocket. "Hello, Matty!"

"We talked about this," says Matt. "Matty isn't a nick-name. Matt is the shortened version of Matthew. That's as close to a nickname as my name logically gets."

"I was trying it out. Just to see if it felt right."

"Well, it didn't feel right," he says.

"I'm guessing coffee with Kenji was not a success?"

He sighs so heavily into the receiver that my speaker crackles. "He's so worldly. Like, he cares about things like apartheid—which I had to discreetly google while he was talking, by the way—and some kind of South American bee-tle that's at risk of becoming extinct."

"Well, I'm sure you'd care about those things too if you knew more about them."

"Faaaaaaaaaith." He says my name in almost the same way Grandma Lou does when she's caught me in a lie. "He wouldn't even drink coffee on our coffee date, because the Bean didn't have any fair-trade brews. And I'd already ordered! So he just sat there and watched me drink my greedy capitalist murder coffee. Which wasn't even that good, by the way."

I giggle. "I'm sorry," I say. And I really am. Matt is aching to be in a relationship. I don't really feel that same urgency myself. I mean, I'm all for a sweaty make-out sesh—not that I've had many or really any—but I barely have time to do my homework, let alone maintain a relationship. I never said anything about crushes, though. I love a good crush. It's almost as good as the fandom high you ride when you first discover a new obsession. "I'm sure he liked you a lot." I wish I could make Matt see what a catch he really is, but I guess we're all a little shortsighted when it comes to ourselves. "And if he didn't, he doesn't deserve to get to know you—"

"Faith!"

I startle at the sound of my name, and my feet float an inch above the floor for a second before I check my adrenaline and plant my feet firmly on the linoleum.

Dr. Bryner crashes through the door and to the exam table on the far side of the room, carrying a stiff-looking sandy-colored mutt. Oh no. It must have been hit by a car. Poor baby's in shock. Either that or Dr. Bryner has a passion for taxidermy.

"Matty, I gotta go. I'll call you on my way home."

"My name isn't Matty!"

I reach into my pocket and hit the end button. "Carley, stay put." The corgi hears the no-nonsense tone in my voice and waits dutifully as I chase after Dr. Bryner.

I take off my soapy apron and use some hand sanitizer. "What's going on?"

Dr. Bryner pulls the stethoscope up around her ears and presses the other end to the dog's chest. "Hmmm." She listens for a moment more before removing the buds from her ears. "Has Skye left for the day?"

I nod. "Just me." No vet techs.

"Help me check his veins, will you?"

"Of course." I look down at the dog, a medium-sized mutt, for the first time. His legs are rigid and his eyes glazed over. If it weren't for the shallow rise and fall of his chest, I'd assume he was dead.

I reach down into the cupboard across from the exam table. "Who brought him in?"

"Good Samaritan," she says, like she's trying to parse out a riddle. "Found the little guy on the side of the road."

I come up with a fresh pack of needles. "Are you sure it was a good Samaritan? He looks like he might have been hit by a car." Sadly, sometimes people bring animals in and know *exactly* what happened to them but aren't so eager to take the blame.

She shakes her head. "No abrasions or cuts. Just some matted fur. A little dehydrated."

"What can we do for him?" If anything at all. I have to wonder if the little guy is in more pain than we know.

"Let's start with some bloodwork. And then fluids. We'll leave him with the overnight crew and plan our next move in the morning. I might call Dr. Gerard at the university to see if he can come by for a second opinion, depending on what we find."

I nod. I like a plan. I remember when I was just six or seven and I told Grandma Lou I wanted to be a veterinarian. She didn't blindly encourage me like most grandparents would. She looked at me seriously and said, *The hardest part about work like that, baby, is that it's not always about helping a living thing live. Sometimes it's about letting them die.* My dad let out this nervous laugh, telling her to take it easy. Grandma Lou and Mom never censored themselves around me, but Dad wanted me to live in a rosy little bubble. Even if it was just for a little while. I don't recall being very put off by what Grandma Lou said. I gave her a toothy grin and jumped up from the kitchen table as I announced that I was equally interested in life as a career unicorn. I guess I was leaving my options open.

These days I'm undecided on veterinarian school. Journalism feels pretty enticing too, but either way, this internship with Dr. Bryner is exactly what my college applications need. And I get to snuggle puppies and kitties. It's a win-win, if you ask me. But moments like these with this poor creature are the kind of things I have to force myself to forget every night before bed. Along with the looming reality of how Grandma Lou and I will even manage to pay for school at all or if I can bring myself to leave her when the time comes. She acts tough, but we only have each other, and I can't imagine leaving her alone, especially as she gets older. For now, the best I can do is handle life one bite-size piece at a time, and this internship seems like a good place to start.

Dr. Bryner is careful to handle the catatonic dog herself. She doesn't want me holding him if and when he wakes up startled. Even the nicest dogs can bite given the right circumstances.

"Could be a seizure," she says, locking him in one of the crates by the exam table, where we keep all the animals who are under medical observation.

"You don't think someone dumped him, do you?" I ask as I make my way back to Carley to give her coat one last rinse before I dry her off.

"It's not right," she says. "But it happens all the time. Sometimes things happen, and these days families can barely pay their own medical bills, let alone those of their pets."

My gut reaction is to say that those people shouldn't have pets, but I guess if I judged worthy pet owners by who could afford a trip to the actual emergency room at a moment's notice, there wouldn't be a very large pool of potential pet owners left to choose from. After the last six months, I've learned that life isn't as black-and-white as I always thought it was.

After I finish up with Carley's bath and then Bumble's, I hover at the front desk to write down my hours for today in my intern folder.

Dr. Bryner plops down in the rolling chair behind the intake desk and crosses her endlessly long legs. I can't say for sure, but I think she's well over six feet tall. She keeps her hair cropped so short, and every few weeks you can see strands of gray curling around her ears. Her deep brown skin and delicate features require zero makeup, and I've even heard some of the vet techs say she used to model in college. "You okay?" she asks. "That was a little intense."

I nod. "Yeah. It was intense, but I'm fine." I mean, I'm sure I'm going to have nightmares about an army of catatonic dogs or at the very least wake up with a guilt hangover over him and every other dog that's too far gone for us to help.

"You've been doing a great job here," she says, rubbing her eyes. "Kit's always harping on me about how I only say something when people mess up, so don't take it too personally if you feel like I'm not giving feedback. But I'll try to remember."

My cheeks warm. There's something about Dr. Bryner that reminds me of my mom. A little moody and a little too serious about the things she loves, but like Mom, her affection feels a little bit like an adrenaline rush, because it's so sparing in the first place.

It's why, ever since Mom and Dad died, I've done everything I can not to hold back with my feelings. Whether it's a friend or Grandma Lou or a podcast or TV show, I love the things I love and I want there to be no mistake about that. They both loved the same nerdy things, especially that first generation of *The Grove*, but Mom was the type who would sit around and debate its merit or value and Dad was content just to love it exactly as it was served to him. I guess I'm more like Dad in that way.

Dr. Bryner wipes her brow with the back of her hand.

"How about you finish up closing duties? I'm good here. I'm just going to stick around and keep an eye on that guy for a bit longer."

"You got it, Doc." I quickly gather up all the trash and take it out back to our alleyway, kicking a loose brick in between the back door and frame so it doesn't close on me.

After I haul the bags into the dumpster, a strong gust of wind swings the lid shut.

A small blue egg falls to the pavement right in front of me, making an awful splatting noise. "Poor baby," I say to myself.

I look up just in time to see a bird's nest plummeting to the ground. Before I even realize it, I push off from the ground with such buoyancy you'd think the earth was one giant trampoline. Holding my hands out, I beg my body to obey my will, and I catch the bird's nest just barely.

I chuckle to myself as I look down to the alleyway six feet or so below me. Cupped in my hands is a tiny nest with three small eggs inside. I know better than to touch eggs or baby birds, but I didn't have very many options here. Floating up to the rooftop, I tuck the nest under the lip of the roof in the hopes that I haven't done any damage to the birds or the nest.

"Good luck, little ones," I whisper. "A hero's work is never done."

I step up onto the ledge of the old office building housing

the vet clinic and let my lungs fill with crisp, early evening air. Except I'm no hero. Not really. Just a total fangirl possessing a recently discovered superpower. I've spent so many years gobbling up TV shows and comics and books and anything I could get my hands on that fed my insatiable desire for there to be something more to this life. Something bigger. Something super.

With no one around to see and no reason to try and control a power I haven't even fully grasped, I swan-dive into the alley and for a moment, I can feel the wind whistling past my ears. It's dangerous and invigorating, and even though I don't know what the heck I'm doing, I never want it to stop. Suddenly pavement is inches from my nose and I bail, somersaulting to the ground, landing square on my back.

I groan and hiss as I wiggle my fingers and toes. At least I didn't lose any limbs in the process, but that's going to leave a bruise. The sliver of blue sky above me is a faint memory all too quickly. A dark blue bird soars overhead, landing on the ledge above and chirping chaotically until she finds most of her eggs safe and sound.

I sit up, eyeing the shattered egg a few feet to my left. "Sorry, little guy." Peter's words echo in my ears. The same words he told me over and over again as he and Kris drove me back to Glenwood, careful to use only back roads. *Can't save them all*, he said. *You can't save them all, Faith. That's the most important thing I'll ever tell you.*

I shake my head, trying to erase the memories. I wish my brain was like an Etch A Sketch and all you had to do was shake your head to start over again.

After saying good night to Dr. Bryner, I head out to my car—well, Grandma Lou's car—a maroon Kia Rio with multiple honor-roll stickers plastered to the bumper. On the drive home I listen to my latest discovery, an out-of-production podcast called *Hellmouth Grove* hosted by two fangirl sisters named Bea and Suze, who spend every episode breaking down all the ways Margaret Toliver's *The Grove* influenced Joss Whedon's *Buffy*. It's meta in the best possible way.

All Paws on Deck is only about fifteen minutes from home on the opposite side of town in Old Glenwood, where the houses seem nice enough on the outside, but you only have to pause a moment for a closer look. Cracked windows, overgrown shrubbery, weeds shooting through cracks in driveways, even a few eviction notices taped on doors, and roofs looking like they might just slide right off. The less desirable streets dead-end into shady apartment complexes where you don't want to get stuck after dark. Old Glenwood is like a storm cloud gradually moving through the rest of the town, choking out the light as it spreads slowly like a disease.

At the same time, though, Old Glenwood isn't all bad. It's not like good people don't live here. I slow to a stop at Ches's street, peering out at the house she shares with her mother and five brothers. For a moment I consider stopping by on a whim.

Ches's mom loves me, along with all her boys and their friends, and she's got an open-door policy when it comes to guests.

But then I notice Matt's Jeep there parked on the street, and I can't help the feeling I might be intruding in some way. He would have said something on the phone if he wanted me to know they were hanging out. I press the gas and head for home and Grandma Lou's tuna casserole.

Matt and Ches are my best friends, but little moments like this remind me that before I came along and made us a trio, they were very much a duo. And I'm okay with that. I try to remember that the bond they share runs just a little bit deeper and that there are some things time can't replace. That's no one's fault. At least that's what I try to tell myself.

When I pull into the driveway, Grandma Lou is outside with the hedge clippers, hacking away.

"Do they look even?" she shouts over her shoulder.

I roll the window down. "Looks great," I lie. Never mind the gaping hole in the lantanas. Normally I can't stomach a lie, but Grandma Lou's sanity is on the line here. "Beautiful!"

She yanks off her gardening gloves and tosses the clippers behind the hedges. I sigh and write myself a mental note to put those away later.

It's not that we have a beautiful, well-manicured lawn that she's dead set on maintaining. When I moved in and Grandma Lou realized she'd have to take good enough care of herself to see me through high school, she traded smoking half a pack of Virginia Slims a day for yard maintenance, and I've gotta say, she was way better at blowing smoke rings during bingo than she is at keeping her flower beds alive.

I throw my backpack over my shoulder and follow her inside to the kitchen, where she washes her hands, and sure enough, a tuna casserole made with spaghetti noodles is cooling on the stove. Grandma Lou is actually a great cook, but the woman loves her canned meats. Dad always said it was a generational thing. Whatever it is, it's definitely not hereditary. My idea of spaghetti Thursday would definitely include spicy red sauce and lots of that to-die-for powdery Parmesan cheese that comes in a plastic shaker.

"Let's sit at the table tonight." She pulls two fresh plates from the cabinet. "Turn off that TV, would ya? I want to hear about your day."

"You got it." I duck into the living room—or as Grandma Lou calls it, the parlor—and my eyes practically water from how loud the six o'clock news is.

"Are you trying to get a noise complaint from Miss Ella?" I call over the news anchor.

"Oh, that old dinosaur already has plenty to complain about."

Digging through the brocade throw pillows on the couch, I search for the remote. "Nice way to talk about your best friend!" I reach my hand between the cushions. There it is!

Behind me the news anchor says, "Cindy Ramirez is reporting live from Glenwood City Hall, where council members are debating the recent uptick of rabid dogs and possible—"

I click the TV off over my shoulder and toss the remote back on the couch. The current rabid dog situation in our town is almost as polarizing as a presidential election, and I just don't have the brainpower for it today.

At the kitchen table, Grandma Lou is waiting with two dishes of casserole and a liter of ginger ale.

I plop into the chair across from her and let out a contented little sigh.

"Let's say grace," she says.

I nod, and we hold hands and close our eyes. We both sit in silence, saying our own prayers. Grandma Lou says that praying out loud is about being loud, not being heard. I don't really pray to anything in particular. I've never had any trouble seeing all that's good and all that's evil in the world, but something about a higher power feels like a game of make-believe that not even I can bring myself to have faith in. But I'm starting to wonder, with all the weird stuff going on, if someone somewhere is pulling the strings. Still it's a nice moment of quiet every night to think about all that we've lost and all that we still have to be grateful for. At the very least, we have each other.

And way too much tuna casserole.

She squeezes my hand to let me know she's done. "Dig in, baby girl."

2

The Hopper County Fair is held on the outskirts of town near the old and now defunct paper mill. The fair is one of my favorite events of the year. It's the kind of gathering that makes me nostalgic for a version of Glenwood I never even knew, a time when there were no bad neighborhoods or Old Glenwood. Only Glenwood. All in all, it's a good way to spend a Saturday.

Grandma and I ride over with Miss Ella, our next-door neighbor and, though she admits it only grudgingly, Grandma Lou's best friend.

As I'm getting out of the back seat in the dusty makeshift parking lot, Miss Ella, who is the epitome of little old white lady, checks to make sure the scarf tied around her perm is securely in place. "You know, Sal down the street told me he heard they were going to have metal detectors this year to keep out those gangs and that they might even fence the grounds with barbed wire to keep those damn dogs out."

I sigh and look to Grandma Lou. *Fake news*, she mouths. And I can't hold back my laugh.

"What?" asks Miss Ella. "You think our safety is a joke?"

I turn to Grandma Lou. "I've got to get to the rescue booth."

She nods. "You run ahead. I'll hang back with this slow-poke."

Miss Ella huffs. "That's a sight I'd like to see. That girl running." Something inside me bristles. I am not a tiny girl. Fat. Plus-size. Curvy. Whatever you want to call it. Not many people comment on my size. Grandma Lou thinks it's because I've got such a commanding and cheerful demeanor, but there's the occasional jerk at school and then there's Miss Ella, who still thinks that a woman's value is calculated by the measurement of her waist. I almost say something back to her, but I don't want to be rude. Besides, if she'd be shocked to see me running, she'd probably have a full-on freak-out if she saw what else I could do.

"Ella, I'm about to lock you in that car with the windows rolled up." Grandma Lou winks at me and I give her a thankful grin before running my fat little butt up to the fairgrounds, swishing my hips for Miss Ella to see.

Ches is waiting for me up by the ticket booth, pacing back and forth, her long black skirt billowing around her combat boots laced with purple tulle instead of shoelaces.

"I told you to wear jeans," I say, even though she looks fab.

She spins on her heel and shrugs. "I know." She groans. "I just woke up possessed by the ghost of Stevie Nicks. And jeans make me obsess about my butt. Is it too round? Too flat? Too wide? A skirt is just so freeing." She reaches into her midnight blue velvet messenger bag and pulls out something lavender. "But at least I brought the rescue T-shirt you gave me."

"Well, that's something, I guess."

She loops her arm through mine. "Come on. Let's go save the puppies or whatever."

Francesca Palmer is the witchy best friend of my dreams. She's tall and lanky with sporadic sprinkles smattered across her ivory skin and chin-length box-dyed black hair and has recently announced that she has decided to "shed" the label bisexual in favor of pansexual. She absolutely wafts confidence, but then she opens her mouth and you realize she's just like the rest of us—floundering and constantly in search of some guarantee that everything is going to be okay. Her self-assurance can be a little intimidating at times, but I've always respected the way she looks like she knows exactly where she's going, even when she's just as lost as everyone else.

We met on my first day at North Glenwood Elementary, when I moved from Minneapolis to live with Grandma Lou, which happened to be on Halloween. We were in third grade, and she and Matt sat down at my lunch table. I was dressed as Sailor Moon, Matt was a Pokémon, and Ches was dressed as Severus Snape. For seven-year-olds, I think our taste was pretty exquisite. Ches asked why I looked so blue, and when I couldn't give an answer because of the tears I was holding back, she offered me her Merrymaking Elixir, which turned out to be grape juice. But it worked, at least until the end of the school day. That night we went trick-or-treating, and our bond was solidified over our shared love of blue Tootsie Pops.

"Matt came over last night. He made me watch some awful Swedish movie that Kenji mentioned on their date."

"I saw his car in the driveway on my way home from the rescue," I say, my voice almost too small to hear.

She chuffs. "You should've just come over! You always do this."

"Always do what?"

"Wait around for someone to invite you. You're our best friend. You need no invitation, Faith."

Hearing her say so out loud has me feeling foolish for even thinking otherwise yesterday, but I can't let go of the feeling that I'm the third wheel sometimes. I shake my head. "It's silly. I just don't ever want to intrude if you two want to hang out on your own."

We pass under the tent where the rescue is located. Dr. Bryner and a few other volunteers are talking over barking dogs to potential volunteers while Kit, a curvy white lady with a passion for all things retro, tries to explain to an inquisitive little girl with light brown pigtails and grabby hands that not even nice dogs like to be tugged on.

"Our friendship," Ches says, "is your friendship."

I squeeze her hand. "Thanks."

"But listen, I can only stick around for an hour or two. I've got to get home to work on that AP Chem paper."

"That's not even due for another month."

"Faith, not all of us can pull a twelve-page paper out of our asses the night before and still manage to ruin the curve for the whole class, okay?"

I grin sheepishly. Nothing feeds me like procrastination and a deadline. I'm not a perfect student, but I'm quick on my feet and I'm clever, so I don't want to say school is a cake-walk, but I don't find it as challenging as some people either. "Fine. Go see what Kit needs over there, and I'll check in with Dr. B. And put that T-shirt on over your clothes at least!"

Carley is waiting for me in her crate. "It's a big day, missy! You want to go on the leash? Maybe make some googly eyes at potential adopters?" I reach down to put her leash on, but she plants herself on the floor of her crate, whining at me and making eyes at her sometimes crate neighbor and partner in crime, Bumble. "All right, all right. I'll take you both out. Come on, Bumble."

In front of our tent, I walk back and forth. Bumble pulls me forward while Carley pulls me back. "Hi!" I call out to passersby. "Are you interested in fostering or maybe even giving a forever home to one of our rescue pups? They're all spayed or neutered and completely vaccinated. For fosters, we cover the expense of food and medical bills."

A few people take cards and some even stop to give Carley and Bumble a head scratch or two before moving on to the row of games at the far side of the fairgrounds.

"No joy like the joy of fostering!" I call out cheerfully.

"Give me all the dogs!" says a haughty voice.

I turn around to find Matt in a Delgado & Sons Bakery T-shirt. I should've recognized his Cruella de Vil voice. "Hey, you! I thought your dad's booth was short-staffed today."

"Benny finally showed up, so Dad cut me loose for a few minutes to take a break."

Matt's family runs the funnel-cake booth every year, and their funnel cake is more than deep-fried dough. It's a religious experience. Call me when your county fair serves a prize-winning bananas Foster Nutella funnel cake. Their family bakery, run by his dad and uncles, is a local chain and a staple here in Glenwood.

I clip Bumble's and Carley's leashes to the dog-walking belt Dr. Bryner outfitted me with so I can give Matt a proper hug.

Matthew Delgado and I are basically the exact same body type. The only differences are his brown skin thanks to his Puerto Rican roots and our, well, differing equipment. But to be totally honest, we've been known to share clothes from time to time, and it pains me to admit this, but he looks better in my skinny jeans than I do. I love Ches, but Matt and I exist on the same wavelength in a way that Ches and I don't. We're both pop culture nerds who aren't afraid to love the things we love. Ches isn't afraid either, but the things she loves are usually medieval fairy tales and feminist think pieces about Wiccan culture. It's the perfect mix, though. Matt meets me where I am and Ches expands my horizons.

"But for real," says Matt, "I had to come over here and see if you really got Ches to wear that pastel T-shirt." He holds his hand above his brow to block the sun. "And holy shit. Will you look at that? Our own little witchy Easter egg," he says loud enough for her to hear.

Ches checks to see that Kit's back is turned before she gives him the finger.

My body tugs to the left as Bumble pulls impatiently at his leash. "Hang on, buddy," I tell him. "Oh my God. We haven't even talked about the season finale of *The Grove*."

Matt's face screws up into a grimace. "I am not happy about how things played out. And are we just going to ignore the fact that Reese is supposed to be a Seer and would have totally known that Parker wasn't actually dead?"

"Oh, whatever. You're just pissed because your prediction—" Bumble tugs more violently, causing me to stumble.

I grab the leash to pull him back. "Easy there." I turn back to Matt. "Like I was saying—"

But I don't get to finish, because now sweet Bumble, the dog who spends all day waiting for belly rubs and treats and who wouldn't hurt a butterfly, is pulling me with such strength that I have to run to keep up and we're leaving poor Carley in the dust, practically dragging her behind.

"Bumble!" I shout. "Bumble! What the heck has gotten into you?"

"Faith!" shouts Matt as he runs after me. "This better count as my workout for the year! Someone tell Coach Grant so he'll get off my ass for once."

As I'm dodging in and out of the crowd, trying not to lose my pants, I unclip poor Carley's leash. "Matt! Catch Carley!"

The faster my feet move, the harder I have to concentrate on making sure they return back to the ground, like I could just shoot right up into the sky with all this building momentum. There's an ache running all the way down to my toes, just begging me to push myself off the ground and soar. Since this summer, my whole body's biology has changed entirely and my head is having a hard time catching up. It's like I went through puberty for the second time, but this time instead of boobs, I gained the ability to fly and enough trauma to last me through college at least.

"Hey, girl!" someone calls.

"Now is not the time for pickup lines!" I shout back.

The path ahead of me clears and I can see the source of the voice, the one person refusing to budge. They're either the nicest person ever or looking for a reason to get run over. "Hey, girl!" they call again, and this time I can hear that they are definitely talking to Bumble and not me.

"Incoming!" I shout as my body collides with theirs, sending us both flying onto the dirt ground.

Bumble finally, mercifully stops, taking a moment to lick my head before greeting our guest.

I sit up. "Bumble, what got into you?"

The person sits up as Bumble collapses into their lap. "Bees," they say before taking off their sunglasses and baseball cap. "She was being chased by bees."

I look over my shoulder to see a small swarm of bees dispersing, people swatting them away.

The stranger who was kind enough to literally stop us in our tracks is small, but has a solid frame with tightly muscled arms and wears an effortlessly cool black T-shirt and slouchy jeans. Something about them is so familiar, like I'm having déjà vu.

I gasp. "Oh. My. God." This is way more impossible than déjà vu.

"I know," they say. "Poor thing."

"You—you're Dakota Ash. *The* Dakota Ash." My chest is seizing. Is this a heart attack? Is this what it feels like?

Dakota stands, shaking the dust off her pants, and holds a hand out to help me up as the crowd around us begins to mill about again, the action mostly over.

I stare blankly at her hand for a moment too long before taking it.

She smiles as she puts her Ray-Bans on again and tugs her red baseball cap back over her short hair, which swoops all to one side, showing off her buzzed scalp on the other side. She's only a year older than me, and somehow, she's cooler and more confident than I can imagine myself ever being, let alone by this time next year. "Maybe don't say that name so loud."

"You're Dakota Ash," I whisper.

She grins, somehow charmed by how big of a fool I am in this moment.

But OH MY GOD DAKOTA ASH. THE DAKOTA ASH. STAR OF *THE GROVE*. I am silently screaming on the inside. I bite down on my lips to stop myself from saying anything I'll regret. Matt is going to die. We both are. RIP us. We'll be buried side by side. Our headstones will read: *They died as they lived: consumed by fandom.*

I say it again. "You're Dakota Ash."

"I know," she says. "And who's this sweet girl?"

I stand there in silence for a moment, begging my brain to compute. That is a question. Deep breath. Questions have answers. Deep breath. That is a question I can answer.

"I'm F-faith," I stutter. "Oh wait. No. This is Bumble.

40

She is very sweet. I mean, I can be too. But mostly Bumble is the sweet one. The sweet girl."

Dakota holds her lips in a tight line, like she's trying not to smile. She motions to my T-shirt. "And is she available for adoption?"

"She is! Bumble is looking for a lifelong companion who will take her on adventures with them like hiking and picnics. She's playful, but the true way to her heart is through belly rubs and rawhide," I say, reciting Bumble's online bio. "She's in perfect health and only suffers from a—"

"Bee allergy," Dakota finishes. "I read about her online." She squats down and Bumble immediately rolls over, baring her belly.

I can't believe I'm talking to Dakota Ash about pet adoptions and that all these people are just walking around us like two pebbles in a stream. She read about Bumble online. How wild is that? And that she's here! In Glenwood! Wait. I have so many questions. "Dakota," I say. "Miss Ash?"

She pops back up. "Dakota. Please."

I nod. "Dakota. I don't mean to pry, and I promise not to, like, call the paparazzi or anything—not that we even have paparazzi in Glenwood—but what are you even doing here? I mean, don't get me wrong. Glenwood is a pretty okay place, but there's not much to see."

Dakota glances over her shoulder before taking a step closer to me. "Can you keep a secret?"

 *3*

Can I keep a secret? If she only knew!

I nod feverishly.

"We're here in preproduction and scouting a few locations for external shots," she says.

"Here? In Glenwood? You've got to be kidding."

She chuckles. "That's television. You go where the budget takes you, and the dollar always stretches a little further in places like . . . well, the Midwest, which is why we used to film just outside Chicago, but we yada yada tax law changes, so we're giving Minnesota a shot."

I take a huge gulp of fresh air. "I don't mean to freak you out, but I'm a really big fan."

Dakota nudges me with her elbow, like she's about to clue me in on some inside joke, like we're just two old friends, when Matt finally catches up, panting. "There you are," he says. "Oh my God, are you okay?"

But then he freezes, his eyes widening like saucers. "Ho-ly. Shit. HOLYSHIT."

My pupils bounce frantically as I try to communicate to him to keep his cool. This moment feels like a firefly—I'm lucky enough to catch it, but if I'm not careful, I could kill it. Trust me, I'm a serious fangirl, and containing my squee is no easy feat, but the last thing I want to do is scare Dakota away.

Dakota clears her throat and holds out a hand. "Holy shit is what my mom calls me. You can just call me Dakota."

His jaw snaps shut and he takes her hand. "Right. Of course. Sorry, it's just that you're—"

Dakota drops down into a squat, nuzzling her head against Bumble's. "Totally hoping that no one has claimed this sweetie," she says.

Something in my stomach flutters. *She likes dogs.* And not just cute little dogs that conveniently fit in your purse. She likes big, bungling dogs who take up half your bed and whose drool leaves little puddles. Dogs who take up just as much of your house as they do of your heart.

"She is," I say, finally remembering that I'm the authority on adoptable dogs here. "She's totally available to a good home. One where she can be active."

Dakota smirks. "Well, I did just rent a place. Nothing fancy. But there's a big yard."

"She'd love it," I say.

Matt clears his throat. "Not to ruin the moment or anything, but I should probably get back to my booth, and I think Ches has her hands full back at yours."

I deflate a bit.

"Maybe you could give me some info on Bumble here?" asks Dakota.

"Gladly!"

The three of us walk back up to the booth, with Bumble attached to my leash belt.

I wait for the throngs of people to recognize Dakota. It's not just in my head. She's a really big deal. *The Grove* has been ongoing since my parents met and bonded over it in high school. Every few years they bring in a new generation of actors, and sometimes a few even come back as adults to play teachers or parents or even villains. It addresses all the sticky issues a good after-school show does on top of having a sort of spooky setting where things aren't what they seem and some townspeople (like Dakota's character) even have supernatural abilities thanks to a mishap with the town's water source that ended up causing a hereditary gene mutation. The more recent seasons have been sexier and darker, which has attracted a whole fresh crop of fans.

So yeah, Dakota Ash, whose style isn't exactly feminine or masculine, is basically a modern-day heartthrob. Between her midnight Instagram confessionals about her sexual identity (lesbian), gender (she/her), racial identity (half white/half Latinx), anxiety (mingled with depression), and favorite off-brand cereal, plus her on-again, off-again relationships with various cast members, if you don't dream of kissing Dakota, you at least daydream about being cool enough to be her friend.

Back at our tent, Matt splits off to find Ches and fill her in, though she is thoroughly unimpressed by all things *The Grove*.

I lead Dakota past the rows of dogs, their tails eager and waiting (the cats get way too stressed outside their element to bring them to events like this), back to a smaller adjoining tent where we have a table and chairs set up for adoption paperwork and foster applications.

Bumble spins in a circle beside us, fussily considering the best spot to sprawl out. After digging her paws into the grass for a moment, she plops down with her chin on Dakota's foot.

A short and quiet "Awww" escapes me, and my head feels fuzzy with heart-eyes feelings.

Dakota grins. "I'm smitten. Where do I sign on the dotted line?"

"Well, actually," I say, "we're pretty serious about finding the perfect home for each pet—and that's not to say you wouldn't give Bumble the perfect home—but what happens next is that you fill out an application, including references, and then we send someone to do a home visit before we approve you."

"Wow," she says. "Well, ya know, I guess I'm glad you're

so thorough. Um, who exactly would be doing the home visit?"

The truth is that answer varies, because we're so strapped for time and resources that it usually falls down to whoever lives nearest to the prospective adopter, but I'm having a hard time figuring out if Dakota is asking because she thinks I'll be discreet and not publish her home address online or maybe she's freaked out about me and doesn't really want a fan all over her house. But I can't ignore the vibe I feel between me and Dakota. Mom would have called it the special sauce—some unidentifiable connection—and hopefully I'm not the only one feeling it, because I think that maybe Dakota Ash might just be interested in being friends with me, Faith Stinking Herbert.

"Me," I say. "If that's okay with you, I could do your home visit. I could even bring Bumble to see how she does. Or we can arrange for someone else if you want." I motion over to Dr. Bryner and Kit.

Dakota nods as she fills in the blanks on her application. "You gotta have Faith," she says, quoting the exact George Michael song my parents named me after as she smiles to herself. (Most people assume my name is religious. They obviously never met my parents.)

"In fact," Dakota adds, "you should probably go ahead and plan on paying a visit to the set too. If that's cool with you?"

OMG. OMG. OMG. OMG. INTERNAL SCREAM. "Oh, yeah. Totally cool. If you think that's necessary." Cool as a cucumber.

She signs her name at the bottom, her signature tight with a dramatic *D* for Dakota and *A* for Ash. "Best to be a hundred percent thorough, right?" Bumble chuffs as Dakota prepares to stand, so she squats down so that they're eye to eye. "It won't be long until you're home sweet home, baby." She gives her a good scratch behind the ears and stands.

I look over the application. "And this is the best number to reach you at?"

"The one and only," she confirms with a wink. "But maybe you could go ahead and give me your number in case I have any questions?"

"Oh, right. Of course!"

She hands her cell over, and I giggle at the fan-art version of last season's poster she's using as her screen saver, except in this version, everyone is drawn to look like bobbleheads.

"What can I say?" she says. "I'm a fan of the fans."

I save my number in her phone and have to do everything in my power not to save it as some sort of pun or *The Grove* inside joke. Plain old Faith Herbert will have to do.

"I'll call you for a home visit as soon as Dr. Bryner signs off on your application."

Dakota looks at my number there in her phone. "I'll be waiting, Faith Herbert."

Bumble stands as she leaves, and I loop a finger through her collar just in case she plans on making another run for it.

A warm thrill rushes through my veins. There's a tingling in my toes as the earth feels less and less solid, like I could just float up out of this tent and fly. I watch Dakota go, forcing myself to concentrate on staying grounded.

Matt and Ches rush through the flaps of the adjoining tent and I plant my feet firmly on the ground—it's maybe the most self-control I've felt over my body in months.

"Tell us everything," Matt demands.

Ches shakes her head in disbelief. "I don't even care about that show, but holy cheezus, that girl was hot."

I lead them back out to our main tent and proceed to put Bumble back in her crate. As we check everyone's water and food, I spill almost every detail except one. I keep one little moment to myself.

You gotta have Faith, I hear Dakota say once more in my head. *You gotta have Faith*.

4

The rest of the weekend feels like that uncontainable buildup of energy you experience when you're at a surprise party and are still waiting for the birthday person to arrive. I know a secret and I'm sure it won't be a secret for very long. Dakota Ash is here, and not only is she here in Glenwood, but I spoke to her and she spoke to me and I think we might be acquaintances. Maybe even acquaintances on the highway to casual friendship?

What even is my life?

On Monday morning, Matt picks up Ches and then me for school. Matt and Ches always drive together, but Grandma Lou usually lets me take her car. Today she's got a few doctor's appointments and some errands to run, so Matt cheerfully scoops me up with an extra chocolate milk waiting for me in the back-seat cup holder.

Morning chocolate milk is something Matt and Ches

have done since they were kids riding the bus together. It's very much *their* tradition, but they're always sure to include me when I'm around. I've known them for over half my life now, but there's just something they share from knowing each other since they were in diapers and Ches's mom was working a second job at Delgado & Sons.

"Well," says Ches, eyeing me from the visor mirror as she smudges her eyelids with deep navy eyeliner. "Did Dakota call you?"

I roll my eyes. Not because I'm annoyed with her, but because I'd been silly enough to hope that she might. "Nah. Not that she has any reason to."

"So what'd you do all day yesterday then?" Matt asks as he peels off down my street. "You were totally incommunicado."

I pop the paper top of my chocolate milk open and take a slurping sip. "I just wanted to get caught up on blog comments and homework." And that's totally true, but I also found myself daydreaming about Dakota and the idea of starting fresh with a friend who I don't have to share.

"You sure you weren't busy with your fancy smarty-pants journalism camp friends?" asks Ches, a touch of bitterness in her voice.

If she only knew! As far as Matt, Ches, and even Grandma Lou are concerned, I spent my summer at Pleasant Oaks Journalism Camp on Lake Erie. None of them know the truth, which is that I spent the summer as some sick science experiment and Peter Stanchek sort of forced me into joining his rebellion, changing everything.

I shake my head to force myself not to think about that. I made the decision to leave Peter in the past, along with everything that happened at the Harbinger Foundation, but I'm starting to wonder if that's going to be as easy as I'd hoped. Since I've been home, I've had my head focused on two goals: (1) Get back to everyday life like nothing happened and maintain a low profile, and (2) keep my feet on the ground.

"Nope, and trust me, journalism camp is nothing to be jealous of," I say, unable to avoid the image of Peter falling off a skyscraper as I jumped right behind him, totally unsure if my flying abilities would be enough to save him and not turn me into a pancake.

My voice must sound distant, or maybe there's just a booger hanging out of my nose, because both Matt and Ches watch me in their mirrors as we sit at a stoplight.

I put on a high-pitched laugh for both of them. "Everyone smelled like broccoli, and the most exciting scandal to rock the place was a dry-shampoo shortage at the commissary."

Matt laughs. "Yeah, definitely not our brand of nerd, Ches."

She sighs as he hits the gas. "Yeah, well, I bet those

nerds don't have to panic over having a high enough GPA and impressive enough application so they can get a crack at a full ride to a state school. And test well! Did I mention test well?"

I twirl my finger through one of Ches's curls. "You're all those things and more," I promise her. Last fall, Ches had a eureka! moment and realized that the only way she'd ever get out of Glenwood was if she got a scholarship and a degree. The only problem? Her GPA was so bad, she probably would have been better off starting from scratch, so she's been on a campaign to save her academic career all through junior year and now senior year. "Besides, we're only three weeks into the school year. Nothing major to stress over yet."

"And hey," says Matt, "Zach from the crystal shop said you'd always have a job there. If you get stuck in Glenwood, you might as well be the town authority on all things metaphysical."

Ches groans, squirming in her seat. "Zach just wants me to go full-time so he can see me dressed like a wench when the shop has a booth at the Ren faire."

"I mean, I would also like to see you dressed as a wench," I offer. "Just at least once."

Matt turns his blinker on as he merges into the student parking lot line. "It's not too late. We could just skip. We could go to the mall."

"Malls are so pedestrian," says Ches. "Nothing exciting happens at the mall."

I squeeze my eyes shut, memories from this summer swarming me like a cloud of bees.

"No mall for me," I say.

Matt groans. "School it is."

As the last bell for first period rings, Mrs. Raburn, a short, stout black woman with her springy curls slicked back into a puff of a ponytail, takes a red marker to her dry-erase board and writes out *NEW ASSIGNMENTS*. Mrs. Raburn is our school newspaper sponsor and journalism teacher. She takes her job very seriously, which I appreciate, because that means she takes us seriously. "Okay, let's get cracking on our next issue."

Rebecca Khan's arm shoots into the air.

"Yes, Ms. Khan?"

"Cross-country season starts this week and since my girlfriend, Clarissa, is on the team, I'll be at all the meets anyway, so is it cool if I cover their first meet for the sports article?" Rebecca, who is half Pakistani with thick black hair that is always braided into a long, smooth braid, smiles sweetly.

Mrs. Raburn's gaze sweeps over the newspaper staff. "Doesn't look like anyone's clamoring to cover cross-country. If there are no objections, it's yours."

Rebecca turns to Johnny Leonard, our editor in chief. "Just have your piece to me by first period on Thursday," he says. "Two hundred words. And I know it's just running through sticks and leaves, but maybe try to find some kind of angle?"

Rebecca gives him a thumbs-up. "Two hundred words and an angle. You got it."

Johnny lets out a chuckle and pushes his fingers through his hair as he jots her assignment down. His brown curls bounce with every movement, and by some miracle, his skin with its olive undertone escaped puberty with only a few acne scars.

I clear my throat. "I think my piece last week did pretty okay." I made a listicle called "The Introvert's Guide to Surviving Homecoming." I'm being modest when I say "pretty okay." It was a hit. Well, Matt and Ches thought it was funny, at least.

Johnny's eyes light up. "It was hilarious!"

Mrs. Raburn tsks quietly. She's not a fan of journalism that includes lists or memes, but if you ask me, reading the news is gloomy enough. Why not lighten it up when you can with a list of internet-famous dogs ranked by snuggle factor? That's the kind of hard-hitting facts I'm interested in.

I clear my throat. "So I was thinking maybe I could do something like a little guide to the school musical for everyone who doesn't get theater?"

Johnny nods. "Yeah. Yeah, that could totally work."

"Like a cheat sheet," I say. "And a frequently-asked-questions section?"

"Why are people always breaking out into song?" Johnny asks in a deep voice, like he's just some random reader.

"How come I don't jeté out of a room when I'm sad in real life?" I say, and snort at my own dumb joke.

Johnny grins and jots down my pitch. The gold chain of his Star of David necklace peeks out from the collar of his T-shirt.

My cheeks flush as I look around and realize that we're the only ones laughing. I begin to shrink back, but then Johnny gives me a brief but dazzling smile.

"Actually," says Mrs. Raburn, "I was thinking you might want to try your hand at something a little grittier, Faith. There's that party drug making the rounds at Shady Oaks Prep. Might be interesting to do a little digging there, no?"

I look to Johnny for some kind of out. It's not that I don't think we should be covering stories like that, but does it have to be me? Especially now, with the chaos of this summer still ringing in my ears.

Beside me, Colleen Bristow timidly raises her hand. "I—I think I could give that a go," she says, her voice almost as small as she is. Colleen, the paper's youngest staff member and copy editor, is a tiny white girl who wears purple-framed glasses and always keeps her mousy brown hair in a neat ponytail.

Johnny looks to Mrs. Raburn, deferring to her. Colleen is supersweet and very thorough, but she's younger than all the other sophomores because she skipped fourth grade. Even though there's nothing wrong with being shy, it's hard to imagine her standing her own ground snooping around a place like Shady Oaks Prep, where the students can sniff out an outsider like a fake designer bag at a flea market.

Mrs. Raburn shifts in her seat. "Maybe we should work up to a story like that, Colleen. Let's get your feet wet with something more . . ." She turns to Johnny.

"Oh, right!" says Johnny. "How about . . ." He taps his pen against his lips, thin on top with a pouty bottom lip. "How do you feel about covering the new vending machines?"

Colleen gives a flat smile. "Sure." She must be one of those girls who's always cold, because she's wearing purple gloves and a matching scarf.

"And maybe you could help Faith with the Senior Spotlights. I think Gretchen Sandoval is our next senior."

I stifle a huff. Senior Spotlights are the worst, mainly because the seniors who get spotlighted are the kind of people who think the newspaper staff are a bunch of nerds who spend their weekends writing fanfic and playing tabletop role-playing games. And while that's actually not entirely untrue, those things are just as cool as being captain of the drill team, which is why Gretchen Sandoval is next on the list for Senior Spotlight.

Colleen catches the grimace on my face. "Um, sure, if that's okay with Faith."

I smile, trying to recover. "Oh yeah! Of course."

After the rest of the workload for this week's paper is divided up, I settle into my little cubicle to brainstorm. Calling my space a cubicle is generous, but I love this little stretch of home buried deep within the halls of East Glenwood High. The computer at my desk is something straight out of a museum and would probably work faster if I plugged a bike into it and started pedaling. Last spring I ditched my plain old desk chair for a school bus bench Johnny and I found out by the dumpsters when we were cleaning out some old storage space the school assigned to us for our newly instated archive after months of begging.

The greatest perk of senior year is getting not just one, but two class sessions back-to-back in the journalism room, both of which I share with Johnny. First period is my actual journalism class and the other is a study hall, which today I'm looking forward to for blog maintenance.

The study hall bell rings as I open a new browser and *Faithfully Yours* slowly begins to load. Johnny plops down beside me and as a gut reaction, I lurch toward the mouse to frantically close the browser.

He chomps into an apple with a loud cracking bite. "'Faithfully Yours,'" he reads over my shoulder.

"Uhh . . ." I scramble to close the screen, but the stupid computer is frozen. Of course it is! Come on, come on. I click incessantly, but the little arrow on the screen doesn't budge. I swear this computer is straight out of ancient Rome.

Johnny plops down next to me. "'My Top Five Predictions

for Next Season. Number one. Grant will discover that Parker is his sister. If you ask me, Grant's whole story arc has been building to this—'"

"Stop, stop! Shhh!" I clap my hand over his mouth, and he grins.

"What?" he asks, his voice muffled with fingers still covering his lips. "Just catching up on the latest *Grove* gossip."

The arrow on my computer races all over the screen as it unfreezes and tries catching up on all the right clicking and window minimizing I'd attempted. All the while, a GIF of Dakota winking at the top of my latest posts stares back at me over and over and over again.

Johnny reaches for the mouse and hovers over my subscriber count in the sidebar. "Holy crap. Faith, is this your blog? You have almost ninety thousand followers! Wow. *The Grove*? Isn't that the one where the kids have weird superpowers but then also can't figure out normal stuff like how to get birth control? I can't believe it's still on the air, honestly."

"It's more nuanced than that!" I tell him. "*The Grove* perfectly blends the paranormal with superhero lore and the everyday dilemmas of American teens. It's iconic!" I nearly shout that last part, feeling a little defensive.

Johnny lets out a low whistle. "Whoa. Stand down. Sorry, I didn't know."

I blush and sink down a bit into my bus bench, the tear in

the seat giving way to yellowing foam scratches against my back. Why couldn't I just have been looking up porn like a normal teenager?

He scrolls and checks out different pages and previous posts as I continue to shrivel right there beside him.

Faithfully Yours isn't a secret, exactly, but it's not something I've advertised. Call it the fangirl in me, but something about keeping my identity a secret from all of my audience and letting everyone speculate about who I really was excited me. A few readers have figured out who I am, and to me, it's like they're the most pure of heart and worthy of such a secret. Just like in *Kingdom Keeper*, a game I wish I could forget playing. And it doesn't hurt that none of my readers have been psycho stalkers, but beyond that, only Matt and Ches know that I'm the puppet master behind *Faithfully Yours: Your One-Stop Fan Blog for All Things Grove*. I used to keep up with all the cast gossip, but honestly, the type of commenters that brought onto the blog disgusted me—the kind of people who would say awful and vicious things about the cast, completely dehumanizing them. So these days it's mostly in-depth recaps.

I groan. It's one thing to be a fan of something. It's a whole other thing to create an internet shrine to it. "It's kind of a secret, okay? So maybe don't print this in the paper?"

He minimizes the screen, and his eyebrows shoot up and down knowingly. "Almost like a secret identity."

I hold my pinky out for him. "Promise you won't tell a soul."

He loops his pinky around mine, and my insides flutter. "I swear. I'll tell everyone it was porn."

I laugh and tug harder on his pinky, showing him my muscle.

"Okay, okay," he whispers. "Your secret identity is safe with me." And then his eyes catch mine, and in a very serious tone, he adds, "All your secrets are safe with me, Faith."

He clears his throat, talking loudly enough for everyone else in study hall to hear so that it's very clear that nothing odd is happening here. No sir, nothing to see here. "So you need anyone to go check out the musical rehearsals with you? I could bring the camera. Maybe we could get a bite afterward and brainstorm some more?"

If Ches were here, she'd scream, *THIS IS A DATE. HE'S ASKING YOU ON A DATE.* But thankfully, Ches is not here. Both Ches and Matt have sworn up and down since freshman year that Johnny has a crush on me, and at first it was so hard to believe. For as much as I love *The Grove* and *Kingdom Keeper* and *Buffy* and Harry Potter and *X-Files* and Wonder Woman and Squirrel Girl and X-Men and every other fandom where I've found friendship and hope, one thing I've never found is someone having a crush on a fat girl.

But Johnny is persistent, and now, with our senior year

looming ahead of us, I can't help but think they're right. It's nice to be wanted, but what's really hard is not knowing what *you* want.

"Let me check my schedule with the shelter," I finally say, giving the most noncommittal non-answer I can manage.

Hanging out with Johnny feels like the highway to normal town, which is just what I need. But thinking back to Saturday, when I came face-to-face with Dakota, her grinning, and me typing my number into her phone, I can't help but wonder: maybe what I need isn't always what I want.

 **5**

After school, Ches and Matt drop me off at the shelter, where Dr. Bryner is shouting at the printer.

"Work! You have one job! One job! I don't get to wake up in the morning and not do my job." She smacks the thing with an open palm and the paper feeder falls off.

The bell above the door jingles as the door shuts behind me.

"Faith!" Dr. Bryner says, her expression a cross between embarrassment and relief. "I . . . am having a disagreement with our printer, as you can see."

I laugh quietly to myself as I dump my bag under the front desk.

"Laugh all you want," she says. "Mark my words. There will come a day when a considerably younger person walks in on you abusing a piece of office equipment."

"Okay, okay," I say. "Let me take a look." I read the error

message and open the top of the printer and yank a crumpled piece of paper out. "Just a jam," I say.

"I tried to—" she starts. "You want to know what? Never mind. I'm a happily married woman with a PhD. I win. Do you hear that, printer? I. Win." Taking a deep breath, Dr. Bryner turns back to me, her face serene now. "Could you please hang up these Missing flyers that came in today and then join me in the back?"

"Sure thing," I say. "Hey, I forgot to ask this weekend, but whatever happened with that dog who came in on Friday? The one that was all rigid."

She lets out a sigh. "Not much. Vitals were fine. The weekend crew kept him on fluids, but he was no worse and no better, so Dr. Gerard from the university came to pick him up today. It was like he was catatonic. We took a picture to keep on file in case any Missing Pet flyers that match come across our desk."

"So what will happen to him?" I ask, unsure I want an answer.

"Well, I'm sure Dr. Gerard will run a more extensive panel of tests and bloodwork, but if they can't do anything . . . they can't do anything."

She doesn't have to say another word. I know just what she means.

As I shuffle through the papers, I'm absolutely stunned by how many pets went missing over the weekend. And it's not even a holiday! Holidays are a little crazy. People forget to lock a gate or fireworks startle a dog enough to run or a cat to dash out the door or a distant family member unaccustomed to pets leaves the front door ajar. This would be a lot for a holiday weekend.

I take the stapler and begin to work on taking down old flyers of pets whose fate is unknown to me and replacing them with new ones. It's the kind of thing that makes you feel like all the weight of the world is resting on your chest and the only news is bad news and you're not sure when it was, but surely there had to be a time when things weren't so bleak, a time when you could leave your front door unlocked, just like every person over the age of forty has sworn to be true.

About halfway through the missing pet boards, my phone vibrates in my back pocket.

The moment I see who it is, my heart nearly pounds out of my chest. I clutch my phone against my breastbone, trying to remind my body how to breathe normally.

"Hi, Dakota," I say as nonchalantly as possible.

"Hi!" she says. "I didn't think you'd pick up. Aren't you in school or whatever?"

I glance at the clock on the wall. "Uh, no. But I am at the shelter. Just about to go check on Bumble."

"Sorry," she says. "Actually, double sorry. I'm just bad at talking on the phone in general and I totally blanked on school hours. It's been a little while since . . . Margaret helps us get on track for GEDs."

"Oh, right." Suddenly, I feel very, very childish. Dakota is basically an adult. I mean, she is because she's eighteen, but as far as I know, she lives on her own and does adult things, like buy cars and washing machines.

"Anyway," she says. "I was thinking you could come over and check out my place—for Bumble, obviously—and then I could bring you by the new showrunner's office and a few of our set locations. Ya know, give you the grand tour."

It's a good thing she can't see my face, because I'd need someone to lift my jaw off the ground. I can't believe she actually called back. It's for Bumble, sure, but I'd convinced myself that our whole interaction was some kind of hallucination. "Well, sure. Of course. Yeah, I would love that."

"This Saturday," she says.

Oh God. I have to wait five whole days.

"I'll text you details," she says. Someone shouts for her in the background. "Be right there!" she calls. "Faith?"

"Yeah."

"I'm really looking forward to seeing you again."

"I can't wait," I say. "To see you again. And for the text." I pull the phone away from my ear and silently scream.

"Cool," she says. "Give Bumble some love for me."

I hang up and do a quick little celebratory dance, letting my feet skim the floor a little longer than is natural.

 **6**

The week moves just about as fast as Miss Ella, which is not fast at all. It helps that I've been busy with the shelter. I beg Matt and Ches to hang out on Friday night, thinking we could see a movie and then spend the night at Matt's.

I decide to walk to Matt's and take mostly alleyways, letting myself take a few shortcuts by flying over a fence or two. I haven't really let myself fly. Most of the flying I've done since coming home from the Harbinger Foundation has been an exaggerated leap or jump or brief soaring before tumbling back to the ground.

It's so unusual for my body to instinctually know how to do something, and yet I don't quite know how to control it. It's like currents of electricity constantly buzzing beneath the surface of my skin, and anytime my mood changes or I'm startled, the currents react too.

Just before I cross the block to Matt's street, I double

back to an alleyway and give myself a running start, pushing myself off as hard as I can.

I soar, my arms spanning out like wings as I spin through the air. The crisp autumn air runs through my veins and I let out a shriek as I tilt my body forward and down, tumbling back to the ground below. I stand up and shake the gravel off my jeans.

"Maybe I'll even land on my feet next time," I mutter, rubbing a hand over my shoulder, which took the brunt of my landing.

At Matt's house, his mom, Mrs. Delgado, answers the front door. Mrs. Delgado is the kind of mom you only see on TV. She's always in her apron with something cooking in the oven, inviting anyone with a heartbeat to stay for dinner. Today is no different. The short woman with round hips, narrow shoulders, and shoulder-length, wavy curls stands in the entryway in jeans and a blouse with a yellow apron. "Faith!" she croons, reaching for my hair and smoothing it for me. "Did you walk through a wind tunnel to get here?"

I chuckle. Um, sort of. "Yeah. It's pretty windy out there tonight."

She clicks her tongue. "Matt and Ches are upstairs."

I race upstairs and find Matt rolling around on the carpet of his bedroom while Ches sits with her legs crossed, encircled by color-coded note cards organized into piles.

"Faith!" he moans. "Thank God you're here! She's making us study. On a Friday!"

Ches looks to me and shrugs. "What else were we going to do? Fart around and watch movies?"

"Um, yes," says Matt. "That's exactly what we were going to do."

They both look to me. Lucky me, the tiebreaker.

"Maybe we could study for a little while and then watch some scary movies or something?" I ask.

Ches turns the page of her notebook to her handwritten review for physics, the one class all three of us share. "I made note cards. We could start there." She chews on the cuticle around her thumbnail and takes a big gulp of the energy drink she brought with her.

Matt looks to me, desperation in his eyes.

I shrug.

Do something, he mouths to me.

"Ches," I say her name sweetly as I try again, "how about we study for a bit and then blow off some steam with a scary movie? We'll even try one of your spooky games."

Matt throws his head backward. Despite his deep, unwavering love for Ches, the boy hates scary movies and is way too superstitious to dabble with her tarot cards or witchy antics.

I throw up my arms. *What?* I mouth back to him. If he wants her to ease up on studying, our best shot at convincing her is with something she loves to do.

Ches stills for a moment and spins to face us. "Two hours," she says. "We have to make it through the review and the flash cards."

"Got it," I say.

"And light as a feather, stiff as a board," she says.

"Not it," says Matt.

"Fine," I say. "Whatever."

Mrs. Delgado is so impressed to see us studying on a Friday night that she makes us Rice Krispies treats with Fruity Pebbles mixed in. The first time I spent the night here after moving to Grandma Lou's after Mom and Dad's accident, I woke up crying and begged to go home. Grandma Lou sleeps about as heavy as a brick, so Mrs. Delgado had no luck calling her. Instead, she stayed up with me all night and we made Fruity Pebbles Rice Krispies treats. I've had a soft spot for Mrs. Delgado ever since.

"So," Matt says, elbowing me as Ches alphabetizes the flash cards we've already gone through. "You excited about your day with Dakota mother-freaking Ash tomorrow?"

When I told Matt over lunch that I was not only going to Dakota's house but visiting the production offices and set, his head nearly exploded. And then after he had a moment to process, he playfully asked if he could be my plus-one. Then I had to very awkwardly explain to him that this didn't really feel like a plus-one situation, but that if something else came up, I'd totally ask to bring him. Since then, he's only teased me about my plans with Dakota once or twice, but I know he's jealous. I feel bad. I wish I could take him with me. And yet, I'm also relieved to have something that's just for me. It still feels weird to not be able to properly freak out about this with him, but I definitely don't want to gloat.

Ches looks up. "That Dakota girl?" she says. "She was super gay for you. I could sense it."

Both Ches and Matt look to me, waiting for me to respond. My best friends are amazing, wonderful people who seem to know exactly who they are and exactly who they like. For me, though, figuring out what exactly my sexual orientation is has felt a little more abstract. One thing I know for sure is I feel a spark with Johnny *and* Dakota. Very different kinds of sparks.

"She's just charming," I finally say. "That's her job, after all. She's America's heartthrob, for goodness' sake!"

Ches snorts. "All right, back to work."

I'm a very good pupil. Honestly, I'll do anything not to bring up Dakota again—for a multitude of reasons. And Matt is well behaved too. Until his phone starts to buzz and whoever he's messaging back and forth is sending him into fits of giggles.

I can feel Ches's agitation growing as I ask her Physics questions. I can practically see her brain misfiring every time Matt chuckles or his phone pings. Then he hits play on a video of a chicken clucking and a woman yelling at it. He turns down the volume, but it's still so distracting.

Ches reaches over and rips the cards out of my hands

before throwing them in Matt's lap. "I'm going to get some fresh air."

Matt stops laughing abruptly as he notices the cards in his lap and Ches slamming his bedroom door behind her before trotting down the stairs.

He looks to me and shrugs. "What?"

"You know what," I tell him.

"Faaaaaith, it's a Friday night. What are we even doing?"

"Not exactly how I'd planned on spending Friday night either, but we promised Ches."

He rolls his eyes. Matt hasn't done a great job of taking Ches and her efforts to turn her grades around very seriously. Even though this is just one instance of him being distracted on his phone, I know it's a lot more to Ches.

"Alphabetize those while I go check on her?"

"Fine."

I walk out into the hall to find that Mrs. Delgado has already gone to bed and downstairs Mr. Delgado is asleep in his recliner. I check out front, but Ches isn't there, so I go around back and find her swinging in Matt's old swing set. Of the three of us, she's definitely the smallest, and still she looks like a giant compared to the playground equipment.

"You want some company?" I ask.

She doesn't answer, which is as good as an invitation to me.

I climb to the top of the slide, which isn't much of a climb at all, and sit there with my legs dangling over the side.

"He was just really excited for the weekend, ya know? I don't think he meant to be rude."

She pumps her legs into the air, clad in forest-green leggings and her Docs. She wears a T-shirt she cut into an oversize crop top that says Witch Please. "He doesn't get it," she says. "I've known him my whole life and he doesn't fucking get it."

"Get what?" I ask. "You can talk to me, Ches."

"You're smart," she tells me. "Like, really naturally smart. I know life hasn't been peaches for you, Faith." She turns to me, nothing but earnest. "I really do, but you're going to land on your feet."

I try not to laugh. If only she knew. Landing is the hardest part, honestly.

"This all comes so easy to you. You went to freaking journalism camp! You're on the newspaper. You don't have to study. And you run a badass blog with legions of fans. And Matt! He charms everybody, and his parents will always be his safety net."

"You're smart too, Ches." I wish I could tell her that she has a safety net too, but the truth is, no matter how great Ches's mom and brothers are, none of them have the means to put her through school or to bail her out if things ever get rocky. Grandma Lou might not have much, but it's more than Ches has to fall back on.

A gust of chilling wind sweeps through the Delgados' backyard. Ches sniffs and pulls the long sleeve of her flannel shirt over her fist to wipe her nose. It's late September and in a matter of a few weeks, we Minnesotans are clinging to our last memories of summer as we find ourselves hunkering down for winter hibernation.

"I mean, look at all this." She motions around to Matt's playground set, his tree house, and this whole neighborhood, which is one of the newest developments in all of Glenwood. "I love Matt. I love him so much. But sometimes things are so easy for him. Christ, Faith. His parents got him a car for his sixteenth birthday. Not even a used one, and with a big red bow just like the car commercials."

I laugh. "And then Matt traded the car out for the color he actually wanted." Maybe that sounds spoiled of him, but there was never a moment when Matt wasn't grateful. He's just never been scared to ask for exactly what he wanted. I remember him saying, *Why should they spend all that money and not get the right color?*

She shakes her head, laughing now too. "Trust me, we've all gotten plenty of use out of that car."

It's true. Matt even let Ches use it as a make-out spot when she had instant chemistry with a girl at an away football game I got stuck covering for the paper last fall.

"But at the end of the day, Faith, I don't have anyone footing my bill. I gotta make it on financial aid and scholarships or I won't make it at all."

The screen door leading to the house swings open with a squeak. The light from the kitchen glows behind Matt, turning him into a silhouette. "Permission to come aboard?" he asks.

I look to Ches and she nods, so I say, "Get your ass out here, Delgado."

Matt takes the swing next to Ches and the rusted playground equipment creaks. This thing was definitely not built to sustain the weight of three fully grown teenagers.

"Break beneath my fat ass!" Matt yells at the swing set. "I dare you!"

The three of us titter with laughter until silence wins out and all eyes are on Matt. "I know why schoolwork is important to you," he says. The chains of his swing twist above him as he turns to Ches. "I'm sorry. I was being a dope. Just texting some guy. No big."

She kicks at the dirt beneath her with the toe of her boot. "It's cool," she says. "Maybe we should call it a night with the studying!"

Matt shrieks with delight and then claps a hand over his mouth. "Sorry."

Ches shoves his shoulder. "Come on. Let's go inside."

Matt stands and offers his arm to Ches, while I slide the short length down the slide and then loop my arm through his other arm. We walk, the three of us a human shield, completely invincible to the cruel, dark world around us. Flying isn't what makes me special. This is. This connection with the people I love most is what I'll fight for to the day I die.

This is what fuels me. Not some greedy foundation or Peter Stanchek or anyone else.

Inside, we pile up in Matt's oversize beanbags with cheddar popcorn and a jar of mini dill pickles (Ches's favorite) to watch *Halloween III* (her choice) as she explains all the "nuances" and behind-the-scenes drama of the Halloween franchise.

Afterward, we live up to our promise to play light as a feather, stiff as a board with her.

"I'll do the lifting," says Matt. "But I'm not down with being in, like, some kind of state and opening myself to"— he throws his hands around, like we're in the midst of some serious spirits—"whatever is out there."

Ches looks to me, and I begin to stutter. "O-oh, Ches, come on. You know I don't know what the hell I'm doing."

She twists her hands together in a desperate sort of way. "Pleeeeeeease."

I push the beanbag out of the way and lie down. "Fine. Fine."

Ches lights a few candles she retrieved from Mrs. Delgado's pantry. "For ambience," she explains. "Faith, cross your arms over your chest."

Matt exhales loudly. "Let's get this over with."

"Okay," says Ches. "Take two fingers on each hand and slide them under . . . right here," she says, sliding two fingers under my hips and two more under my arm.

Matt does the same.

"We're going to start chanting, 'Light as a feather, stiff as a board,' but it's less about the chant and more about concentration," she says.

"What about me?" I ask. "Do I chant?"

Ches rocks back on her knees. "Hmm." I've stumped her. "Well, I guess you can, but for you it's more about relaxing your body and opening yourself up to cosmic energy. So I guess just do whatever you're comfortable with."

I nod and close my eyes.

"Ready?" Ches asks.

"Let the demonic possession in my childhood bedroom begin," Matt says.

"Light as a feather, stiff as a board," they chant, rocky at first and then finding their rhythm in unison. "Light as a feather, stiff as a board, light as a feather, stiff as a board."

I chant along with them quietly, like when the music is so loud that you just sing along because no one can hear you, and if no one can hear you, there's nothing to be embarrassed about.

And then I start to feel it. I'm still firmly planted on the floor, but I feel the temptation to take flight quaking in my bones. Energy thrums from the tips of my fingers to the tips of my toes, and I have to really focus in on the weight of my body, grounding myself.

"Light as a feather, stiff as—"

"It's not working," says Ches, breaking the chant.

Heaviness returns to my body as quickly as flipping a switch. My eyes shoot open.

It was working, I almost say.

"Damn it," she says. "I just . . . I can't do anything right! Why can't this one thing that I love so damn much just work for me?"

"Let's try it again," I say. I cross my arms over my chest. "Come on." I grin up at her. "For science."

"You heard her," says Matt.

The three of us reassume our positions.

"Light as a feather, stiff as a board, light as a feather, stiff as a board, light as a feather, stiff as a board."

My voice joins theirs, but this time I'm more confident. Louder. All three of us are.

With my eyes closed, I let out a deeply held sigh. My mind quiets as I let my body take over. The electricity rippling through me flickers and flickers until something in me sparks and I begin to float. No, I begin to fly.

It's an inch. And then two. And then three. This is the most control I've felt over my body in months.

"HOLY. SHIT," Matt says.

It takes everything I've got not to open my eyes and not to fly right out the window. I wish I could share this one thing with them, and even though no one explicitly told me not to, there's no easy way to tell my friends that a) super-powers are real, and b) I have one. It's not like we know every little thing about each other, but this secret feels huge enough to span an ocean.

Ches gasps. "Oh my goddess. Faith, are you okay?" I can hear the elation in her voice, even though she's trying to remain in control of the situation.

My heart swells, thinking about how she'll probably remember this moment of magic for the rest of her life. I know it's technically a lie, but Ches needs this. She needs this little win.

And maybe I need it too. But this is for her, I remind myself.

Slowly, I ease myself back onto the carpet, their fingertips still pressed against me, and open my eyes.

It's quiet for a moment as they pull back from me, each of us stunned.

Ches claps her hands together with glee and Matt rushes to turn on the lights and blow out the candles. "I think I need to chug some holy water."

I touch a hand to Ches's knee. "You're one badass witch."

7

Grandma Lou agreed to let me take the car for the day and said that Miss Ella owed her a favor in case she needed a ride anywhere.

I head over to Dakota's place, a small two-bedroom house near the center of town. The whole street is lined with seventy-five-year-old bungalows that have been rehabilitated and are painted all sorts of bright colors. There isn't really any part of Glenwood that's hip, but if there were, this would be it.

After parking beside Dakota's bright white Tesla, I lift my fist to knock on the door, but Dakota's already there, swinging the door open.

She grins and gives me a one-armed side hug. "I saw you pull up. Come on in!"

I step inside to find that, like her car, the interior of Dakota's home is all white. "Wow, this place is really . . . white."

"I . . . yeah. I didn't really grow up in the brightest place, so something about crisp white makes me feel calm."

"Should I take my shoes off?" I ask, half-joking.

"Oh, no, no. Just because I like white furniture doesn't mean I'm good at keeping it that way. You should've seen the cleaning bender I went on before you got here."

I open the folder I've been holding to my chest with her application for Bumble. "I guess we should get this part over with."

"Oh, yeah," she says.

Somehow being around Dakota in my official capacity as a shelter intern is less complicated than just being around her as plain old Faith, so armed with my folder and pen, it's easier than I expected to take command.

I check out the backyard, which has a brand-new fence tall enough so that Bumble won't be able to jump it, and I talk to Dakota about how all her beautiful furniture might not stay so beautiful, but she's not at all bothered by that. I ask her where Bumble will sleep, and Dakota tells me that Bumble will sleep in her bed or in the many dog beds she plans on buying. I also sit down and talk through diet options for Bumble and possible health issues she should be on the lookout for down the road. We even talk about what will happen when Dakota travels or goes back to California, where she and most of the cast live when they aren't on location, and Dakota assures me again and again that she's in this for the long haul.

"Well," I finally say as I'm signing off on the home visit paperwork, the two of us seated about half a cushion apart on her cozy sofa, "I think Bumble will be very happy with you, and all your references checked out. So if you'll have her, she's all yours."

Dakota beams and reaches to hug me, but then stops. "Are you a hugger? Can I hug you? I'm so excited!"

I laugh. "Definitely a hugger!"

She squeezes me tight. "Thank you, Faith. I'm so excited to call Bumble family."

"And I'm sure your family will love her too!" The words are out of my mouth before I can stop them. No one in the *Grove* fandom or the media in general know much about Dakota's family, because she goes to great lengths to make it very clear that her family is not up for discussion.

"I'm sorry," I blurt. "I know family is a sensitive subject."

She waves me off with a gentle eye roll. "Don't worry about it. Seriously. I just don't like to make my family public business or whatever."

"Oh, I totally get it. I've got some family stuff too that I don't like to talk about much, and . . . well, I can't imagine the whole world thinking that just because you're on TV, that gives them the right to know all sorts of private information about you."

She leans back, one arm propped against the back of the couch, and looks up at me, her eyes hooded and her swoop of bangs adding another layer of protection. "I don't mind talking about them with friends." She pauses. "And I'd like to think of you as a friend."

My breath hitches. "I'd like that too."

Pushing a hand through her hair, she squeezes her eyes shut for a moment. I can see then all the reasons why she's a good actor. It's not that I'm feeling duped or manipulated, but it's the way she truly speaks with her whole body. "My story isn't special. I know it's not. I grew up in a forgotten suburb of Chicago. My mom loved me, but not as much as she loved getting high, and my dad . . . well, who knows who the hell he is? I've got a sister. Different dad. She lives with her grandma. She's got a good life, and I help out with, like, stuff. But the truth is I was barely scraping by when Margaret Toliver met me. Shit, *discovered* me. She plucked me out of obscurity. She saw something in me no one else had before."

I want to ask her how and where and when. I want to know everything. I'm greedy and I want to gobble up every little detail of her life. I want to feel like I've known her my whole life.

"My parents died," I blurt, like I've got to somehow return the family trauma secret.

She places a gentle hand on my shoulder. "Oh, Faith. Oh, I'm so sorry."

I nod. Her hand burns through my T-shirt, warming me. "School had just started and we were driving to some con over the weekend. Mom and Dad were going as Mario and Luigi and I was going to be Princess Peach. We'd worked on our costumes all summer, staying up late at night with our hot glue guns." The memory of us all out in the garage with a box fan while Mom ran inside to fetch Popsicles. The whole street was dark, but our little garage burned bright.

"That sounds amazing," Dakota says. "You'd make a really good Princess Peach."

"My parents let me wear my costume in the car. I never wanted to take it off. I even wanted to sleep in it." I shrug, trying to swallow back any tears. It's been so long that it's almost easy for the memory of it all to feel like a movie—something I clearly know and remember, but not an experience I can feel and inhabit. "It was a really bad storm. Dad was pulling off the highway when we hydroplaned. The car flipped and . . . people kept telling me it was instant. I know that's supposed to make me feel better."

She lets this all sink in for a moment, not trying to fill the silence with cooing or some awful nonsense about everything happening for a reason.

Dakota touches her hand to my leg. "I can't imagine what that must feel like. For everything to just change in a moment."

"I guess we both have a few dings and bruises."

Dakota glances up from under her swoop of bangs, giving me a look I've never seen on *The Grove*, one that feels like it's meant for me alone. "Margaret always says the broken have ways of finding each other."

And maybe that's how we heal, by finding one another.

"I think this calls for a field trip." She stands up and tugs at my hand. "We deserve some fun, Faith Herbert."

Dakota's Tesla SUV is pretty much the closest I'll ever get to riding in a spaceship. It even drives itself. The future is here.

The production offices and part of the more permanent set are in the warehouse district, close to Ches's house.

As we pull up, Dakota's excitement builds. She points out different people and waves to a short white guy with a round tummy, blue hair, and a lip ring who she explains is Margaret's assistant.

The warehouse doors are open, with two huge trucks backed up to the bay. There are people everywhere. Not Hollywood-looking people, but the kind of people who wear cargo pants because they actually need the pockets. They shout at each other and run up to help lift things without being prompted, while cracking jokes.

"The cavalry has arrived," says Dakota.

"Wow."

She nods, recognizing my awe. "Takes a lot of people to pull this thing off. Trust me," she says, "even the worst TV shows take an army."

Suddenly my appreciation for every TV show and movie I've ever seen takes on a whole new level.

She guides me in through a small side door that has—
"Oh my God! '*The Grove* Production Offices'!" I read it off
the decal on the door. Immediately my cheeks flush red.
"Sorry," I say. "Fangirl moment."

Dakota yanks my phone out of my hand. "Passcode," she
demands. I reach over and punch in my four-digit code and
she pulls up the camera and snaps a quick selfie of us with
the production office sign behind us. "It's real now," she
says. "It's been selfied."

I follow Dakota, pretty much floating, as she takes us
down a narrow hallway lined with glass doors leading to
bland offices. Dakota opens the door with her name on it
and the title *Assistant Producer*. The only thing inside beyond
the desk stacked with papers and a mini-fridge is a life-size
cardboard cutout of herself from last season's promo photo
shoot. The cutout has a comical twirling mustache inked on
her face and a huge olive-green puffer jacket draped over the
shoulders.

"I make a very good coat hanger," Dakota explains.

"No lies detected," I respond.

"But I spend most of my time in my trailer. I'll save that
for the end of the tour."

Two doors down, we pass Margaret Toliver's name, and
I suck in a breath through my teeth.

"Now she," Dakota says, "is totally worth fangirling
over. But she's not in today. Next time," she promises.

"I don't think I could handle a set visit *and*

MarTo"—Margaret's internet shorthand name—"in one day."

We pass through a makeshift conference room/what appears to be a former lunchroom to the open warehouse, where diorama-like sets I know so well are configured like little matchbox scenes.

"Lots of shows still film on lots in LA," Dakota explains. "But Margaret swears Hollywood kills her creative energy. She likes being in the thick of it."

"The thick of what?" I ask.

Dakota shrugs. "Middle America. Why work so hard to isolate yourself from the audience you're trying to serve?"

"That's so smart." I can't hide the awe in my voice.

"Can't take credit for that one. Just another Toliverism gem."

Dakota walks me through each of the main five characters' bedrooms. There's Parker, the volleyball jock from a blue-collar family who lives in a well-kept but modest house. Greta, the rich girl who just wants to go to art school, lives in a huge mansion, is closer to her childhood nanny than either of her parents, and has an on-again, off-again relationship with Reese, who's played by Dakota. Reese lives with her financial adviser dad in a lush town house. Neither of them are over the death of her mother, and they communicate by slamming doors. Reese is also a bit of a playgirl, which the media has also framed Dakota to be. Then there's Cody, Greta's twin brother and the golden boy who's never good enough. Lastly is Reese's best friend, Dylon, the rehabilitated bad boy who lives above the motorcycle shop where he works.

"We've got each room set up in here, but we'll be using spots around town for exterior shots like movie theaters and shops and for places like Dylon's new shop."

"Since the old one burned down last season," I say.

It's like I'm standing in the middle of a dollhouse where the fourth wall has been entirely removed. "This is incredible. What's up there?" I point to a whole other floor that probably once housed supervisor offices so that whoever ran this factory could check out the whole place with just a quick glance.

"Oh, that's nothing right now," Dakota says. "We'll probably rotate a few sets up there. Maybe for some hospital scenes or something."

"Hospital scenes?" I ask with a raised eyebrow. "Was that a . . . spoiler?"

"Nice try!" she says. "I'm a seasoned pro. If I didn't spoil Parker's faux death last season, there's no chance I'm spoiling what we've got in store for next season. Besides, you wouldn't try to get me in any trouble, would you, Faith?"

I laugh nervously, because as much as I'm a purist and hate spoilers, last week, before I met Dakota, I would have jumped at the chance of getting an itty-bitty spoiler of next season. But something that feels like guilt settles in the pit of my stomach. I would never write about all this stuff Dakota is showing me on *Faithfully Yours*, but maybe . . . I don't know. Maybe it was wrong of me not to at least tell her who I am. Surely she's at least heard of my blog. The official *Grove* social media accounts share my recaps all the time. Dakota even posted one of my memes on her Instagram once. Plus, if I don't tell her soon and she finds out later, all of this could blow up into a much bigger deal than it is.

Dakota leads me past the prop department, where a white woman about my size with wild curly hair wearing nothing but overalls and a fluorescent yellow sports bra sits on the floor surrounded by papers organized like a crop circle. "Corissa!" Dakota shouts. "This is my new friend, Faith." Dakota turns to me. "Corissa is a good person to know. You make nice with Corissa and Doug over at craft services and your life will be at least ten percent better for it."

"Hi, New Friend Faith!" She doesn't even look up.

"Nice to meet you!" I call back.

She glances up to me then. "Oh, hey, you gotta tell me where a girl can find some decent plus-size clothes in this town! It's like a fashion desert out here."

I laugh. "That's one way of putting it. There are a few good places in the Twin Cities," I tell her. "Even a really cool resale shop called Cake."

"Mmmm," she says. "My kind of store. Come hang out with me some time, New Friend Faith."

"Uh, um, yeah. Grool. I mean, great. Or cool."

She laughs, sliding a pencil behind her ear and returning to her papers. "Grool."

"Bye," I say so quietly only I can hear myself. "She's so cool," I tell Dakota as she leads me outside.

"Yeah," she says. "And hot." She holds her hand to her heart.

Something in me hisses. Jealousy? Is that jealousy?

"Sadly, taken, though," Dakota adds.

I press my lips together to keep my smile hidden.

But wait. She said Corissa was hot. And yeah, Corissa totally was hot. I've never actually heard someone describe a person who looks like me or Corissa as hot before, though, and so that has me wondering if maybe . . . to someone out there . . . I'm hot too.

Out in the field behind the warehouse is a circle of trailers. All that's missing is a campfire at the center.

Dakota's name is on her trailer in glittering gold letters with a star below, and inside the star, *Reese* is spelled out in cutouts.

"And this," Dakota says, "is home sweet home."

Inside is a makeup chair, a couch, a flat-screen TV, and a built-in kitchen table beside a counter with a sink and microwave.

We both plop down on the couch with fizzy waters from the mini-fridge.

Dakota holds her arms out. "Well, what'd you think? Everything you ever dreamed of?"

My heart flutters. "Everything and more. I'm just amazed by all the people and how they seem like one big happy—"

"Family," Dakota finishes. "That's the best part, I think. We yell. We fight. We cry. We're our best and worst selves. But we're family."

Something about the way she says it causes a lump in my throat. "Family," I whisper. I've got Grandma Lou and of course Ches and Matt, but there will always be a Mom-and-Dad-shaped hole in my heart.

"Wait till I bring you on set when we're actually shooting. I don't know if your fangirl heart will be able to handle it."

"I have to confess something," I say, the lump in my throat building into tears. I feel so stupid. Why am I even tearing up?

Dakota takes my drink and places it next to hers on the coffee table and then turns her whole body toward me. "Faith, what is it? Is everything okay?"

"There's something I haven't told you about me," I tell her.

Her expression darkens a little. Oh no. This . . . this was a mistake.

I close my eyes, trying to center myself in the same way I did when I dove off the roof of the vet clinic the other day.

"I'm Faith. That's still me. But I'm also the person behind *Faithfully Yours*. I don't know if you've heard of it. It's like a Grover fan blog, but not like gossipy. Mostly recaps and . . ." I can feel myself rambling. "And I just . . . please know I would never actually share anything that you've showed me today . . . or, oh my gosh, anything you've told me about your family. That goes in the vault, Dakota. You have to know that."

She says nothing as she runs a finger over the tear in her jeans.

"Dakota, I'm so sorry. I should've said something. That was wildly unethical of me." Mrs. Raburn would kill me if she knew I'd done something so awful like this. I should go. I begin to stand. "And I just . . . I understand if you never want to see me again. I can find my own way back to your house to get my—"

Dakota takes my hand, tethering me to the couch. "I know." She laughs and hides her face with her other hand. "Oh man. This is embarrassing."

"Huh? I mean, yes, I am mortified, but you have nothing to be embarrassed about."

Dakota shakes her head. "I have a confession too, Faith." I lean back into the couch.

"Okay . . ."

"I guess you could say I'm a fan of your work."

 **8**

"It started out with me reading your recaps of old episodes when Margaret hired me. One of the PAs actually mentioned *Faithfully Yours* to me."

"Oh!" My whole body warms with pride, and I feel a prickling in my chest like I could cry from relief or joy or something.

"And then . . . I don't know. You were just so charming and funny. You seemed to *get* the show on a deeper level, so I did some sleuthing. . . . God, this is going to make me sound like such a stalker."

Please stalk me, Dakota Ash, I nearly blurt. But then I slap my own internal hand. Bad, Faith. Stalking = bad. But there's something about knowing she thought of me or—heck!—that she knew I existed in the first place. It evens the playing field a little.

She shakes her head. "And then I found a whole Reddit

board dedicated to figuring out who you are, and before you know it, I'd put some dots together."

I sit there silently, a slow smile overtaking me.

"I didn't go to the fair knowing you'd be there. I saw Bumble independently. And then there you were. Barreling toward me."

"There I was." I giggle. "Being tugged along by a sixty-pound mutt." Something about rehashing the first time we met makes me feel like we're old friends with a long, storied history between us.

"So I guess this makes us even," she says.

In a way, she's right. Something about knowing this also makes me feel like I'm on even ground with her, helps me feel a little more at ease.

As we drive back to Dakota's house, we sail through Glenwood with the windows down and the Tesla's seat heaters on, protecting us from the chill without saving us from it entirely.

Even getting into Grandma Lou's car doesn't return me back to reality. New friendship always makes my heart thud. Sometimes I feel things so intensely, it scares me. It's like showing up to a costume party and finding out you're the only one who actually wore a costume. But Dakota seems like she's all-or-nothing too, and something about it almost feels a little dangerous.

By the time I get home, it's dark enough that Grandma

Lou should already be cozied into her recliner with only a lamp on as she shouts the answers to *Jeopardy!* reruns she's seen so many times, she's got them memorized.

But when I pull into the driveway, nearly every light in the house is on, a warm glow spilling out into the street.

I walk in and the smell of cigarettes hits me like it did after I came back this summer, but then the scent was stale and old, like it'd been there all along and I'd just gotten used to it over time. This smell is fresher, more recent.

I drop my keys on the coffee table and leave my coat on the hook by the door.

"Grandma Lou?" I call.

"In here!"

In the kitchen, I find my grandmother standing at the sink with a cigarette hanging from between two fingers as she sprays down a pan with the other hand.

"Grandma Lou?" I ask again, and some dormant part of me is scared she's going to turn around to reveal herself to be some kind of creature who's been living inside my grandmother's body for months, my grandma Lou long gone. "Grandma Lou!" I shout.

She whirls around then, surprised, as she drops the spray nozzle in the sink. "Oh, Faith," she says. "You startled me."

I see then that she's wearing her old uniform, the one she wore five days a week for thirty-three years when she worked the assembly line at SuzyCakes, a packaged snack cake company almost as old as she is.

Confusion tugs at me. What is she doing? Maybe she was just stressed and needed a cigarette. Maybe she's having a tough time making ends meet and she's gone back to working a few hours a week. It could be that she just wanted to try on her old uniform to see if it fit, like people do with wedding dresses. Heck, I even do it with old Halloween costumes.

"I wasn't expecting you, baby."

Something about the melody in her voice makes me sick with terror, like I'm in one of Ches's horror movies.

I glance at the clock on the wall. Ten o'clock. I guess I'm normally out later on weekends with Ches and Matt.

Her brow furrows for a moment as she focuses in on me, and then her whole face relaxes as she shakes her head. She looks down at the cigarette in her hand, like it's a loaded gun.

"Here," I say, taking it from her and stubbing it out in the sink. "It's been a long day. What do you say we get some rest?"

She nods to herself. "A long day."

I guide her upstairs with a hand hovering behind her.

As I lie in bed that night, I try as best I can to redirect my brain and remind myself of what an incredible day I had with Dakota and how Matt is going to freak out when I tell him all about visiting the set. Maybe I can even bring him with me next time.

But tonight's events with Grandma Lou linger like a fog. I feel it in the pit of my stomach, something I can sense, but I'm not brave enough to speak it out loud—scared that if I do, it might just be true.

9

I sit in the courtyard on Monday at lunchtime with Ches and Matt. Ches sits beside me, leaning on my shoulder as she mumbles to herself between flash cards.

Matt points at me with a Twizzler. "Okay, one more time. From the top."

I've told Matt about my set visit two times already—once over the phone on Sunday, once on the way to school, and again just now. I can't blame him, though. If the same thing had happened to him, I'd want to hear every detail over and over again until I'd absorbed it all into my own memory.

His excitement at the thought of being so few degrees of separation from the cast of *The Grove* outweighs his jealousy from last week.

My phone buzzes and I see an image of Homer Simpson shrinking back into green bushes. Below the image, white text reads: *season 13 cliff-hanger drops and MarTo be like:*

I giggle and Ches peers over my shoulder. "Oh, so Dakota's sending memes now?"

"Let me see!" says Matt.

I oblige him, and he just shakes his head. "What is your life?"

My phone vibrates again.

DAKOTA: Are you much of a texter? I'm a chronic
texter. Stop me if it's too much.

ME: I'm a serious texter, but maybe we should have a
safe word?

She sends me a picture of a car-wash sign a few blocks from her house. The sign is bright blue and reads *Scrub-a-Dub*.

ME: Scrub-a-Dub?

DAKOTA: Perfect. I can't imagine invoking it, but just in
case I over-meme you.

ME: I have a very high meme threshold.

DAKOTA: I guess I should test that out.

I slide the phone into my back pocket, Ches shifting beside me. My cheeks ache from smiling so hard.

"Wow," mumbles Ches. "Someone's crushin' hard."

"Okay," I say to Matt. "So on Saturday afternoon, I went over to her house. The furniture and everything inside was all—"

"White," Matt says. "So chic."

A gust of wind blows through the trees, shaking the

first few leaves of fall free. I continue on, telling Matt the whole story for the third time, and he's the perfect audience, squealing and shrieking in all the right places. Even Ches puts her flash cards down to listen.

Dakota and I text back and forth regularly over the next few weeks, finding funny videos and memes to share, and when those run out, she shares frustrations about next season's script and she even asks about school, which seems trivial in comparison.

On Thursday, as I'm sitting in journalism, my phone buzzes.

DAKOTA: Big plans for Saturday night?

Oh, I type back, just saving the world. I smirk. I wish.

DAKOTA: Interested in taking a break from life as a superhero for a night?

As my fingers hover above the screen, trying to find clever enough words, she sends another text.

DAKOTA: Season twenty-one kickoff party is at some club in Minneapolis.

DAKOTA: I can put you on the list if you want to go.

UM YES, I almost shout while everyone else works quietly beside me. I instantly think of Matt. It's no set visit, but this might be even cooler. Besides, I'm sure Dakota would love Matt. And Ches! They're by far the cooler, more charming two-thirds of our tripod.

I begin to type, Could I bring my friends Matt and Ches? Matt's a big fan and super funny, and I bet Ches would read your tarot if you wanted.

Then I add, Not at the club. That might be weird. Just in general.

DAKOTA: Okay.

DAKOTA: I'll add them to the list. I'll text you the address on Saturday.

Johnny plops down beside me, and I pull my phone to my chest, buzzing with excitement and a tiny bit of dread. Matt is going to be so excited, but maybe I asked to invite them too soon. I don't want Dakota to think I'm using her.

"Doing secret website things?" Johnny asks. "Texting your secret lover?"

I snort. "What? No."

He grins sheepishly. "Good."

I'm flattered, yet I find myself scooting away from him a bit.

"Your listicle on the play was hilarious," he says.

"Thanks. I didn't really have time to go by a practice because of work."

"It didn't show at all," he assures me.

"Is Faith Hubbard here?" asks a dry voice.

I look up to find Gretchen Sandoval standing in the doorway, her long blond hair scooped into a floppy bun at the top of her head and her short red cheer shorts barely visible under her baggy Glenwood Turkey Trot 5K T-shirt.

She sort of looks like a mess, but in that way only tradition-ally hot girls get away with, which is silly, because I want to show up to school like I just rolled out of bed too. When fat girls do that, they're called slobs. Note to self: Who cares if people call me a slob? I can be a cute slob like Gretchen if I want.

"It's Herbert," I say as I make my way over to her.

"I'm here for my interview," she says without looking up from her phone.

"Hi, Gretchen," Colleen squeaks, standing up from her desk near the door. She turns to me. "She's here for her Senior Spotlight today."

It would have been nice to have time to prepare, I nearly respond in a snippy tone. Instead, I hold back a sigh and say, "I don't have any interviews scheduled for today."

"Oh," Colleen says, "I thought I told you I set this up for today. Mrs. Raburn wanted me to help you so I could learn the ropes."

I glance over to my desk and the epic pile of work I need to get to before the bell rings, and I have to admit I'm a little annoyed that Colleen scheduled this without even checking in first. "I'm sorry, but I just have way too much going on right now. Could we reschedule you, Gretchen?"

Gretchen huffs and crosses her arms over her chest. "Are you serious? I rescheduled winter dance committee for this." She turns to Colleen. "Thanks a lot, dumbass."

I roll my eyes. What a troll.

Gretchen stomps off and Colleen says, "Oh wow, Faith, I'm so sorry."

"It's fine, it's fine, but maybe don't schedule me for things without asking first?" I say as sweetly as I can.

She nods feverishly.

I settle in back next to Johnny.

"That was weird," he murmurs.

I sigh. "Is it awful that she drives me nuts?"

"Colleen or Gretchen?"

I let out a low chuckle. "Well, both, I guess."

He clears his throat. "Hey, I was thinking we could go to the tech rehearsal dry run next week to take some photos, and maybe you could do a review in listicle form."

"Sure," I say. "Count me in."

He holds his palm out like it's a notepad and makes a fake check mark with his pointer finger. "Counted."

He's a total nerd. A very cute nerd.

After school, I ride home with Matt and pick up Grandma Lou's car before driving to work. Grandma Lou is lying down and taking a nap, so I leave her a note on the fridge to let her know when I'll be back. Outside, I take the steps two at a time, practically floating to the car.

"You know," Miss Ella shouts from the mailbox as she thumbs through junk mail. "Your grandmother stood me up for cards this morning and then had the nerve to come over and borrow some creamer this afternoon. She didn't even apologize! I've got a bone to pick with the woman."

I roll the car window down as I shut the door behind me. "I'm sorry, Miss Ella. If it means anything to you, she's taking a nap. I'm thinking she's not feeling too good today."

Miss Ella grumbles and waves me off.

At work, Dr. Bryner is huddled in a circle with the morning-shift vet techs, both of whom should be gone by now, leaving just a small window of time that the doctor is here by herself. "I just can't imagine what happened to them." She chews on the cap of her pen. "I guess I can imagine."

"Vigilante assholes," says Marcos, a short guy in royal-blue scrubs.

"They weren't hurting anyone," says Cheryl.

"Who knows?" Dr. Bryner asks. "Maybe those awful developers did something with them."

"With who?" I ask, dropping my bag on the counter.

Dr. Bryner looks up to the ceiling, like the answer to my question is there or like . . . or like she's trying to hold back tears. "The feral dogs at the edge of town, in the woods by Russo's Creek, went missing."

"What?" I ask. "How do we know for sure?"

"Kit goes running over there, and she hasn't seen a dog in two weeks, so I gave Cooper Mills a call. He's the guy over at the humane society who works on the catch-and-release program. He went out there every day for four days. With food even. And nothing. Not even a bark or a yip."

"Maybe they went somewhere? Like for the winter."

Marcos shakes his head. "I've lived in this town for

thirty-five years, and that pack has been a year-round Glenwood staple. Something happened to them."

He grips Dr. Bryner's shoulder and Cheryl gives her a quick hug before the two of them put on their coats and pass the torch to me.

"Are you okay?" I ask Dr. Bryner. I've never seen her so startled before, and it actually freaks me out a little bit.

She nods and then shakes her head. "I've lived here my whole adult life. I know it's ridiculous. We make tough choices every day. We see the best and the worst, but those dogs . . . something about seeing them when I'd go for a walk. They were free. And now they're gone."

I know exactly what she means. Obviously, I love domesticated animals. If Grandma Lou would allow it, I'd have a whole zoo in our house, and someday when I have my own apartment, I will. I usually feel bad for animals I see out on the streets, and I've been known to dedicate hours of my life trying to catch a stray cat, but those dogs had been out there for years and they thrived. Everyone in town had an opinion on them, and most of the horror stories surrounding them were urban legend, but how could they just disappear?

I spend the next few hours cleaning cages and sorting through more missing animal alerts that have come through.

When I get home, Lyla Peterson, the woman who lives at the end of the street with her husband and daughter, is walking down the sidewalk with a stack of papers and a stapler.

I park in the driveway just as she presses her stapler into

the utility pole outside Grandma Lou's house. "Hey, Mrs. Peterson," I say. "Everything okay?"

She sniffles and taps under her eyes with the heel of her palm. "It's Gus-Gus," she says. "We let him outside to do his business this morning and he got out."

"He was in the backyard?" I ask.

"Yes." She hands me a flyer, and on it are three big pictures of Gus-Gus, a floppy Saint Bernard who is adored by the whole street.

"Did he dig out?" I ask. There's no way he got over the fence. They've got a tall and fairly new fence.

"The latch on our gate was open. It was like someone let him out. But why would anyone ever do that?"

"I don't know," I say, my words slowly dripping out as I try to piece this puzzle together in my head. The overstuffed bulletin board at work lingers at the forefront of my brain. "Can I have a few of those?" I ask. "I'll put some up at the shelter and look around the neighborhood."

"Of course," she says, wiping another tear.

"Maybe leave some clothes with your scent on the front porch," I tell her, "so he has an easier time finding his way home." I reach into my bag and jot down a few names on a scrap of paper. "Here. Try these groups online. They're like missing-animal back channels for the whole Twin Cities area."

"Thanks, Faith," she says, taking the paper.

"We'll find Gus-Gus. I swear," I say, offering a promise I know I might not be able to keep.

 **10**

I love a good montage. Makeover, training, whatever. I love them all. Getting ready for this party with Matt would make the ultimate montage, though. He brings over a suitcase full of clothes while Ches sprawls out on my bed, reading us our latest star charts while Matt swatches lipstick colors on her forearm. She came over dressed since she's smaller than Matt and me and can't wear our clothes.

After Matt settles on the perfect navy lipstick for Ches, he and I toss shirts and jeans and skirts back and forth until our wardrobes (his admittedly much better curated than mine) blur together in a pile on the floor.

"I think this is it," I say, twirling in front of the mirror in a glittery black jumpsuit that definitely belongs to Matt. The top is sleeveless and fitted and the cropped wide legs add the perfect amount of volume.

Matt nods in appreciation. "I love you enough to let you wear something I've never even worn before," he tells me.

"Where were you going to wear a disco jumpsuit?" Ches asks.

"To coffee. The grocery store. Target. Does it matter?"

"Oh and hello, ladies!" says Ches, cupping her own boobs.

I look down at the deep V. "Is it too revealing?" I ask, unable to hide the desperation in my voice.

"Only if you think it is," Matt chimes in.

"You're like superhot right now," Ches confirms. "But yeah, what he said."

"Maybe you *want* someone to see a little skin?" Matt asks.

My cheeks flare with heat, and I tip face-first into my bed to hide my reaction.

I've always had a crush on Dakota, but it was just a crush on a famous person. I could fill a book with all the crushes I've had on famous people. I really like having crushes, okay? But this is all too real suddenly. I've had a crush on Johnny for the last few years, and that always felt so much more terrifying than swooning over some random famous person, because Johnny could actually find out how I felt about him. But now that's the case with Dakota too. She's more than just a person on a poster, and whatever this is that I'm feeling for her is electric.

I've tried for the last few weeks to tell myself that it's just the thrill of meeting someone I admire so much, but I think I'm just foolish enough to believe that Dakota has feelings for me too. And that thought alone makes all my feelings for her even more intense.

Ches rolls over on her side next to me and brushes a stray hair from my face as I peer at her from the corner of my eye. "Does it hurt?" she asks, like it might delight her just a little bit. "The crush?"

I prop myself up on my side and Matt wedges in behind Ches. I've never had a girlfriend or a boyfriend, and the only kisses I have under my belt are ones from each of them. We were fourteen, and they were just baffled when I told them I didn't know if I liked girls or boys or both or all. They each volunteered to kiss me, like that might somehow settle it, but that only left me with more questions. The only thing I knew for sure was that I liked kissing but probably not with either of them.

"She's such a big deal. There's no way she could actually like me. Besides, I think what she really needs is a friend. And there's Johnny too. You know I've had it bad for him for ages."

Matt huffs. "Johnny's been putting the moves on you slower than a turtle for the last three years. If he wanted all of that," he says, motioning to my body like it's something to be coveted, "he should have acted by now."

Ches sighs and takes my hand. "He's not wrong. But there's also nothing wrong with taking it slow, I guess."

Matt stands and whips a silk scarf around his neck. "Pfft.

Slow? Dakota's an Italian sports car and Johnny's one of those old-timey unicycles. No competition."

Ches lets him pull her to her feet. "Are you two done playing *America's Next Top Model* or whatever? Can we get this show on the road?"

We trot down the steps and Grandma Lou has the three of us pose for a picture, like we're going to the prom. Even though it's against the laws of being a teenager, none of us protest, because this party is probably a bigger deal than our prom ever will be.

As we drive into downtown Minneapolis, hulking sky-scrapers and fancy hotels stretch over us like the impossible structures they are. We circle the same few blocks over and over, shouting over one another as we hunt for a parking spot. Finally, Ches spots a five-dollar lot that we all agree is our least scary option.

We trudge the few blocks to the Tipsy Toad, and we each groan with exasperation the moment we see a very small but informative sign that reads *Complimentary Valet*.

"Should I go back for my car?" asks Matt. "Do you think it will be safe back there? The parking attendant looked like his brain was made of static."

"I'm sure it'll be fine," says Ches. "Besides, there were way nicer cars to steal in that parking lot."

I shrug. "She's not wrong."

"I'm choosing not to be insulted by that," he says.

We wait in a line of the hippest people I've ever seen gathered in a hundred-mile radius of Glenwood. Sometimes I feel so sequestered in our little suburb that it's easy for me to forget that the Twin Cities can be pretty cool if you know where to look.

With just one person ahead of us in line, I text Dakota to let her know we're here. For a quick moment, my anxiety spikes. What if we're not even on the list? Maybe there was a mistake, or maybe Dakota forgot to add Ches and Matt to the list.

Ches elbows me in the ribs.

"Name," the bouncer demands. I get the feeling it's not the first time he's asked me.

"Faith Herbert," I tell him. "I should have plus two. Ches Palmer and Matt Delgado."

He glances down at his list. "ID," he says.

The three of us flash our ID cards, and he slashes big black *X* marks on the tops of our hands.

"Subtle," Matt grunts as he replaces his ID in his wallet.

"What's up with the *X*s?" I ask.

"We're minors," Ches says. "It's basically a giant neon sign over our head that says, 'No Drinky Drinky.'"

Inside, Matt disappears for a moment and returns with three cups of fizzy water, one for each of us. He raises his clear cup with its thin black stirring straw. "To sobriety!" he says.

"Sobriety!" Ches and I echo.

My phone buzzes in my bra. (Screw absolutely every women's clothing manufacturer that doesn't include pockets in their designs.)

DAKOTA: Come find me by the velvet rope

"Ooh! Come on. Let's go," I tell Matt and Ches.

Matt shrieks with excitement. "Our patron Grover beckons! Exsqueeze you," he barks at a flock of petite girls in short, stretchy dresses.

We weave through the crowd, the music—mostly techno remixes of pop songs—vibrating and strobe lights bouncing off the brick walls of the crumbling industrial building. At the back of the club, in a quieter corner, is a platform of small plush sofas roped off from the rest of the partygoers.

Dakota stands beside a tall bald man, and my heart stops. She wears a crisp, fitted, iridescent maroon suit with no shirt underneath the jacket. Whoa. She looks amazing. Delicious. Can you call people delicious? Is that appropriate? Whatever. I remind my heart to start beating again.

"There you are!" she calls, pulling me to her for an embrace.

As she steps back, she tugs at my wrist, and before I even know what she's doing, she's placed a black plastic band around my wrist that reads *Production Only*.

"Hey!" Dakota shouts over the music to Ches and Matt.

Matt holds out a hand. "We met, sort of. At the fair.

Briefly," he says. "I'm Matt. You have exquisite taste," he says, motioning to her suit.

"And this is Ches," I tell her. "What's this for?" I ask, holding up my wrist.

"That's the VIP band," she tells me, and then looks to Matt and Ches. "I'm sorry. I could only get one."

Then I notice the sign beside the tall bald man. *VIP Access Wristband Required.*

"Oh." I shake my head. "I totally don't need this. Maybe we could all just hang out here by the dance floor for a little while."

Behind me, I can feel Matt and Ches shrinking back.

Dakota's eyes dart around. "I know this is going to sound like I'm just really full of myself, but I really just don't want to go out there and get mobbed by people, ya know? Maybe you could just hang out in the VIP section." She looks to Matt and Ches again. "Just for a little while."

Matt doesn't say anything. It's Ches who finally nudges me forward. "We want to dance anyway," she says, and winks at me. "Text us if you can't find us."

"You two are the best," Dakota calls after them, and tugs my arm. "Thanks, Nigel," she tells the bald man.

We sit down on one of the couches. On the other side of the VIP section is Meredith Souza, who not only plays Parker on *The Grove* but is also Dakota's former flame.

I try not to stare at her, but my brain is having a hard

time fathoming that Meredith looks exactly like she does on-screen. Not a hair is out of place.

Dakota leans over and whispers in my ear, as though she can read my mind. "When you're a robot, it's pretty easy to look that perfect, but trust me, it's not worth being a robot."

I snicker, but I sort of feel a little bad too. Meredith's jutting cheekbones are glistening with highlighter, perfectly blended into her medium-brown complexion. Her hair is formed into long, perfectly sculpted waves, and her black figure-hugging minidress gives way to lanky legs. She's both delicate and severe, but most of all she appears to be incredibly bored. Even though the boy and the girl, neither of whom I recognize, on either side of her are talking her ear off, I don't think she's blinked once. In fact, if you looked closely enough, you might even think that Meredith Souza, America's sweetheart, is actually miserable.

"She looks miserable," I tell Dakota.

"Between you and me," Dakota whispers, "she wanted out of her contract this season. She thinks the show is beneath her."

That causes me to bristle as I recall all the people I saw on set who come together to make this show happen, and on top of that, all the loyal fans who've made Meredith who she is.

Corissa, who I remember from the set, sits down beside us, her loose curls dusting her shoulders and her slinky copper dress hugging her thighs all the way down to her knees.

"Whoa," says Dakota. "You clean up nice."

"You look beautiful," I tell her.

Corissa reaches behind me and checks the tag on my jumpsuit. "This jumpsuit, though. I have to have it!"

I feel myself clam up a little, not wanting her to see whatever size it is that I'm wearing, like it's some big secret that I'm not skinny. It reminds me of a short phase I went through in middle school, where I would cut all the size tags out of my clothes so that I didn't have to be reminded of my size and so that no one would accidentally see the number inside my jeans while I was getting dressed for gym. But what was I trying to hide? It's not like my classmates were looking at me, expecting to find some thin little thing hidden beneath my clothing.

Still, for as far as I've come, Corissa's confidence is so brazen it makes me a little nervous. But in a good way.

Beyond the ropes, a familiar frame parts the crowd. My whole body freezes. I'd recognize that disheveled head of hair anywhere.

Peter Stanchek.

 **11**

I stand up abruptly, like I've just heard a signal on a frequency only I can pick up.

Peter Stanchek. My vision blurs, and I feel like I might lose my balance as it all comes back to me. The procedure. The adrenaline rushing through my body like every drop of blood in my veins was on fire. The days spent wasting away in that cell, thinking I'd never see Grandma Lou or Matt or Ches again.

I'd sat in my cell for nine whole days, before a mousy woman with red-framed eyeglasses came in and explained the procedure to me. Nine whole days without natural light or even the sound of anyone calling me by my name instead of a number. I couldn't see much from the vantage point of my room, but from what I could tell, they were working their way down the hallway to me, and once other kids left their rooms, they rarely came back. The sight of their empty rooms chilled me as I was wheeled down to the lab.

I remember the feeling of the cold metal table along my spine as I lay there in the lab with electrodes attached to my head and chest. Toyo Harada, who I'd only briefly seen on my first day, was the man in charge.

He stood in the far corner of the room, talking to Peter. The sight of Peter stung. When we'd first met at the mall, he was boyish and funny, but ever since we'd arrived here, he'd barely even looked at me. Never mind speaking to me. Peter, in jeans and a ratty old Cubs T-shirt, was part of the Harbinger Foundation, but he didn't wear a uniform and he didn't cower at a mere glance from Harada. I didn't know if I should fear him or respect him or despise him.

Watching from the corner of my eye, I noticed the way he chewed nervously on his cuticles. Just like Ches does before she's about to walk into a test.

"I'm not your show pony," he said.

"Peter, you've made that very clear." Harada's voice was low and sharp. "But your options are to watch my team attempt the activation or to do it for yourself."

"You promised me this would be safe," Peter said.

"My team has done everything in their power to minimize the risk, but our subjects know that some risks are unavoidable. We're very up-front."

Except they weren't entirely. I knew it could be dangerous, but the lady said it was like getting your tonsils removed. It would most likely be fine, but still, anything could happen.

It was only later on that Peter explained I stood a 50 percent shot at best of surviving.

Peter looked to me, and I smiled, trying not to be awkward. There's no chill way to smile when you're waiting for someone to decide if they'll perform an experimental procedure on you.

The hard line of Peter's jaw softened.

"Besides," said Harada, "it was you who scouted her."

"I'll do it," Peter finally said. "But I'm not some wish-granting machine, Harada. Just because I can activate anyone doesn't mean we should attempt to activate everyone."

Peter walked straight toward me and braced himself above me so that, from my point of view, his head was upside down, reminding me of the iconic Spiderman/Mary Jane upside-down kiss in the rain. I shook the thought from my head as quickly as possible. I really do crush hard and fast. Also, I don't think I could ever crush on the guy who basically catfished me into going to an underground lab run by a bunch of morally ambiguous people where I could potentially die.

"Okay," Peter said. "Faith?"

I nodded. He said my name. He said my name instead of the number on my uniform and intake bracelet.

"This shouldn't hurt, but you might feel some pressure."

He closed his eyes and pressed his forehead to mine. My whole head filled with static. Every thought or memory I'd ever held was zapped from my brain.

I could've been out for twenty minutes or twenty days. I didn't know. All I could hear was the incessant, buzzing static.

The only thing to pierce through the noise was Peter's voice. "It's not working." Peter's breath warmed my cheeks. "Shit," he muttered. "It's not—she's not a psiot."

My whole body was blanketed in a fog, and all I wanted was to reach through and tell him I could hear him. I could hear everything. It was like those horror stories you hear about people being totally conscious during surgeries even if their bodies appeared asleep. But that wasn't the worst part. The actual nightmare was that I wasn't special. I wasn't gifted. I was totally, 100 percent normal.

"I'll be right back," I tell Dakota and Corissa.

"Faith?" asks Dakota. "Faith? Are you okay?"

"She looks like she's just seen a ghost," mutters Corissa.

"I'm fine," I tell them as I stumble over their legs, ducking under the velvet rope and practically jumping off the platform.

I try to follow Peter's dark head of hair through the crowd. A door swings open on the other side of the bar and he's gone.

I throw myself into the pulsing crowd. A hand grasps for my arm.

"Faith!" Matt shouts through the crowd, but I don't even turn around.

What the hell is Peter doing here? Corissa was right. I've seen a ghost.

I push through the door and am met with steep concrete stairs leading up to another door. Racing up the stairs in the stupid red velvet high heels Matt talked me into wearing, I push the door open with the momentum of my whole body.

A rush of cold air jolts me. I find myself on the roof. The only other person here is a tall white blond girl with stringy hair in a red leather dress, hipbones protruding from her body and black liner smudged around her eyes. She shivers as she puffs on the joint dangling from her fingers. Around her wrist is a black VIP wristband. I look a little closer. "Swan?" I ask. "Swan Belle?"

Swan's parents fell in love very publicly at the height of their musical careers, and the whole thing ended tragically when Swan's mother died in a plane crash. Her dad, Raymond Belle, is a big record exec these days and rumored to be in an on-again, off-again relationship with Margaret Toliver.

"Tell Marge I'm not coming down. For Chrissake, I don't give a shit about the cast toast." Her words slur a bit as she swings her legs over the ledge of the building.

"Look at 'em," she says, pointing down to the line of people waiting to get in. "All these grubby little people waiting to get their taste of Hollywood." She cups her hands around her mouth. "It tastes bitter!" she shouts, even though none of them can hear her.

Swan has had many failed attempts at becoming a serious actress, so I'm sure *The Grove* wasn't exactly her first choice of jobs. And she doesn't even play a main character. Just Parker's nagging cousin, who makes an appearance a few times every season.

She turns back to me, eyeing me up and down. "And who are you? Someone's assistant?"

I stand a little straighter. "A friend of Dakota's."

She barks a laugh. "I should have known. She's got a thing for strays."

I let whatever assumptions or insults she's attempting to hurl at me roll right off. "Have you seen a guy up here? Dark hair. Tall."

She holds her arms out, swinging her legs around again with her back to the street below. "Just me and you. No dark and tall strangers to be found."

Something about the way her body sways and how she's perched here on this rooftop makes me nervous. I don't want to leave her up here alone. "Hey, maybe we could go back inside? It's pretty cold and you don't have a coat."

She rolls her eyes and stabs her finger in my direction. "I knew it! I knew Marge sent you for me!" She sways backward, and I stumble forward to steady her. "I'm fine," she says. "Tell Marge to stick my joint up her ass."

There's not much else I can do. It's not like I can physically restrain Swan Belle. "I'll be sure to pass the message on," I tell her.

I walk across the rooftop back to the door as Swan pushes herself up from the ledge, but she's not so steady on her feet, and suddenly she's tipping backward. Everything happens in slow motion and at warp speed all at once.

I rush forward, and adrenaline sweeps me off my feet as I soar to her.

She screams but nothing comes out, and the panic in her eyes as she loses her balance and falls off the edge of the roof is one of the most raw things I've ever seen.

I can see the headlines now. It would be reported as a suicide. *Swan Belle Takes Her Own Life*; *Swan Belle Succumbs to Depression*; *Swan Is Roadkill*.

Swan Belle might be miserable, but she's definitely not making an attempt on her life. At least not tonight she isn't.

I loop an arm around her waist, and for a moment we hover in the air and I can't help but think of the bird's nest a few weeks ago and how I survived the same crash that killed my parents and how all of humankind is a walking contradiction of fragility and resilience.

Swan is suddenly very aware and very alert. There's no mistaking the horror and awe in her eyes as we float above the unknowing crowd below.

"Holy fuck," she whispers, her voice much more sober than minutes ago.

"Hold on," I tell her, trying to focus on one thing at a time, and right now that thing is getting both of us safely back on that roof.

With her wrapped around me like a koala, I direct us back onto the roof. I stand there for a minute, carrying the weight of her before I say, "You can let go now."

"Oh, right," she says, clumsily getting to her feet. Then, as if the events of the last sixty seconds have just caught up to her, she's gasping for air. "You—you just—you . . . ," she stutters, unable to get the words out.

Yeah, I think, *I flew across the roof and saved you. Spit it out.* But I'm caught between the thrill of actually having saved someone's life (because OH MY GOD THAT WAS BADASS) and using my powers for good and the sheer terror that she knows who I am—sort of—and she knows that I can fly. Peter never gave me any rules. He wasn't really the kind of guy who gives the newbie a Superpowers Orientation for Beginners, but instinct and years of pop culture have taught me that the best thing I can do is keep my recently acquired talents to myself.

"That—that shit was nuts!" she shouts. "Are you like a fucking superhero? What the hell was that?" She laughs to herself in a maniacal pixie kind of way, and her words slur just enough that I can see she is still very drunk and very high.

I don't have many options here. *Think fast, Faith.*

Spreading my legs a little, I brace myself, Swan still

babbling, and rear my fist back. And then I punch Swan Belle square in her temple, knocking her out cold with one blow.

"Ow!" I howl, hugging my fist as I stumble to catch her before she hits the ground. "Ow, ow, ow!"

I sit there with her head in my lap. She's not so bad when she can't talk, and with the life she's had, I'm sure I'd be pretty awful too. Ches's older brother, Tyler, taught me, her, and Matt how to punch the summer before seventh grade. I was resistant to the idea, but Tyler insisted. *A supposed witch, a fat girl, and a gay kid*, he'd said. *You three could use a lesson in self-defense.*

But now what the heck do I do? And why is it so freezing up here? Calm down, Minnesota winter. Jeez.

I check my phone. The blue light flickers as notification after notification pops up. Oh crap.

MATT: Where are you?

CHES: Matt's getting antsy

CHES: And this party is really not my thing.

MATT: Did you ditch us?

MATT: This is so not like you.

CHES: I think we might go home. I don't feel good
about leaving you here, though.

CHES: That bald security guard said he would get you
home.

MATT: Really not cool, Faith. Can you just please
respond so I know you're not dead?

CHES: Okay, we're leaving. Call us if you're stranded.

Matt's pissed, but he'd turn around if he has to.

CHES: TBH, my feelings are kind of hurt too.

MATT: Whatever, Faith. Have fun with your new famous friends.

Oh man, I feel awful. I fire off a quick group text to both of them. I'm sorry!! I type. I'm alive. Will call you both later. Love you.

This still doesn't solve the problem currently sitting in my lap. As if on cue, Swan Belle begins to snore. I can't just leave her here.

Careful not to jostle her too much, I rest Swan's head on the rooftop and head back inside and downstairs. It takes me a moment, but I find Dakota hovering outside the VIP ropes.

"Faith!" she shouts. "What happened to you? I've had Nigel looking all over for you."

"I'm sorry," I gush. "I thought I saw someone I knew and then I had to get some fresh air." I lean in closer so that only she can hear. "I didn't want to make a scene, but I think that Swan Belle might have gotten a little too inebriated and passed out on the rooftop. Looks like she took a pretty serious tumble."

Dakota shakes her head. "She's going to get hurt one day." She takes a few steps back, and Nigel leans over as she relays the news. I watch as a chain of people pass the news all the way to Margaret Toliver, who sits by herself in an ornate armchair. She wears a crisp white suit with a silk blouse underneath, and her dark purple lipstick is almost black in this light. She might be the coolest person I've ever seen in my entire life.

Margaret whispers something to the woman who's just shared the news with her, and soon a quiet flurry of security guards and publicists are on the move.

Dakota turns to me. "Thanks for being so discreet. Margaret will appreciate it too. For more reasons than one," she says, practically confirming the rumors about MarTo and Raymond Belle, or as the paparazzi call them, MarMond.

"I've got to get home," I tell her.

"Let me take you," she says. "Nigel says your friends left you." She doesn't bother hiding the distaste in her voice.

I guess, yeah, when I think about it, it was sort of crummy of them to just leave and not even wait for a response. I hadn't disappeared for that long. "This is your party," I shout over the music. "You can't leave."

"At least let me get you in a car. The whole production staff has a black car service on hand for the night. Come on. I'll walk you out."

Dakota says something to Nigel, and he leads us out the back into an alleyway, where a sleek black car is waiting for me.

All manners, Dakota opens the door for me while Nigel

stands watch. "You'll text me when you get home?" she asks.

The driver, a round older man with a dust-colored beard, turns down the smooth crooning music on the stereo. "Where to, Ms. Herbert?" he asks as the door shuts behind me.

I give him my address and spend the whole drive trying to wrap my head around everything that happened tonight. What happens when Swan wakes up? What if she wasn't as wasted as I'd hoped? I've got to do something about Matt and Ches. And Peter Stanchek. I'd recognize him anywhere.

When I get home that night, Grandma Lou is asleep in her recliner with a half-eaten melted bowl of ice cream beside her. I can't help but chuckle. She'll be annoyed to have wasted the ice cream.

On the TV is the ten o'clock news rerun.

"The authorities are reporting an alarming string of missing persons cases from the suburban community of Glenwood. Officials say the only definitive link between the cases is that the missing are all part of Glenwood's homeless community. Officials also admit that it's hard to say when the disappearances began, since there are few ways to track the activities of those who have gone missing. Most recent among them is Horace Freemont, whose family is speaking out."

The screen splits in two. One half shows a reporter in the studio, and the other half is on a dark street, with another reporter standing next to a well-kept-looking man in a black down jacket and a green polo tucked into khaki pants.

"Ken Thurgood here with Horace Freemont's son, Bruce Freemont." He turns to the man, white air puffing between them. "Bruce, what would you like to tell the people out there?"

"My, uh, my father has been missing for two weeks. My sister, Virginia, brings him food and toiletries every once in a while. She usually finds him down under the Cooper Street bridge with the, uh, other homeless population." He takes a deep breath and then looks directly into the camera. "I . . . we just want to know he's safe, wherever he is. If you know anything about him or any other missing homeless people in Glenwood, please call the police hotline."

Ken points to where the bottom of the screen would be. "You can find that number below, folks. See something—anything—call the number. No detail is too small. Isn't that right, Nadia?"

The woman in the studio nods as her image retakes the whole screen. "Awful stuff, Ken. Just awful. Let's get those folks home. Or—" Her voice falters as she realizes what she's just said. "Back. Let's get those folks back."

I turn the TV off as she closes out the show, still tripping over her words, and wake Grandma Lou.

She's startled at first and then looks immediately to her melted ice cream and balls her hand into a fist. "Well, damn."

"Come on," I say. "I could use some ice cream too."

We sit at the kitchen table as she recounts some neighborhood drama Miss Ella has gotten herself embroiled in, and I give her a very brief recap of the party.

Sometimes I wish my world could stay this small. Just me and Grandma Lou and some midnight ice cream.

12

The most I've gotten out of Ches or Matt was a K from Matt and a glad you're okay from Ches, but since Saturday night my texts and calls have gone unanswered. I write every possible worst-case scenario in my head, and all of them end with a friendless senior year.

On Monday morning, Grandma Lou gets up to take me to school—something she hasn't done since Matt got a driver's license. I offer to drive us there so we can stop at the doughnut shop for apple fritters and coffee. I walk out to the driveway, ahead of Grandma Lou, and chuck my backpack into the back seat, when a car honks from the street.

Matt rolls his window down and dangles a carton of chocolate milk. "Going somewhere?" he asks.

"I didn't think . . ."

"What?" he asks. "You didn't think we'd ride to school together like we do every other day because you ditched us at some crazy party?"

I bite my tongue to stop myself from saying that they sort of ditched me too by not waiting just a little longer, but I'm just too overwhelmed with relief at the sight of him and Ches in the passenger seat to point fingers. I've got plenty of flaws, but needing the last word isn't one of them.

"I really am sorry," I say to both of them.

Ches grins. "Yeah, the sad puppy GIFs got me good."

Matt sighs. "And Ches might have helped me realize that my temper got the best of me."

I grab my backpack and pop my head into the house, letting Grandma Lou know that there's been a change of plans, which she doesn't mind since she's barely even finished her coffee.

As we're pulling out of the driveway, Matt asks, "Where were you anyway? On Saturday night?"

"I, uh, saw someone I knew."

They both look at me in the rearview mirror. I could tell them. For all I know, Swan Belle knows my secret and is telling everyone who will listen. I can only hope her reputation as a party girl follows her closely enough that her memory of that night won't be trusted. But I'm not ready for how everything will change if I tell Matt and Ches.

"Just someone from when I was a kid. Before I lived with Grandma Lou."

They don't ask any more questions. Something about a person from my past life when both my parents were still alive silences them.

Journalism moves at a sluggish pace. While Johnny sits with me at my desk as we discuss the layout of the paper, Colleen edges into the conversation.

"Uh, hey," she says. "Faith?"

Johnny and I share a look. "Yeah, Colleen?"

"I was thinking maybe we could partner on that prep school drug piece Mrs. Raburn mentioned a few weeks ago." Her voice squeaks on that last word.

"Uhhh . . ." Again with this prep school story? I feel bad shutting her down, but—

"Actually, Colleen," Johnny says, "I really need you on copy edits right now. I think we missed a few things in the last issue, so it might be best if you weren't distracted with another story."

She clears her throat and nods.

I motion to the red suede gloves on her hands. "Cute gloves."

"Thanks," she mutters, and backpedals to her desk.

The moment I'm sure she's out of earshot, I whisper to Johnny, "I feel so bad. She's so sweet, but—"

"Don't feel bad. Mrs. Raburn doesn't even think she's ready for a story like that yet." He touches my arm. "You were totally nice. Nothing to feel bad about, I swear."

When lunch finally rolls around, I track down Matt and Ches in the courtyard, where they're both soaking up the last bits of autumnal sun. Ches spends the lunch hour poring over her world lit textbook and filling in reading journal entries, while Matt and I sit huddled beside one another, swiping through a dating app he just downloaded.

"His facial hair is a little too unruly," I say as Matt swipes. "And he just looks a little . . . I don't know, racist? Can you look racist? He just looks like the kind of guy who's going to show up to a Halloween party in a racist costume."

"Oh, totally," says Matt. "He's got culturally insensitive written all over him." He swipes again.

"Now he's cute," I say.

Ches looks away from her notes for a quick moment to check out the guy on the screen. "Not his type."

"Ches is right. A little too cute," Matt says. "I like 'em a little rough around the edges."

Grant Vincent sits down beside Ches and slings an arm over her shoulders. She rolls her shoulders back, wiggling out from beneath him like he might be covered in some kind of contagious slime. And he very well might be.

"What's cooking, weirdos?" he asks.

Matt rolls his eyes. "What do you want, Grant?"

Grant was expelled from Shady Oaks Prep last year and brought all his bad behavior here with him to East Glenwood, where the population density alone allows him to get away with much more than he ever could at his old school. He floats from group to group, taking on whatever habits and appearances will help him blend, while he conducts whatever skeevy business he's into now. Last I heard it was stealing broken computer equipment from the school district and selling it for parts. Oh, and have I mentioned he's rich? He doesn't get into trouble for any other reason than liking the taste of trouble. Basically, if you looked up *entitled white dude* in the dictionary, you'd see a picture of Grant.

Grant stretches out, bracing himself on the bench and throwing his head back, the sunshine pouring over him. "Senior year is shit. Take this test. Write this paper. Fill out this application. Write this essay about why you're so special even though you're not, you're just like every other sad sack who bought into the lie that they have to go to college to make anything of themselves." He laughs to himself, like he's in on some kind of joke and the only way to get the punch line is to be an insufferable rich kid.

"Wow, what a ray of sunshine you are!" says Matt.

Grant leans forward, his elbows on the table, all business. "Let's be real for a sec."

And that's when I see it—the charisma that so many people fall for. It's the reason why he was on his sixth strike at Shady Oaks instead of his third. It's why teachers think they can save him, and it's why one day he'll leave this place and be successful without even trying. Just the thought of it has me boiling with anger.

"The pressure is unreal. And we're supposed to have all the answers." He shrugs. "I don't have all the answers, but I have this one."

He takes a tiny plastic baggie out of his pocket with four

multicolored pastel pills inside. Engraved on each tablet is *A+*. "Adderall's cooler older sister," he says.

The pills themselves are so cute they almost remind me of those little conversation hearts you get on Valentine's Day.

"Get that shit out of here," says Ches, brushing him away. Matt picks the bag up for a closer look.

"I guess this one's not a believer," says Grant, pointing to Ches. "Yet. But here, take some." He pulls out another plastic bag and hands it to me. "Consider it a sample." He stands and gives a grand bow. "You know where to find me. And you too, Sabrina the Teenage Witch."

Ches slams her book shut once he walks away. "You two better throw that shit away." And without another word, she stuffs her books into her bag and stomps away.

Matt pockets the drugs. "We can't just leave them here."

I nod. "You're right. I'll, uh, flush them later." Leaving them here to be found by any random person seems irresponsible. And what if a teacher saw us leave them here? Then we'd really be in trouble.

After lunch, I head into the bathroom and stand over the toilet with the pills in my hand, but instead of flushing them, I put them back in the plastic bag and drop them into my backpack. I don't want them. And I definitely have no intention of taking them, but I'm pretty sure this is the drug Mrs. Raburn mentioned. Curiosity gets the better of me, and I can't throw them away.

13

On Wednesday, Dr. Bryner gives me the day off so I can go see a dress rehearsal for *Fiddler on the Roof* to write up my piece tonight for the paper releasing on Friday. I'm a firm believer in loving what you love and not being even a tiny bit ashamed of it, but I've just never really been a musical-theater person unless you're counting "Once More, with Feeling," the musical episode of *Buffy*. Johnny, a reformed stage kid whose parents put him in a kids' show choir at age six, is the perfect companion for my nearly private showing of *Fiddler*. (He swears up and down that true theater junkies refer to it as just *Fiddler*.)

I meet up with Johnny after school at his car, a dusty old Subaru. The plan is for us to go get some food and make it back for the five o'clock curtain, which I'm told is theater speak for showtime. When I asked him over text message if that was the same as call time, he sent a long message explaining call times and something about actors saying, "Thank you, five!" when their stage managers yell call times. Rituals, I've come to learn, are very important in show business.

Johnny drives us to a burger place called Greasy Spoon, where we both order at the counter, agreeing to split cheese fries since we can both agree on our preferred toppings, because Johnny and I rightfully believe that green onions are an abomination. I sit in a booth by the window overlooking the parking lot, while Johnny fills rows of little paper cups with ketchup.

When he slides in across from me, an air of awkward energy hangs over us as we both realize this is the first time we've hung out outside of school.

"So show choir?" I finally ask.

He picks up his phone and scrolls for a minute before settling on a photo of a little boy with meticulously parted hair in black tuxedo pants, tap shoes, a purple vest, and a matching bow tie. All that's missing is the shirt underneath his vest.

"Wow. You look like a *Magic Mike* dancer."

"Well, you try being the only boy in show choir when the recital song is 'It's Raining Men.'"

"You must have been pretty popular," I tell him.

"Until Seth Frasier came along, I was like a boy unicorn."

I laugh. "Of course Seth came along and stole your spotlight." Seth Frasier is *the* theater kid. He competes in all sorts of competitions and stars in every show, and on top of that he's really, really hot. Not just theater hot, but real-world hot. He's the kind of person you 100 percent know will be famous one day.

"What kind of horrifying activities did your parents make you take part in?" he asks.

The moment the question leaves his lips I can see the regret in his eyes.

"Sorry," he blurts. "I didn't . . ." He shakes his head.

"People don't ask me about them enough," I tell him, saving us both from this moment with some actual truth. I smile at the thought of distant memories. "I took piano for a little while and then I tried hockey once, but the thing they dragged me to that actually stuck were cons."

"Like conventions? Like Comic-Con-type stuff?"

I nod. "Yeah. If you can imagine it, my parents were even bigger nerds than I am. It was like when I was born, not only did they have this daughter that they loved, but they also had a really great reason to expand their cosplay arsenal. I guess there's a lot of fun to be had with a stroller or a baby strapped to your back. And when I got older, it was like we just got to celebrate Halloween more than everyone else."

"Sounds like they were probably the coolest parents ever."

My chest tightens and tears press at the corners of my eyes. "They really were. There are, like, great cosplayers out there who could be professional costumers, but my parents were a little more homespun. It was always a team effort and always homemade if we had the time. And my parents are actually why I love *The Grove* so much."

"Man," he says, "that show really has been going forever."

"You want to know what really sucks?"

"What?" he asks.

"How for them, they never got the answers to some of their biggest fandom questions. Book series they thought they'd get to finish or movie franchise cliff-hangers or TV show plotlines or MMORPGs they left unfinished. Something about it all feels like the highest crime you could commit against a true fan. Even worse than spoilers."

The waitress swings out the kitchen doors, our order balanced in her arms. "Did someone say spoilers?" she asks. "I'm a season behind on *The Grove*, and dodging spoilers with the whole cast in town is like dodging bullets." She laughs to herself. "That's what I get for cutting out cable, though. Trying to save money where I can." She looks down at Johnny and me as though she's suddenly realized we're here and weren't actually talking about Grover spoilers. "Right. Well, you two enjoy your burgers."

"Have you seen any of the cast?" Johnny asks. "Like, around town?"

And it's then that I realize I haven't told Johnny about Dakota or the set or the cast party.

The waitress leans down a little. "That girl, the gay one, what's her name . . . Dakota! She's done a few take-out orders, but I haven't actually seen her yet. Apparently, she's a vegetarian, because she only orders the black bean burgers and double-checks every time to make sure we don't fry our fries in animal fat. Vegetable oil only," she assures us before heading back to the kitchen.

"Can you believe that?" Johnny asks. "The whole show relocated here? To Glenwood? What are the chances? That's wild."

"You have no idea," I tell him. It was hard to keep Dakota from Matt and Ches, but keeping her from Johnny feels just as necessary as making sure the peas on my plates don't touch anything else. Because peas are gross. Not that Johnny is gross, but he is very clearly in the school corner of my brain, and something about blurring the lines between him and Dakota feels complicated.

We talk about the print schedule for this week and who hasn't been pulling their weight in journalism and how Colleen is just so darn awkward.

As we're walking back out to his car, Johnny turns to me, the sunlight streaming through the sagging trees above us, ready to be free of their dying leaves. "We should go to the corn maze next week," he says.

My heart skips a beat. That definitely sounds like a date. Even I can't deny it.

"Or we could go with a group of friends," he quickly adds.

"Sure. A group could be fun." Okay, totally not a date.

Dutifully, he opens the passenger-side door for me just as a white Tesla parks beside us.

The door swings open before the car is even fully parked, and a voice calls, "Faith?"

I watch as Johnny's expression morphs, going through all the phases of realizing a) it's a famous person, b) a famous person I know, c) Dakota Ash, d) THE Dakota Ash, and then finally, e) Dakota Ash knows Faith Herbert—by name! "You—you two know each other?" he stutters.

I feel immediately guilty for not saying so earlier.

"Old friends," Dakota supplies.

I shake, doing my best to hide my blushing cheeks. "It's a long story, but yeah we're . . . friends."

I stand there with the both of them presented in front of me like two clear, but very different, paths. There's Johnny, who makes me feel good about who I am right now in this moment, but then there's Dakota, who has me wondering who I might become. I've always hated love triangles. They're always just all this unnecessary filler, but right now, this actual physical manifestation of my very own real-life love triangle is too real.

Mentally, I tap the brakes. *Whoa, there, Faith.* Who's to say either of these people even like you back? This whole love triangle could just be a round-trip ticket to the friend zone.

Still, the way Johnny and Dakota are sizing one another up makes me think that maybe I'm not imagining all this.

"Dakota," I say, snapping myself out of my own spiraling thought process, "this is Johnny. We work on the school paper together."

"And we're also friends," Johnny adds, overenunciating. "Really good friends. Like, for years now. Right, Faith?"

I nod. "Freshman year and counting."

Dakota smiles, completely unfazed. "You two just leaving?"

"Yeah, headed to do some things for the paper," I say.

Dakota gives me a long hug and then shakes Johnny's hand. "Good to meet you, John."

"It's Johnny," he calls as she jogs inside to pick up what I presume is an order of black bean burger and fries. "It's Johnny," he says again for only me to hear.

As we drive back to the school and park at the auditorium, something in Johnny changes. His chest puffs out, like he's been challenged for the first time. "We should definitely go to the corn maze," he says as we settle into our seats in the dark theater a few rows behind the director's table, which has been propped up on top of a few rows so that the drama teacher can sit and take notes with a few other crew members.

I sit with my notebook in my lap and the pen Grandma Lou put in my stocking last Christmas, with a little light that shines down on your paper. Some gadgets are just genius. The theater seats are tiny and my hip overflows a little into Johnny's seat, pressing against his thigh, but he doesn't make any effort to move like some people sometimes do, like my fatness might be some kind of disease they can catch. Because I never really know the politics of armrests, I take a gamble and wedge my elbow into the back of the armrest, my free hand hanging loose over my leg while Johnny takes the front. He angles his arm so that our pinkies brush every few seconds, until he hooks his pinky around mine, his hand slowly enveloping mine as I hold my breath.

A quiet gasp slips from me. Johnny and I so often fumble around each other, mumbling apologies when our skin grazes, but him taking my hand so deliberately makes me feel like there's light pressing against my rib cage and I might just burst right here in this dark theater.

By some miracle, my body remains whole. We sit there, watching *Fiddler on the Roof*, Seth Frasier in the lead role, of course, as I take a handful of notes, which turn out to mostly be doodles of flowers and hearts. Our hands stay linked together until halfway through the curtain call, when someone runs through the doors at the back of the auditorium, fluorescent light streaming in from the lobby, and shouts, "Gretchen Sandoval is missing!"

A moment later, our phones light up with an emergency alert from the school district, notifying everyone of a missing student and a hotline number for anyone who has tips or information for the police.

I see the horror on Johnny's face, every true-crime documentary he's ever obsessed over playing back in his head.

My phone buzzes with texts from Matt and then Ches. Gretchen is the holy trinity: popular, beautiful, and rich. All the missing pets. The feral dogs. The homeless people. It was as though none of it mattered too much, but Gretchen . . . people care about girls like Gretchen going missing. If Gretchen can go missing, none of us are safe.

14

News of Gretchen is everywhere. Her name crosses state lines and quickly becomes the biggest story in a five-hundred-mile radius.

There are search parties. Men and women in fluorescent vests with dogs spread out across every cluster of trees overnight and on into the next day. As the days go on, the volume of volunteers begins to thin. Pictures of Gretchen pop up everywhere. Two in particular are used over and over again. One of her holding the family dog in her lap while she sits on a porch swing, and another of her sitting in her drill team uniform on the football field for a yearbook picture. There's no scowling or eye rolling like I sometimes remembered her doing at school. Only angelic, glistening smiles. In the blink of an eye, she's a two-dimensional version of the fully realized person she once was—a totally perfect and wholesome girl who everyone misses dearly instead of the less-than-pleasant person she was in real life.

We have a vigil organized by the women in Gretchen's grandmother's church. I stand with Matt and Ches, each of us holding candles with little paper halos around the base. There's singing and praying and crying. Only Matt is brave enough to say what Ches and I are thinking when he whispers, "Is it awkward that we're here and didn't even really know her?"

At the vigil, my gaze catches Johnny's and his lips twitch as he tries not to smile. I get it, though. Not really an appropriate time, but the thought of our fingers clasped in that dark theater gives me goose bumps.

No one talks about the missing animals or the missing homeless people. Only Gretchen. She's the story that sells. Pretty, popular girl from a well-off family goes missing from her own gated community. Based on what the police have pieced together, Gretchen drove her car to the park in her very secure neighborhood. The rent-a-cop patrolling the neighborhood found her car later that night with the interior light on and her purse in the passenger seat, but her cell phone was missing. Her phone was later found in a porta-potty on the other side of the subdivision still in development, but they say the fact that she took her phone leads them to believe she went willingly. At first.

The week after Gretchen goes missing, Matt, Ches, and I sit huddled around our table in the courtyard, sharing every rumor and conspiracy we've heard.

"Honestly," says Ches, half a sandwich in one hand and

a stack of note cards in the other, "I wouldn't be surprised if it's true."

Matt leans in. "She wasn't all that nice. Her underlings killing her off is the most believable thing I've heard yet."

I take a bite out of my peanut butter and banana sandwich, and with my mouth still full, I say, "Johnny said his parents mentioned some kind of insurance scam that her whole family's in on. Sounds like they're not as well off as they made it seem."

Matt waggles his eyebrows. "Speaking of Johnny—"

"There's not much to say," I tell him. "He's been all business lately."

Ches nudges me. "And what about Dakota?"

"I told you guys. I ran into her with Johnny, and it's been radio silence ever since. I mean, it's not like she isn't busy. She's got plenty of things to worry about without adding me to the list."

"Oh!" says Matt. "I heard someone say Gretchen had an internet lover and they ran off to the Maldives."

But my brain is still stuck on Dakota. I check my phone, just like I have over and over again for the last week. But nothing.

I take the weekend off from the shelter, since Johnny and a whole bunch of us are set to go to the corn maze on Saturday.

"Bye, Dr. Bryner!" I call from the front desk as I'm gathering up my things to leave.

"Did you get those adoption applications processed? The ones I left in receiving?"

"Yep," I call back. "And Kit left a message for you. Said she tried your cell and wants to make sure you didn't forget about dinner with the Patels. To talk to them about a fundraising event? Remember?"

"Shit," she mutters quietly so that I can barely hear. We've been running on a shoestring budget for years, but one of the grants that's kept us afloat is about to disappear, so while Dr. Bryner runs around looking for funding, we've been covering for her here. It wouldn't be such a big deal, but we've had a huge influx of adoptions in the last two weeks and only a few missing animals trickling in, and endless calls from people looking for lost fur babies.

Something about Glenwood feels different. Almost apocalyptic with chaos. Driving past the woods around Russo's Creek, you can see the daily search party reconvening for the night at their headquarters tent, the dejection and weariness clear in the way their shoulders slump and their brows furrow.

The streetlight outside Grandma Lou's flickers, like it's about to die out, and it's enough to distract me so that I only notice the white Tesla in the driveway the moment I put my car in park.

I run inside, not even bothering to grab my backpack. And there's Dakota in my kitchen, wearing Grandma Lou's

Cranky and in Charge apron, straining a bowl of pasta over the sink while Grandma Lou sits at the kitchen table sipping her black coffee, no cream.

"Told you she'd be here!" Grandma Lou chimes. "Faith, you didn't tell me you knew the girl from your shows." She turns to Dakota, waving an arm out ahead of her. "She's got a huge poster of you and all your friends taped to her ceiling. You kids are the last thing she sees before bed every night."

My stomach drops to the floor, and everything feels too hot all of a sudden. Obviously, Grandma Lou has never heard of playing it cool.

"Is that right?" asks Dakota, a smirk curling on her lips.

"It's a Friday night." Surely she has better places to be. "What are you doing here?"

"I have today and tomorrow off." She shrugs as she pours the pasta back into the pot and carefully considers the ingredients lined up on the counter. "We've been going nonstop since filming started, and I wanted to spend some time with you. Maybe even get to know the legendary Grandma Lou."

Grandma Lou raises her coffee cup. "Cheers to that!"

"Is that okay?" Dakota asks, reaching past me for a measuring cup.

"Yeah . . . of course."

"Here," she says, dipping a small spoon into what looks to be a green pesto sauce, "try this. Does it need more salt?"

I open my mouth and she slides the spoon over my tongue. "It's perfect."

Her gaze pins me in place, and I think I could suffocate. But maybe it wouldn't be the worst way to go. Death by Dakota Ash's gaze.

"It better be!" Grandma Lou pipes up. "The girl's some kind of mad scientist over here with this recipe. Pine nuts! Who puts pine nuts in spaghetti?"

Dakota grins, and I can tell that she's absolutely charmed with my grandmother. "You'll thank me later, Grandma Lou."

My heart swells. Something about the idea of two of my favorite people getting along makes me giddy. "Put me to work!" I say. I want to ask Dakota where she's been, but I love this moment too much to let it go.

I'm given instructions to shave some fresh Parmesan cheese, and soon we're all gathered around the kitchen table with a meal so perfectly plated, it could be in a magazine. The only thing that gives it away is Grandma Lou's old yellow plates with green and orange flowers and little bluebirds.

"All right, all right," Grandma Lou says. "The fancy spaghetti was worth the wait."

Dakota tells Grandma Lou all sorts of insider stories about famous people she's come across and who has weird or gross habits or who doesn't tip and which ones are all bark and no bite. Grandma Lou tells Dakota a few of her favorite dirty jokes, the kind that make Miss Ella huff and use words like *unladylike* and *untoward*.

After dinner, I do the dishes while Grandma Lou and Dakota shout *Jeopardy!* answers at the TV, and the sound of them both hollering and laughing is sweeter than my favorite song.

After we each have a bowl of strawberry ice cream, Dakota turns to me, every bone in her body serious, and says, "Now, I've got to see this poster."

I groan and do my best to stall as she trudges up the stairs behind me. "This is so awkward. Why? What's the point? You know I'm a mega fan. It's just a poster."

"What if I want to sign it?" she asks, dodging past me, taking a lucky guess and swinging my door open to reveal my room.

My room isn't too big and it isn't too small. The roof slopes down on the side where my headboard is, and on the other side are my dresser and desk. It's not like I put posters on the slanted ceiling so I can stare up at the cast of *The Grove* as I fall asleep, but it doesn't hurt. And while this is plenty embarrassing, I'm at least relieved that I didn't get around to hanging up my solo poster of Dakota that I ordered online over the summer.

Dakota flops down on my bed, and I plug in the twinkle lights that outline my ceiling.

"Wow," she says, her voice breathy. "This is a great room."

"Pretty childish compared to the whole house you have all to yourself," I can't help but scoff.

She looks down at her feet as she says, "Turns out being an adult is pretty lonely."

"But don't you have tons of people with you all the time? The cast is like one big happy family, I thought?"

Her expression hardens. "A family built on business."

I walk around to the other side of my bed and lie down, patting the space beside me.

Dakota kicks off her shoes and joins me, our shoulders pressed together. "It's a family with conditions. We all love each other, but what you've got with Grandma Lou—and your friends, Matt and Ches—that's different. I don't really have that with anyone."

After a long moment, I practically whisper, "You can have that with me."

She turns to look at me, and we're so close our noses nearly brush. "Are you sure your friends don't hate me?" Her voice comes out husky as her eyes travel from my forehead to my nose to my lips to my eyes.

I'm this close to asking her to stay still enough for me to count her eyelashes.

And then she's lunging toward me—no, past me. "What are you doing with this?" she asks, grabbing the A+ out of the ring dish on my bedside table. "Faith, you don't take this shit, do you?"

"Me? No. No, definitely not." I'd seen Dakota do tons of antidrug ads, but I didn't realize she took it this seriously.

"I've seen this shit circulating around town." She closes her fist around the baggie of pills. "Swan, I think. That's who I saw had it." She shakes her head. "Don't mess with this stuff. Drugs like this . . . it feels like it starts out small, but suddenly you need it to get by and you're doing whatever you can . . . betraying whoever you have to . . . for your next fix."

And then it hits me. Her mom. Stupid, stupid, stupid Faith. Of course she would freak out about a good friend doing any kind of drug after all that she went through with her mom.

"Dakota." I take her fist in my hand, realizing then how small her hands are. "Some dumb kid at school was handing these out as samples. Trying to drum up business, I guess. My journalism teacher was talking about something like this circulating at the prep school, so I just pocketed it to take a closer look and forgot about it. I was never going to actually take it. I would never."

"You promise you'll flush them?" she asks.

I pry her hand open and take the pills, hopping off the bed and walking straight into the hallway bathroom. I don't think twice before dropping them into the toilet bowl and flushing.

I march back into my bedroom and hold up my hands like I do when I'm giving the puppy at the shelter treats and I run out. "All gone."

She gives me a relieved smile. "What are you doing tomorrow night?"

"The corn maze just outside of town."

"Oh yeah? We were thinking about scouting out that place to film the Halloween episode."

"You should come." I don't even think about what I'm saying until it's too late.

"I think I will," she says.

And just like that I've got two dates on the same night. Maybe I can fly back and forth between the two. That seems like a totally responsible use of my powers, right?

 **15**

The next morning as I lie in bed, I send a Mayday text out to Ches and Matt in the hopes that the two of them can help me juggle Johnny and Dakota.

> **ME**: MAYDAY! MAYDAY! 911! I sort of invited Dakota on my date with Johnny.
>
> **ME**: Well, it's not officially a date.
>
> **ME**: But it's sort of a date.
>
> **MATT**: It's totally a date.
>
> **ME**: There are other people going. It's a group thing. Really, I was just expanding the group.
>
> **CHES**: It's definitely a date.
>
> **CHES**: And!
>
> **CHES**: This is basically an IRL love triangle.
>
> **MATT**: I wish love triangles just meant that all three people live happily ever after all together forever and ever amen.
>
> **MATT**: Nay, GAYMEN.

I groan and let myself levitate a little above my bed.

ME: This isn't helping.

MATT: You're rollin' in the deep, girl.

CHES: Are you quoting Adele?

CHES: I can't believe I even asked.

ME: Like I said, NOT HELPING.

I yank my phone off the charger and shuffle down the hallway. Downstairs Grandma Lou is tangled in the long, spiraled cord attached to her old phone as she curses into the receiver. "Damn phone company. Got their gosh-dang wires crossed." She hangs up and tries again.

"Morning, Grandma Lou. You want some eggs?"

She lets out a *tsk* noise. "Don't mess with that stove. I don't want you burning yourself."

I side-eye her. "I, uh, think I can handle turning on a stove."

"Give me just a minute," she says, exasperated like when I was a kid and would beg over and over again for her to make me French toast. "Let me just try your father once more."

Her mention of Dad, like he's just down the street right now, knocks the wind out of me. The carton of eggs slips from my fingers and immediate tears prick at the corners of my eyes. Because Dad's dead and I don't know exactly what's happening, but something's wrong with Grandma Lou. Something is very wrong.

The eggs hit the linoleum, shell and yolk everywhere. The sound of it doesn't even startle her.

"Grandma Lou," I say, my voice too high and chipper. "Dad's gone, remember?"

Angrily she tries his number again before slamming the receiver down.

"Grandma Lou?" I ask again, stepping over the splattered eggs.

Fear bubbles up inside of me. Real fear. The kind of fear I felt when I was at Darlinda Green's slumber party in eighth grade and her older brother was sleepwalking. I saw him in the kitchen on my way to the bathroom. He stood there, completely zoned out, opening and closing cabinet doors and drawers. I thought he was possessed. I ran as fast as I could to Darlinda's bedroom and slammed the door behind me, my breath ragged as I stood with my back pressed to her door, like I might somehow hold back whatever evil lurked on the other side.

"Your brother," I gasped. "Something's wrong with him."

Then Darlinda gathered us all around as she spoke of her brother's sleepwalking like it was some kind of urban legend reserved for campfires. "And my dad says that no matter what, you can't wake him up. He could freak out and do something really violent."

A shiver spread among us, and we all stifled our screams as his shadow passed beneath her bedroom door and he went back to bed.

That same eerie feeling nearly strangles me now, and whatever's wrong with Grandma Lou, I'm scared of what might happen if she snaps out of it too quickly or what might happen if she never snaps out of it at all. "Grandma Lou, are you okay?" Maybe she just woke up too fast or maybe she's having some kind of migraine.

She sits down for a moment, looking back and forth between me and the phone and then the eggs on the floor. "I . . . was just trying to . . . the eggs," she says. "I oughta clean that up. Let me find the mop."

"You sit," I tell her. "I've got it."

"No, no." She pushes past me. "You get us some toast going. I just . . . I need to clean this up."

The house is too quiet. I prepare toast while Grandma Lou mops, and it takes only a minute or two before the silence is too much and I turn the radio on to the oldies station, thankful for the reprieve from my own thoughts. Neither of us talks about it. We just let the moment evaporate until it's almost like it never happened at all.

That night me, Matt, and Ches all ride together to Hopper Family Farms Corn Maze. In October, the maze is open seven days a week, but on Saturday nights, it turns into a haunted maze with kids from the theater department dressed as all sorts of monsters. Last year Rasheed Hakim caught Ches off guard when he jumped out from the cornstalks, dressed as a chain-saw-wielding serial killer, and she clocked him right in the nose.

At the corn maze, we park in a dirt field. As the three of us walk to the ticket booth, I get a text from Dakota.

DAKOTA: Running late, but I'll text as soon as I'm there <3

Well, maybe that will give me some time to spend with Johnny first, and then I can catch up with Dakota later. This doesn't have to be awkward. There are tons of people here. I just happen to have very confusing feelings about two of them.

"You guys! Faith! Matt! Ches!" Johnny waves us over from where he stands in line with a few of his friends, Carson from journalism and a few other guys I vaguely know who start a new band every few months, recycling names and concepts faster than I can keep up. Last I checked they were an acoustic experience interspersed with the xylophone, and they called themselves Cleo's Patra.

Johnny gives me a quick hug and squeezes my hand once before letting go. "The line's moving pretty fast."

"Oh good," I say. "I think we're meeting a few more people here later too. I hope my cell phone works in there."

Carson cranes his head around. "Looks like they're sending people in two at a time and we've already partnered up, so how about Johnny and Faith and then Ches and Matt?"

Matt looks to me, giving me a chance to object, but I don't really see a way out of this. Of course I want to be alone with Johnny, but I was really hoping for more of a big-group-of-friends vibe when Dakota showed up and less of a stuck-in-a-dark-corn-maze-with-one-of-my-crushes vibe.

"Cool!" I shrug. "I'm sure we'll all find each other eventually anyway."

Carson gives us the thumbs-up before returning to his conversation.

"Are you nervous?" Johnny quietly asks.

"A little," I admit. "Ches is more into this stuff than me."

"No punching the staff this year," Matt tells her.

She throws her arms up. "I can't help it if I have really good reflexes!"

The line curls forward and we head into the maze two at a time. As Matt and Ches veer off down a path and leave us, I hear a delighted shriek.

Johnny holds his arm out for me. "Ready?"

I loop my arm through his, and the bored-looking kid dressed as a bloody scarecrow lets us through to the path on the right, leaving zero chance that we could catch up to Matt and Ches, since every couple is sent down one of three different paths.

The cornstalks loom all around us, and it takes only a few seconds before the noise behind us fades away and it feels like we're out in the middle of nowhere all on our own. What I've always loved most about Minnesota is that it doesn't take very long at all to get lost and find a place where you can really see the stars. Out here, arm in arm with Johnny, the maze is almost romantic enough to—

I shriek as a zombie with a torn shirt and a gash in the side of his head cuts through the stalks directly in front of us. I freeze and scream, and the zombie boy homes in on me, identifying me as the weakest link.

Just as I'm feeling backed into a corner, Johnny takes my hand and yanks me toward him, and we run off down the row to a split in the stalks.

"Right or left?" he asks.

"Right! No, left! Left!"

We slow to a walk as we realize that *oh yeah, that's just some high school theater kid in makeup and he's not actually going to chase us because he has to reposition himself for the next schmucks.*

"Why is that so scary?" I ask. "I know it's just some kid."

Johnny laughs. "Your brain playing tricks on you. Realizing something isn't real takes a minute, and even when you know it's not real, there's nothing there to remind you it's not."

A roaring sound interrupts me before I can respond. We both look over our shoulders, and in coveralls and a Jason mask, some maniac comes racing toward us with a chain saw in their hand.

"What the hell!" I shout as Johnny yanks me forward, both of us running. "How is this supposed to be fun again?"

We watch over our shoulders as manic Jason chain-saw

person gets closer and closer. Adrenaline buzzes inside of me and every muscle in my body tenses as I try to keep a handle on myself. Not really the best time to let myself get swept up in flight.

I scream, and even though Johnny's playing it cool, he can't hide how slick his hands are with sweat. We're both so distracted by what's behind us that we run straight into the two deranged clowns waiting for us at the split in the maze.

Upon collision, my hand and Johnny's become separated.

"What do we have here?" says one of the clowns as he snaps a huge pair of rusted hedge clippers open and closed. I really hope those are plastic.

I shriek and close my eyes. Why am I such a baby? For a girl who can freaking fly, I'm a little too easily spooked by a bunch of theater kids on a power trip in a corn maze.

"Just leave us alone!" I shout with my eyes still shut and now plugging my fingers in my ears. "La, la, la, la, la, la!" I think I once heard that bears retreat when you make yourself big, so maybe this clown will leave me the hell alone if I just shout right back at him.

After a moment, I unplug my ears and am greeted with silence. "Johnny?" I open my eyes and spin, kicking up dirt around my feet. But no one's there. They're all gone. The chain-saw maniac. The clowns. Johnny. They're all gone. The clowns must have chased him down one of the paths. I stare down the path we were on. No chain-saw maniac in sight.

Maybe I could just go back the way we came. I shake my head, feeling a little silly as I realize two asshole clowns and who knows who else are probably watching me from behind the stalks. We went left last time. No, right. No, left.

Actually, Johnny probably wasn't even paying attention to which way he was going. Or maybe he'll come back for me. Maybe I should just wait here. No, that's dumb. *Make a decision, Faith.*

I go left. And then I stop in my tracks and turn around. I guess I'm going right.

The maze is even quieter without Johnny. Too quiet. I make it down a few rows and take enough turns to quickly realize that I'm definitely not going to find Johnny anytime soon.

"Oh shit," I mutter as I turn down a row and find a creepy girl in a hospital gown sitting in a wheelchair at a dead end. "Nope."

But she doesn't move.

A breeze blows through the stalks, rustling them like paper. Her stringy hair moves with the breeze, and still the girl doesn't budge.

"You don't scare me!" I shout. Except she totally does.

She must be freezing in that gown.

"Did you hear me?" I shout again. "YOU. DON'T. SCARE ME."

The girl doesn't flinch. Is she even breathing?

"Hey!" I call to her. "What's your deal? If you're trying to scare me, maybe you should try a little harder."

Another breeze comes, and this one sends a chill up my spine. Her hair blows in front of her face and her gown ripples in the wind, but still she sits slumped in the wheelchair.

I walk slowly down the row of cornstalks. If one of these theater kids is trying to trap me down here and give me a real scare, it's working. The closer I get, the more I can make out her chalky pallor.

Something is not right.

I pick up the pace until I'm standing right in front of her. Suddenly I'm reminded of Darlinda's brother, and I have to hold my breath just to pick up her finger and then her whole hand from where it rests in her lap. She doesn't stir at all and when I let go of her hand, her whole arm flops back down. I wish I could run back and just make my brain believe she was a really lifelike dummy.

Be brave, Faith. The words ring through me so sure that I could swear they were in my mother's voice.

I squat down in front of the girl and brush back her stringy hair to find two green eyes staring right back at me. No, right through me.

Gretchen Sandoval.

I scream and then clap my hand over my mouth, my chest heaving and tears welling up in my eyes. I'm consumed by dread and terror, my whole body paralyzed.

Gretchen Sandoval. It registers in my head all over again. I stumble backward like she might lunge right for me, dust kicking up all around me, and then suddenly, as though it's a response I can't control, my feet leave the ground and I'm flying.

 **16**

Even though I've just found a possibly dead girl slumped over in a corn maze, and even though I'm flying up above the rustling stalks, the first thing that strikes me as I take in the scene below is how few people take a minute to just look up. They'd see the stars, for one, but more importantly they'd see me, which would be disastrous.

For me flying is a lot like breathing. It comes naturally and I can do it without any trouble, but controlling it . . . well, that's going to take some practice. I haven't actually flown this high up before without crash-landing.

I hold my hands out, like that might somehow give me some bit of control. Like Ches does when she meditates, I close my eyes and clear my mind of everything—Dakota, Johnny, Matt, Ches, the shelter, Grandma Lou and whatever's been wrong with her lately, and even Gretchen Sandoval below. I concentrate on one thing and one thing only—gravity. I feel the weight of my body and try my best to train my thoughts on nothing else.

But the past clouds my memory and I see it all play out like an out-of-body experience.

At the Harbinger Foundation, after Peter announced that my activation had failed, I was wheeled back to my room. I had been passed out for hours, plagued by nightmares of endless underground tunnels and whispering people in lab coats hunched together. I woke up to sirens blaring and a strobe of red-and-white lights.

"Security breach," a robotic voice repeated over and over again. "Activate code yellow protocol."

I stumbled out of bed and to the wall of glass windows looking out into the hallway. Guards and scientists darted down the hallway, not a single one bothering to spare a second glance at me.

Suddenly, my glass door shattered. Startled, I jumped backward, but my feet never touched the ground.

I looked down to find Peter standing in the doorway, shards of glass at his feet. "Holy shit," he said. "You—it worked."

I looked down at my hands and the floor below me as I hovered in the far corner of the room. "Am I—am I awake right now?"

"Uh, yeah," Peter said. "And we gotta move it. You know how to land that thing?"

I closed my eyes, trying to concentrate on something—anything—and in seconds I crashed to the floor face-first.

"There will be plenty of time to practice later!" Peter pulled me up by the arm. "We gotta get out of here."

"Wait. Get out of here? You're the reason I'm here to begin with, Peter!"

He threw his arms up, checking the hallway on either side of him. "Well, now I'm getting you out of here, but can you, like, hurry?"

I tripped to my feet and raced after him in my bare feet and Harbinger Foundation uniform. "Did you break the door?" I asked. "How did you do that?"

"Would you believe me if I said with my mind?"

I followed him into an elevator that I didn't even know was there. "So what you're saying is that you're basically a superhero?"

Peter chuckled and reached into his pocket to check his phone. "Shit." He looked to me. "Faith, do you trust me?"

"Why do people ask that just before they're about to do something super stupid?" I nodded. "But yeah, I guess I don't really have many options."

"When we make it to the roof, I need you to jump off the ledge," he said in an even voice.

"What?" But there was no time. The elevator dinged as the doors opened, and we were confronted with a whole crowd of very buff, very angry-looking people and Toyo Harada.

"Go!" Peter shouted as his chest bucked out and he began floating toward Harada like a moth to a flame. Harada's arm was extended out, pulling Peter toward him using some sort of psiot ability.

There was no time to think or second-guess myself. Fueled by fear of what would happen when I jumped and what would happen if I didn't, I sprinted to the edge of the roof and flung myself over the edge into the night sky. At first, my body plummeted a few stories before some sort of innate instinct inside me switched on and I began to descend to the ground. "Woo-hoo!" I howled. I couldn't help myself.

It was the most incredible thing I'd ever experienced until my body somersaulted to the ground. I needed control then. And I need control now.

Pushing those memories aside, I force myself to concentrate. It's hard. Most other times I've flown there's been a rush of adrenaline and things have happened so fast that I haven't had to find it in myself to measure my movement.

I glance down again. There isn't exactly a lot of space to crash-land in a corn maze. It requires a little more precise maneuvering.

Closing my eyes, I focus on my breathing until every person, thought, and memory in my head has dissolved. All that's left is the weight of my body. *Slowly*, I tell myself. *Steady*.

After a minute, my toes scrape the dirt until my feet are

flat on the ground. I let out a sigh of relief and open my eyes before rushing toward Gretchen. I immediately check for a pulse, my hands searching her neck and her wrist until I quickly realize that I don't actually know how to check for someone's pulse. Maybe if I become a superhero I should consider taking a first aid class or something.

Holding my ear close to her lips, I hear a slow, rasping breath. Thank God.

I pull my phone out to call 911—and no service. Someone has to be around here somewhere. I'm in a haunted corn maze crawling with high schoolers . . . which leads me to wonder how she even got here.

"Help!" I scream. "Help!"

But other than distant sounds of laughter and shrieks, no one responds.

"All right, girl," I say to Gretchen. "Stay with me. We're on the move."

I don't know who decided to dump her in this wheelchair, but they've made my job easier.

I release the brakes and take off. Gretchen's body flops with every bump and rock we roll over. I take turn after turn, just praying that some loser will jump out and try to scare me. Surely one of them has to know the way out.

I stop for a minute to catch my breath and try to get my bearings. "Help!" I scream once more.

Just ahead, the stalk rustles free of the wind. "You!"

I shout, and jump back to get a look at who's back there. "You!" I shout again. "I've got a seriously injured person out here. I need your help."

"I'm just a freshman," says a voice. A white, freckled boy dressed as a creepy ventriloquist's doll with fake blood seeping down from the corners of his mouth steps through the stalks.

Then he notices the girl in the wheelchair. "Whoa. What happened to her? Did she get punched? I heard that happened to someone last year."

Ches's reputation precedes her.

"Do you know how to get out of here?" I ask.

He digs into his pocket and unfolds a paper with a hand-drawn map. "I'm not supposed to share this with anyone unless there's an emergency."

"Well, I'm pretty sure this is a freaking emergency!" I don't even realize I'm yelling at him at first.

I pull back Gretchen's hair and take a deep breath. "I'm sorry. This is Gretchen Sandoval."

It takes a minute for what I've just said to sink in. "Holy shitballs. I totally thought she was dead."

"Well, she might be if you don't move your ass."

He turns the map in his hands. "I'm, uh, not so good with directions."

"What's your name?" I ask, my patience wearing thin.

"Benjamin."

I snatch the paper out of his hands. "Benjamin, you push. Follow me."

We take a couple wrong turns, but after a few long minutes, the thrum of voices gets louder and louder.

Finally, we burst through a back entrance to the maze and run around to the side, where I find a group of employees clumped together. "Someone call 911!" I gasp.

Everything after that happens in a hazy rush. People swarm us and then there are sirens. I don't let anyone separate me from Gretchen. I don't trust anyone else with her. Not until paramedics drive through the crowd and arrive on-site.

A kind-looking but gruff older woman in a uniform and with a satchel of supplies slung over her shoulder looks me right in the eyes. "We've got her from here."

"Don't go far," another paramedic says. "That puppet kid too. The cops will want to know everything you can tell them!"

Someone walks me over to a folding chair, and I sit there, waiting, when my phone buzzes.

"Hello?"

"Oh my God." Dakota sighs into the phone. "She's all right," I hear her say to someone else.

"Where are you?" I ask. "I'm on the outside of the maze. There's a bunch of people."

"On my way to you." The phone cuts out.

It's only a few minutes before Dakota is crouched at my side, her hands folded in my lap. "I snuck behind the police tape," she tells me, wearing a baseball cap and sunglasses even though it's dark outside. "I ran into Matt and Ches outside the maze. They were waiting for you to finish."

I shiver and she runs her hands up and down my arms, trying to warm me.

"Faith, do you know how long you were in there for?"

I shake my head, all of it catching up to me at once. Getting separated from Johnny, finding Gretchen, flying . . .

My phone rings again. "It's Matt," I say.

"Faith? Faith Herbert?" A tall black woman with a sleek bob in black jeans, boots, and a down jacket holds her hand out for me to shake. "I'm Detective Wallace. Do you have a moment?"

I look down to my phone.

"I can answer that for you," Dakota says gently.

"Okay."

Dakota takes my phone, and Detective Wallace pulls up another folding chair from the ones the corn maze workers use for smoke breaks.

Things feel suddenly quieter as I realize the ambulance is long gone. One by one, though, news trucks begin to pile up.

"Is there an adult I can call for you?" Detective Wallace asks.

"I'm basically eighteen," I tell her, even though my birthday isn't for another few months. As if my brain isn't cluttered enough, I'm suddenly worried about someone calling Grandma Lou while she's in the midst of one of her . . . episodes.

"Basically eighteen isn't eighteen," she assures me.

And when I don't respond, she says, "Well, listen, you're not a suspect or anything. Can you just tell me exactly what happened? Are you cold?"

I nod.

"Can someone get this girl a trauma blanket?"

After I'm wrapped in a foil blanket and sufficiently resemble a burrito, I tell Detective Wallace exactly what happened. Well, except for the whole flying part. I keep that bit to myself.

"What happened to Johnny? Did he make it out?" I ask.

Dakota touches a hand to my shoulder, and I realize she's been standing behind me this whole time. "He made it out. That's how we all knew something was wrong. He looked for you for a long time," she says.

"And you are?" Detective Wallace asks.

"Dakota Ash. I'm, uh, here with the TV show that's in production."

"Oh." Detective Wallace nods. "I've seen you folks around."

"And she's a good friend of mine," I add.

Dakota squeezes my shoulder. "Detective Wallace,

would it be all right if I got Faith home? It's been a long night. I'm sure her grandmother is worried."

Detective Wallace eyes me thoughtfully before handing me her card. "I'll probably call this week with a few more questions."

"And what about Gretchen?" I ask. "Is she okay?"

Detective Wallace lets out a long sigh. "Can't imagine what might have happened to her. I wish I could tell you she's going to be just fine, but the truth is I don't know." She stands and I do too.

I almost find myself telling her about the stray dog that was brought into All Paws a few weeks ago and how his condition reminds me so much of Gretchen's, but I feel silly for even thinking the two could be linked. For all I know, that dog was hit by a car or something.

"And Faith," she adds. "The department will be making a statement soon, but we'll be leaving your name out of it. I wouldn't talk to the press if I were you."

"That's something we can agree on," Dakota says.

"Okay." I nod. "Thanks for the, uh, space-suit blanket."

That gets a brief smile out of her as she walks past me to a swarm of officers.

Dakota takes the blanket, which hangs limply in my arms, and stuffs it in the trash. "Matt and Ches left already. They wanted to stay, but the police were trying to clear the place out." She coughs into her fist. "Johnny too."

"Okay." But I'm more worried about the swarms of

reporters forming in the distance. There's no way I'm going to be able to make it past them without an onslaught of questions and cameras in my face. I get it. They're doing their job, but I just wish their job tonight wasn't trying to get an on-camera interview with me.

Dakota recognizes the hesitation written all over my face. "Yeah, I'm not really looking forward to that wall of reporters either." She scans the scene. "Gimme a minute."

It only takes Dakota a few minutes to return with a scruffy guy in a Carhartt jacket who works for the actual farm. "Faith, this is Kevin. He's going to take us through a back path on his golf cart."

"Thanks," I tell him.

He grunts. "Follow me."

Kevin leads us to the most tractor-like golf cart I've ever seen, bright red with huge wheels. There's only enough room for a driver and a passenger, since the back is meant for hauling equipment.

Dakota motions for me to get in, and after I do, she hops up, hovering above my lap. "Do you mind?" she asks.

"Of course not," I tell her.

She sits down in my lap. "Promise you'll hold on to me?"

"I swear."

Kevin hops in and we're off.

Dakota's body rocks back against mine and I loop an arm around her waist, and despite how exhausted I am, something in me hitches with excitement.

"I got you," I tell her, my voice raspy.

"I know," she says.

Kevin whips us around the maze so quickly that there's nothing scary about it. He takes us right past the mass of reporters to the parking lot, where Dakota's car is one of the last vehicles standing.

My hair whips in the wind and I rest my head against Dakota's back. If this is it, if this is as far as our friendship goes, I'll always be thankful for this night when she swooped in and took care of me in a way I haven't been taken care of since my parents were alive. It's not that Grandma Lou and Matt and Ches don't love me. It's just that none of them have ever made me feel quite like this, like I could just turn my brain off and let someone else take the wheel.

When Kevin drops us off, Dakota fishes her wallet out of her back pocket and hands him a few bucks. He nods a thanks and takes off the moment our car doors shut behind us.

"Dakota?" I ask.

"Yeah?"

"Can we just drive around out here with the sunroof open for a little while?"

"Are you okay?" she asks.

"I just need some time," I tell her. "I just need some quiet time to process, I think."

"Yeah," she says. "I can give you that."

 **17**

Gretchen's face is everywhere. Footage of the corn maze and the ambulance carrying her speeding down the dirt road leading to the highway dominates the top of every news hour.

I called Grandma Lou on my way home from the corn maze and told her everything. On Sunday morning, she let me sleep in until noon and even then, all she did was open the blinds and bring me toast and orange juice in bed. It all reminds me too much of the weeks following Mom and Dad's death and how she just let me mope for a while and sit in my feelings before nudging me out of my room and back to normal. Most people want you to get over things too fast. It's like your sadness makes them uncomfortable. It's an inconvenience. But not Grandma Lou. Maybe it was losing her husband (my grandfather and my dad's dad) so early in life or maybe it's just the way she was built, but Grandma Lou's never shied away from the hard stuff.

Later that day, Matt and Ches come over and I rehash it all. Instead of asking me a bunch of questions, they pile up in my bed with me and watch reruns of *The Grove* from my parents' generation.

Ches doesn't even bring over homework. She just holds my head in her lap and braids my hair over and over again while Matt and I mouth along to some of the more iconic scenes we know by heart.

That night before they leave, Ches digs in her bag and comes up with a small bundle of twigs and sage. "To smudge your room," she explains. "It'll help. Do you mind?"

Matt smirks, forever a nonbeliever.

"Of course not," I tell her.

Matt and I sit perched on the edge of the bed while Ches lights the edge of the bundle with a lighter and then blows it out, before using the smudge stick to outline the door and then the perimeter of the room. Finally, she takes the empty jewelry dish on my dresser that Miss Ella gave me for my thirteenth birthday and places the smudge stick on top. She lies down on the floor and reaches beneath my bed with the dish and smudge stick.

"For restful sleep," she calls from beneath the bed frame.

Matt looks to me and we both share a smile. "I love that little witch," he whispers.

I nod. I do too. I really do. Ches isn't one for sweeping affectionate gestures or fancy gifts, but this is a specifically

Ches way of letting me know she cares, and it means so much. Even if it is just a bundle of twigs and sage beneath my bed.

On Monday morning, as I'm waiting for Matt and Ches, the chilled morning air laces through my hair.

I watch as Miss Ella, her housecoat wrapped tight around her shoulders, shuffles down her walkway to pick up her paper. She beckons me with the rolled-up newspaper, and I step over her flower beds.

"Something's up with Lou," she says, not bothering to sugarcoat it. "Her brain's all wrong."

Defensiveness boils up in me. But she's right, and the thought makes me nauseated. "I think she's just getting forgetful."

Miss Ella eyes me pointedly. "I'm doing my best to keep an eye on her, but you might want to start driving that car to school during the day. I can take her wherever she needs taking."

Something in me crumbles at that little bit of kindness. "I just . . ." I can't make myself finish for fear of crying.

She grips my arm with her free hand. "Sometimes these things are slow as lava and other times they're as sudden as an avalanche. Let's hope for lava."

I nod as Matt honks his horn.

"I'll take the car tomorrow," I tell Miss Ella.

I'm quiet the whole way to school, and thankfully, Matt

and Ches take it as a result of the weekend I've had, but question after question plagues me. What if Grandma Lou really has Alzheimer's or dementia? Are those even two different things? Can we keep it a secret long enough for me to turn eighteen? I don't think I could bear leaving her. Has Grandma Lou made legal arrangements? The kind that Mom and Dad never had. In fact, if I didn't have Grandma Lou as next of kin, who knows what would have happened to me?

As I'm getting out of the car, Ches catches me by the wrist. "You okay?"

"We can skip if you want," offers Matt.

Ches gives him a look.

"You and I can skip," Matt clarifies.

I take their hands. "I'm good." I'll tell them about Grandma Lou. I will. But for now I just want to get through today.

Johnny is waiting for me at the entrance to the school. I'd texted him to let him know I was fine but ended up ignoring his requests to come over yesterday. It was easier to cocoon myself with Matt and Ches.

I let go of Matt's and Ches's hands, so that I can give Johnny a hug. I can feel the anxiety and worry radiating off him.

"I'm so sorry we got split up," he says.

"It's okay," I tell him, just like I did over text message. "It really is."

We walk into school with Ches and Matt close behind.

"Did you have to talk to the police?" Johnny asks.

I sigh. "Yeah. It was fine. Have you heard anything about how Gretchen is doing?"

"Still in a coma," he says. "Well, not a coma, but whatever state she was in when you found her."

Matt and Ches wave as they head past us toward their lockers, and I pull Johnny into a little alcove a few steps before the journalism room.

"Johnny." My voice drops to a whisper. "Her eyes were glazed over . . . and it was like . . . nothing was left inside of her. It was like . . . it was like a Dementor from Harry Potter had attacked her." A chill runs up my spine.

"It's all linked," says Johnny, voicing the creeping thought I'd had in the back of my head. "It has to be. The missing people. The missing dogs."

"There was a dog a few weeks back. At the shelter. A Good Samaritan brought him in. He'd been dumped on the side of the road, but his whole body was rigid and he had that same glazed-over look about him. Like he'd seen a ghost."

Johnny's eyes go wide. "Where's that dog? What happened to that dog?"

I shrug. "Dr. Bryner took him to the vet school at the university for more testing. We couldn't really do much for him."

Johnny deflates a little as the bell rings.

"Let's get to journalism, and then after that we'll sit down and make a list of everything we know."

I nod fiercely. I knew I wasn't just imagining things, and knowing Johnny feels the same way reinvigorates me.

We walk into journalism a few seconds late and Mrs. Raburn's shoulders slump a bit as we do, like she was expecting someone else. "This is just . . . has anyone seen Colleen? She's been out for a week now."

"A whole week?" asks Johnny. "How is that possible? She hasn't missed a day since . . . well, ever. Right?"

As I sink into my seat, I realize just how possible that is. We're on an A/B schedule, so we only meet every other day, and then there's the fact that people like Colleen are just easier to miss than others. She's soft-spoken and keeps to herself. In fact, I've never even seen her talk to anyone else outside a classroom setting. Like those homeless people, it's all too easy for someone like Colleen to fall off the radar.

Mrs. Raburn picks up the phone on her desk and calls the office. "Yes, Ms. Keagan? Yes, according to my attendance records I've got a student who's been absent for a week. A Colleen Bristow. Have we made a phone call to her guardians yet?"

Johnny looks right at me and I know we're both on the same page.

Mrs. Raburn hangs up the phone, and in a too-cheery

voice that immediately leaves a taste of distrust in my mouth, she says, "Well, Ms. Keagan is on it. Probably just a case of the flu that's overstayed its welcome."

And just like that, she continues with business as usual.

I've got a lump in my throat, and I spend the first part of class just going through the motions as I wait for Mrs. Raburn to release us to our workstations.

Something's out there. Something sinister is out there in Glenwood, and it's stealing people and pets and it's doing something to them. Any of us could be next. Or maybe Colleen already is.

When Mrs. Raburn is done divvying up assignments, Johnny sits down next to me, his notebook open in his lap, with a list of everything he knows.

- missing pets
- missing wild dogs
- missing homeless people
- Gretchen Sandoval missing
- Faith finds Gretchen
- catatonic dog dropped off at All Paws on Deck
- Colleen missing?

"We have to find Colleen," I tell him.

"When's the last time you remember seeing her?"

I think—really think—and I've got nothing. "I can't remember," I finally say. "I remember her saying she wanted to work on that story Mrs. Raburn tried to assign me, and I know I saw her after that, but I just can't remember. What about you?"

"I think I ran into her in the parking lot later that week. She was kind of frazzled, you know?"

"But she always was."

He nods. "Do you even know where her parents live?"

I shake my head.

We huddle together around my computer and do some sleuthing, starting with looking up Colleen on Instagram. Unfortunately, Colleen is about as quiet online as she is at school, but after scrolling for a while, we find out her sister is not.

Below a picture of a pudgy baby dressed as a pumpkin for Halloween, the caption reads:

He gets it from his mama. Carla Bristow:
@ColleenBristow @HankBristow @JuanitaBristow.

And then below an old wedding photo of a young man and woman, the caption reads:

Carla Bristow: RIP Mama and Dad. Not a day goes by that we don't think of you. Another year without you here. It will never feel real.

Below that is a stock photo of a lit candle with a scrolling script that reads *In Memoriam*, and the next photo is an old family photo of two parents, a teenage girl in a soccer uniform, and a little girl, who I'm guessing is a young Colleen, with a book shoved under her arm.

"Did you know her parents were dead?" asks Johnny.

I shake my head. "Didn't know she was part of the club." My chest tightens as I think about how much I probably have in common with Colleen and how all I ever had to do was ask her about herself just once. I'm a little disgusted with myself when I think about how much I fuss over being Matt and Ches's third wheel when people like Colleen are basically friendless. I feel like such a jerk. "We've been in journalism with her for two years," I say.

He sighs. "Trust me. I'm feeling like a pretty big dick right about now."

I click on Carla's profile and scroll through the pictures. It looks like she's got a boyfriend or a husband and a young daughter now.

"Do you think Colleen lives with them?" I ask.

"It would make sense." He taps the screen. "Stop."

I scroll back one photo and squint until I see what he's looking at. "I know that apartment sign," I tell him. "It's over by Ches's duplex."

"What are you doing after school?" he asks.

"Home to get my grandma's car and then work."

"You got time to run by here first with me?"

"Let's do it."

After school, Matt is searching for Ches. "She's been such a flake lately," he says.

"Well, I'm about to flake on you too. I've got to do something with Johnny."

He raises his brows knowingly.

I snort. "For the paper, you perv."

He shoos me away, and I run toward Johnny's car. As we drive to Colleen's apartment, we go over and over the list of what we know, hoping that one of us might somehow think of something new.

"I think I have a cousin who lives here," says Johnny as we pull into the apartment complex.

The buildings are all various shades of beige, the wood thick with coats of paint after having weathered many Minnesota winters. It's not the prettiest place to live, but it has a little pool and gym by the rental office, and there are lots of signs cautioning drivers about children at play. Nothing about the place screams luxury, but it's definitely safe.

"How do we find Colleen's sister's place?"

"Drop me off here," I say. "I'm going to see what I can get out of the rental office."

I take a quick glance in the visor mirror and apply some fresh lip balm. I know that sometimes people look at me and they underestimate me. They see a cherubic blond girl who would probably be easily taken advantage of if she wasn't careful. And you know what? Sometimes that's true, but sometimes it pays to use people's misconception to your advantage.

Hesitantly, I walk through the door to the rental office, where an old man sits with his feet propped up on the desk, a beat-up paperback with a sinking battleship on the cover splayed across his chest. A light snore whistles out from between his lips.

"Excuse me? Sir?" I ask in my most girlish voice.

He grunts but doesn't wake up entirely.

"Sir?" I ask once more, and kick the desk.

That gets him. His whole body fills with electricity, limbs flailing. "Whose? What?" Then he looks up to me and sniffs, kicking his legs off the desk and shoving an empty sandwich bag into his paperback to keep his place. "Uh, yes, ma'am, how can I help you? Is this about the hot water in building C? I've got maintenance on it."

"Oh no," I tell him. "No, I'm actually just looking for my friend. Um, my parents just, like, dropped me off here and I'm supposed to meet her for a school project. But I just got, like, really confused with all the building numbers. Oh gosh! I mean letters. And I can't remember her apartment number and she's not picking up her phone."

He sighs. "We, uh, really don't give out that kind of information."

"I guess I could just call my parents and maybe you can talk to them?"

He looks at me for a long moment. "What's your friend's last name?"

I clutch my hands to my chest, really driving home the clueless fat girl act. "Oh, mister, thank you so darn much. It's Bristow," I tell him.

"Ah, yeah, Carla. Just saw her the other day with that boyfriend of hers." He flips through a few papers and hands me a map of the complex after circling building D and jotting down *26*. "D twenty-six."

I run off with the paper before he changes his mind about me and rush around the corner to where Johnny is waiting for me. "We're in business," I tell him. "Building D. Apartment twenty-six."

Johnny circles for a few minutes until we find non-reserved parking. As we're walking up the stairs to the second floor, he clears his throat. "Uh, I'm the kind of person who gets nervous placing take-out orders over the phone, so . . ."

"I'll do the talking," I tell him.

We follow the numbered signs until we find number twenty-six. I pocket the map the rental office guy gave me and knock on the door.

At our feet sits an old doormat from last Christmas that reads *Santa, stop here!*, and beside the door is a potted plant that could either use a little more or a little less sunshine. I'm not really sure.

After a few minutes without an answer, I try the door once more.

"Coming!" a drowsy voice calls.

Carla, who I vaguely recognize from the picture on Instagram, looks way more tired and run-down than she does in any photos on her page. Her thick, wavy brown hair is piled into a knot at the top of her head, and she wears a sports bra and plaid boxers rolled at the waist.

"I'm not buying whatever you're selling," she says, and begins to shut the door.

"We're not selling anything," I tell her, wedging my shoulder between the door and the frame.

Behind her a baby begins to cry.

"We're friends of Colleen," I say, "and she hasn't been at school for a week. We were wanting to check on her and see if she needed anything."

That wakes her up, and she stares at me and Johnny for a moment as the words sink in.

A sob echoes behind her.

"Uh, yeah. Come in."

We follow her in and Johnny shuts the door behind us.

Quickly, she moves a basket of laundry from the sofa and throws a few teething rings in the corner. "Sit down," she says, and steps into the hallway, returning with a plump baby boy with ringlet curls and light brown skin bouncing on her hip.

Johnny and I sit, but Carla stays where she is. "He'll cry if I sit down," she explains, stifling a yawn. "I work nights, so our schedule is kind of weird." She looks to the baby and presses a kiss to his temple.

"Colleen is supposed to be staying with our aunt. I guess that was . . . like a week ago?"

And I realize that here with Carla, even though she obviously loves her sister very much, it's easy for Colleen to slip between the cracks. With an overnight job, a baby, a boyfriend, and bills to pay, Carla's plate is plenty full.

"Can you call her?" I ask.

"Can you?" asks Carla, her tone turning suspicious. "If you're friends, wouldn't you have her number?"

Johnny coughs into his fist. "We work on the school newspaper with Colleen, but I wouldn't say we're friends-friends."

"More like acquaintances," I supply.

Carla twists her lips and rests her free hand on her hip.

"We wouldn't be here if we weren't concerned," I tell her. "Neither of us knows Colleen very well, but she's your sister and you've got to admit, it's pretty out of character for her to ditch school for a whole week."

She nods and unplugs her phone from where it sits charging on the kitchen counter. "She always was the nerd in the family."

I bite my tongue. I want to tell her we're not so different and that I know what it feels like to see your whole world change shapes in a matter of seconds. But it's pretty obvious that Carla has it way harder than I ever have. I lost my parents, sure, but I didn't have anyone to take care of. Lots changed, but I still had Grandma Lou.

Carla wedges the phone in the crook of her neck and when the baby begins to cry, she retrieves a teething ring from the refrigerator and he immediately quiets. "Aunt Jill? No, no. Theo's mom is watching him for us tomorrow." She's quiet for a moment and nods. "Hey, uh, is Colleen there? She didn't pick up her phone the other day." She says that last bit more to herself than anything else, and I can see the panic quickening as her brow furrows.

"No, no. She didn't come back last week. That's not like her." She pauses. "Aunt Jill, I have to go."

She looks directly at me and Johnny. "Shit. Shit. Shit. Shit. Shit. You're sure she hasn't been at school?"

"Has the school called you?" I ask. "Mrs. Raburn called the attendance office this morning."

"I don't know," she practically shouts. "Who even picks up the phone from numbers they don't recognize anymore?"

She dials a number. "I need to report a missing person." And then she begins to sob.

Johnny and I stay. I call into work and text Grandma Lou that I'll be home later. A policewoman and a detective show up within an hour. I take the baby, who I find out is named Louis, while Carla talks to the police. Most missing minors are runaways, they say, but because of current local events, they're taking any missing persons cases very seriously. Carla is barely aware of what they're talking about, so Johnny fills her in on Gretchen, the homeless people, and the animals.

The detective eyes him when he mentions the animals. That's something the authorities haven't publicly linked the missing people to yet, and the way the detective looks at him makes me think we're onto something.

We wait with Carla until her boyfriend gets home, and we leave her with both of our numbers.

"Colleen's a smart person," Johnny tells us as we stand in the doorway, the sun sinking past the horizon. He says it with such confidence, and I don't doubt that Colleen was— no, is—smart, but we barely even knew her well enough to know, and hearing him say so makes me feel like we're nothing more than imposters.

On the drive home, we're both stunned into silence. How could this happen right under our noses? What would have happened if Mrs. Raburn hadn't asked around about Colleen this morning? How much longer would it have been before anyone even knew she'd gone missing?

All of Glenwood looks sleepy and unassuming in the autumn dusk as Johnny weaves through the streets of my neighborhood, but it only takes a closer look to notice the menace in the way the shadows of every building, sign, and person stretch out across the streets and yards as the setting sun swallows us all in chilly night.

 **18**

All it takes for Colleen Bristow to become the most popular girl in school is for her to go missing. Suddenly everyone has some sort of connection to Colleen.

She was in my algebra class.

Colleen was always the kind of friend you could really confide in.

Her locker was below mine.

We did a group project together last spring.

I was crying in the bathroom once and she gave me a tissue.

One time I sat with her at lunch.

She was always so funny. I swear, she had the quirkiest sense of humor.

I can't believe she's gone.

I didn't know Colleen all that well, and I know everyone is just trying to cope with the trauma of disappearing people, but the way everyone flocks to the counselor's office to cry over Colleen—simply replacing Gretchen's name with hers—leaves a sour taste in my mouth.

There's a candlelight vigil for Colleen and for Gretchen, who is still unresponsive. Now that people know she's alive, though, there are mean jokes whispered back and forth about how Gretchen's such an awful person that maybe it'd be best if she can't talk back for a little while longer. Gretchen might not be the nicest, but it all makes me uneasy to think what people would say about me if I ever disappeared.

Rumors circulate about the possibility of a curfew for everyone under the age of eighteen, but by Thursday morning all that's old news.

Dr. Bryner gives me the day off because she has to close the shelter early, so I make plans to meet up with Matt and Ches at Starfish and Coffee, a Prince-themed coffee bar. (We Minnesotans take our love for Prince very seriously.)

The three of us sit in plush purple velvet armchairs by the window, Matt claiming the one with the perfect view of the barista with a blue streak in his hair and a double lip ring.

"How old do you think he is?" he asks.

"Nineteen?" Ches guesses.

I shrug. "Honestly, the lip ring and hair are really throwing me. He could be like our age or he could be thirty-five."

Matt nods. "And do I want to date someone who's thirty-five and still working at a coffee shop in Glenwood?"

"I think the better question is, would it actually be a good idea to date someone who's thirty-five?"

Matt swats a hand in my direction. "Details."

Ches rolls her eyes. "Tell that to my twenty-year-old brother who dated a fifteen-year-old girl who lied about her age."

I let out a hissing sound. "Not good."

"Yeah, her parents were going to press charges until the girl finally fessed up to lying." She shakes her head. "I mean, don't get me wrong. My brother's an idiot. But dating high school girls isn't really his thing."

My phone pings.

DAKOTA: Hey

My toes wiggle inside my Converses as I send back a short hi. Dakota and I are in the habit of texting back and forth every day and even saying good night every night, but I still get a little rush every time she texts first.

Grant Vincent strolls past us and sinks into a neighboring sofa.

Ches's whole body tenses, her back arching, and I think she might very well growl at him. "Such a tool," she mutters.

"Ignore him," says Matt. "He's total scum."

My phone pings. Dakota again.

DAKOTA: We're shooting at the corn maze tonight.

Thought you might want to come by and say hi.

I've always felt like it's a good idea for me to revisit places where traumatic things have happened so I can make new memories.

DAKOTA: That probably sounds silly.

I respond immediately.

ME: No, no. Not at all silly. I'll be there.

"I've gotta go," says Ches, shooting to her feet abruptly and grabbing her bag.

"Wait," says Matt. "We were supposed to go back to my place, I thought."

"Too much studying to do," she calls over her shoulder.

"But don't you at least need a ride?" Matt asks, but she's already gone. He looks to me. "That was weird, right? Was that weird? She's been, like, impossible to pin down lately."

I reach for my bag. "Probably just school stress."

He takes the other strap of my bag and catches me in a tug-of-war. "You're not ditching me too, are you?"

"I'm sorryyyyyyy," I tell him. "I thought going to your house was more of an abstract plan. Like, I didn't know we actually committed to it, and then I forgot."

He sighs and drops the strap of the bag. "It's for Dakota, isn't it?"

I stand and nod. Matt's warmed up to Dakota a bit, and the way she literally swooped in and saved me at the corn maze helped a lot.

"Can you just decide if you want to kiss her or not?"

Blush burns my cheeks. "Could you be a little more discreet?"

He guffaws. "Uh, yeah. No. Me? Discreet? Never." Then he sighs and waves me off. "Fine! Have fun."

I give him a quick kiss on the cheek and run out to Grandma Lou's car, which I sort of parallel parked on the side of the road. I say sort of, because it took me about ten minutes too long and I'm a foot or two into the street, but luckily no one clipped the side-view mirror.

I feel bad leaving Matt, but I think there's something to what Dakota said about making new memories. I wonder how many times she's found herself in this position, having to cover up old scars.

I follow the roads to the corn maze until they turn from paved to gravel to dirt. There are signs directing all cast and crew to park in the same parking lot where we did on Saturday night. After I park, I text Dakota, and minutes later she shows up in a large Mercedes van, swinging the door open for me.

"Whoa," I say as she swings the door shut behind me.

"Faith, this is Benita," she says, introducing me to the driver, a short Latinx woman with bouncy curls. "Benita is our on-set driver. So when we're on location, we usually park our cars a little ways away off-site, and we've got Benita here to shuttle us back and forth."

"Nice to meet you, Benita." I lean back and buckle my seat belt, but the moment it clicks into place, Dakota announces that we're here.

"Oh, okay. That was fast." And sort of pointless, if you ask me.

As I'm hopping out of the car, Dakota whispers, "Margaret likes keeping people employed as often as she can, even when their job isn't entirely necessary."

And after all the crazy crud that's happened in the last few weeks, that just makes me happy to know—that not only are there good people left in the world, but Margaret Toliver, one of my idols, is one of them.

"Come on," says Dakota. "You made it just in time for lunch."

"So late?" I ask.

She laughs. "Not really your average nine-to-five job."

Dakota leads me into a tent and to the back of the line of crew members, extras, and even a few actors I recognize from the show.

She sighs. "I'm so glad I'm not on camera today."

"You're so good, though," I tell her.

"Oh, it's not that. It's that I just kind of have to psych myself up to be on camera and watch playback of myself. No matter how many times I see myself on TV, it never gets any easier, and I always find new things to be annoyed by. My voice. The way my hair is styled. You name it."

Hearing that even Dakota suffers from days when she doesn't like the look or sound of herself makes me feel like maybe achieving your dreams doesn't always fix all your problems. The thought is both comforting and disappointing.

At the front of the line, Dakota hands me a plate. "I really like the craft services team we hired out here," she says.

There are all kinds of options—vegetarian, gluten-free, vegan—but the general theme seems to be a taco bar.

I pile two tortillas with portobello mushrooms, peppers, onions, sour cream, cheese, and salsa. At the end of the food tables, a woman fills whatever spare room is left on my plate with chips and guacamole.

"I feel bad eating this food," I say. "I don't actually work here."

Dakota leads me to a few spare seats on the other side of the tent. "Trust me. You haven't gotten the full-on set experience until you've visited a craft services tent."

We settle in, and Dakota runs back to the line to grab us each a drink. When she returns, *the* Margaret Toliver is at her side with a plate of nachos. She's a tall white woman with thick thighs and a narrow waist. Her brown waves are unruly, with streaks of gray. Her hair is the kind of effortless that most people spend thousands of dollars and endless hours trying to achieve. Her bare skin is free of any blemishes, and she has delicate, shallow smile lines that I've never noticed in pictures or interviews. Oh my God. MarTo. Here. In the flesh. My insides tighten and convulse. She . . . she means so much to me. I have to tell her.

I stand up and my folding chair tips over behind me. Do

I curtsy? Bow? I open my mouth, but exactly zero intelligible words come out.

"Faith," Dakota says, mercifully intervening, "this is Margaret."

"People around here call me Marge," she says, and drops her headset on the table, a rumpled white T-shirt that says The Future Is Nonbinary tucked into her high-waisted jeans. "Mind if I join you two for lunch?"

"I'm Faith," I finally spit out, and extend my hand. Marge! She said I can call her Marge! My toes tingle, begging to take flight.

She shakes my hand. "Good to meet you, Faith." And then she leans across the table. "Just breathe. I clean my cat's litter box just like everyone else."

And from that information all I glean is: "You have a cat?" She has a cat!

She sits down, so I follow her lead. "Back at home in LA. He's a gray tabby named Frank." She blows out a forlorn sigh. "I wish I could take him on the road with me when we're filming, but that cat barely lets me drive him down the street to the vet. I guess I'll just settle for being Bumble's godmother for now."

I can't help but clutch my hands to my chest and let out an "*Awww*." Animal people are good people. It's just science.

Margaret shoves a fully loaded nacho into her mouth and swipes her tongue at the guacamole left behind at the corner of her lips. "Dakota tells me you're a pretty spectacular person."

"I can vouch for her," says Corissa as she joins us, playing a crossword puzzle on her phone. "What's a synonym for 'helicopter' that's ten letters and ends in a *D*?"

"A whirlybird!" Margaret and I say in unison.

Margaret gives me a knowing smile.

"Season two," I explain.

"Episode nine," Margaret says.

Corissa and Dakota look at us both like we have sprouts growing out of our ears.

"Oh, come on," I say. "You both work for this show but haven't seen every episode?"

Corissa takes a swig of her drink. "Marge knows I love her, but the early stuff is a little dated even for me."

Margaret shrugs.

"I like to keep my headspace in the present," Dakota says, very obviously spewing bullshit. "I don't want to get distracted by what was, when I need to be what is."

Everyone is silent for a minute, even neighboring groups, until Margaret begins to laugh so hard she has to hide her face with her napkin. And then we're all laughing.

Dakota rolls her eyes. "There are only twenty-four hours in a day, okay? Do you know how many hours of *The Grove* exist?"

"Hours?" I say. "More like days!"

"Exactly!" says Dakota.

Margaret dabs at the tears streaming down her cheeks. "At least Corissa was honest. You had to go and pull some art-house crap out of your ass."

"Honestly," Dakota says, "we should just hire Faith as a continuity adviser. She knows this show better than anyone I've ever met."

"Is that a challenge?" asks Corissa.

"Trivia! Trivia! Trivia!" Dakota chants, attracting attention from neighboring tables.

Margaret grins. "Well, Faith, is that a challenge?"

I let out a wild giggle, aware of our new spectators. "Sure! Why not?" If I win, I get bragging credits for the rest of my existence. If I lose, I lost to Margaret Toliver, and I think somehow that might be even cooler to brag about than winning.

Sam Portman, who plays one of the dads on the show, is the first to find a website that claims to have the hardest *Grove* questions known to humankind.

How did this become my life? I can't think of anything I wouldn't do to share this moment with my parents. They'd totally lose it. Even Mom, who could keep her cool in just about any situation, would be a giddy mess under this craft services tent as I go head-to-head with Margaret Toliver to determine which of us is the ultimate Grover.

We agree on five questions—there's a show to be made,

after all. And in true trivia form, we jot our answers down and turn them over to Sam to be graded.

Dakota watches over his shoulder, and the minute he's done, she screams, "It's a tie!"

Everyone cheers, and someone yells, "All right, all right! Back to work!"

Margaret looks over our answers. "We both missed one question—the same one." She lets out a low whistle. "Well, kid, you ever want a job in showbiz, you know where to find me."

I laugh.

"No. Really," she says, crumpling up the papers. "Trivia questions aside. There's just something about you I like, and that's half of showbiz: finding people you actually like."

"Uh, thanks," I manage to say. "I don't mean to be a total sap, but I just wanted to say that . . . your work—all of it—means so much to me. It got me through some really tough times. And I'm sure you hear that a lot, but—"

She reaches across the table and takes my hands. "It never gets old." Her eyes are intent and unwavering on me. "I can't tell you how much it means to me to be a small part of your life. Of your story. Thank you, Faith. Truly."

I swear in this moment it feels like she and I are the only people on the planet. I've never been a religious person, but if Margaret Toliver were a religion, call me a convert. I feel every single one of her words with my whole being. This woman is an icon, and I'm blessed to just exist at the same time as her.

My eyes are beginning to water, and I finally squeak out a word. "I'm the thankful one."

She stands to leave, and before craft services has a chance to clean our table and while Dakota isn't looking, I swipe the two crumpled-up pieces of paper and shove them in my pocket. This has been a day I'll never forget.

I tag along with Dakota for a while longer as filming resumes. I even sit beside her and Margaret in one of the cast's director's chairs while we watch the scene play out on monitors and listen on headsets.

When the sun begins to set, the crew resets the scene, and I hop down from my director's chair, which was not made to accommodate people with hips, by the way.

As I gather my bag to leave, Margaret beckons me closer. In a voice so low I can barely hear it amid the thrum of the crew, she says, "Dakota told me what you did for our Swan at the party a few weeks ago. I wanted to thank you. Personally. And also thank you for your discretion. Swan is . . . experiencing growing pains."

"I just hope she's okay."

Margaret looks at me in a discerning way. "We take care of our own. Again, thank you."

I try to hide the glowing in my cheeks, but it's the same giddy feeling I've gotten since I was a kid when a teacher says

I've done something right or good in front of the whole class. Except that Margaret isn't just some teacher. She's my hero. Forget flying or Peter's mind-control mumbo jumbo. Margaret has real power, and she knows how to use it for good.

On the way home, I'm riding a natural high, imagining all kinds of futures I've never even thought to consider for myself. I'd always planned on going to a state school or community college and maybe one day I'd get a job at a small-town paper. But that doesn't have to be it. That doesn't have to be all there is. Heck! Maybe I could even work on the show that's meant so much to me my whole life and guided me through the darkest times. Maybe I could be more.

By the time I get home, the streetlights are flickering on and it's dark enough that Grandma Lou should be turning on the front porch light at any minute. She doesn't really get all the eagerness over *The Grove* and all the other franchises me and my parents loved so much, but she was always happy to listen and watch our excitement. Even now when I talk about *The Grove*, she patiently puts the TV on mute and listens as I explain fan theories or why meeting Dakota was such a big deal.

"Grandma Lou?" I call as I shut the door behind me and flick the lights on. The house is eerily still. "I'm home!"

I peek my head into the kitchen but find it dark too. No leftovers or takeout. Just our dishes from breakfast. "Grandma Lou!" This time I yell. "Grandma Lou!" I scream.

Taking the stairs two at a time, I race up to our bed-rooms, hoping to find her there in her room, taking a late nap. But our rooms are empty. So is our shared bathroom.

My heart races and I have to remind myself to breathe. I retrace my steps, checking every corner of the house, like she might be playing some sick game of hide-and-seek. The backyard is empty except for a flat sheet left on the clothes-line and a laundry basket full of folded laundry.

Inside, I look for clues . . . hints . . . anything that's proof my worst fears haven't come true. I stand in the entryway, where her wallet and cell phone—an old flip phone—sit on a console table beside her coat.

Grandma Lou is missing. She's just . . . gone.

 **19**

The first thing that hits me is how cold she'll be without her coat. I know it's a silly thing, but an October night in Minnesota can be pretty brutal, especially without any layers of warmth. I take my keys, my cell phone, and Grandma Lou's coat.

I run over to Miss Ella's house. Maybe I'm freaking out for no reason. With Halloween tomorrow night, the whole street is lined with pumpkins and scarecrows, casting ominous shadows out into the street.

After I ring the doorbell twice, Miss Ella finally makes it to the door. She wears a fluffy housecoat and a long T-shirt nightgown that says Do Not Resuscitate. Morbid, but okay.

"Have you seen my grandma?" I ask before she can tell me I've been driving too fast down the street or that I should wash my hair with eggs to make it shinier.

She tries to wave me in.

I don't budge. "Have you seen my grandma?"

She shivers dramatically. "Gonna make it all drafty in my house." After stepping outside and shutting the door behind her, she says, "Haven't seen Lou since this morning. She went grocery shopping with me, and that was the last we saw each other."

"She's gone," I say, my lip trembling, unable to stop myself from hyperventilating. "She's not there."

Miss Ella cups my arm. It's the most comforting, human thing I've ever seen her do. "Okay, okay. Let's not panic just yet."

I gather the too-long sleeves of my jacket into my fists and wipe away my tears as I follow Miss Ella inside. We sit at her kitchen table while she calls a handful of mutual friends and even the bingo hall they both frequent, but all she comes up with are dead ends.

"Thanks, Clarence," she says before hanging up and turning to me. "I think it's time to call the police."

After finding Gretchen and then learning that Colleen was missing too, the thought of having to be the adult in this situation and calling the police has anxiety coiling through my rib cage like overgrown vines.

"I'll make the call," she says, and quickly punches 911 into the phone attached to her wall.

I squeeze my eyes shut, doing everything I can to keep my breathing under control. She couldn't have made it that far. I've had her car. I've been driving it every day, just like

Miss Ella said I should. Grandma Lou wasn't happy about that, but she didn't fight me on it either.

"Yes," says Miss Ella. "I'd like to report a missing person. A missing elderly person, actually."

She pauses for a moment as the operator asks a few questions.

"Well, no, she's not been diagnosed." Miss Ella's gaze cuts away from me when she says, "But she's been forgetful lately and, well . . . I expect something's not right with her."

Dread seeps through me. What if this has nothing to do with Grandma Lou and her memory and the episodes she's been having? What if this is even more sinister than that?

Miss Ella lets out a big sigh as she hangs up. "They said to call again if she doesn't show up by morning."

"What? She's . . . Missing. *Missing.*"

"I guess with everything going on lately there's been an uptick in missing persons calls, and from what they said, a lot of them have been mistakes. So since Lou doesn't have a documented history of dementia or Alzheimer's, they want us to wait until morning."

"But you told them! You told them she hasn't been herself lately."

"I'll tell you what," Miss Ella says. "How about I stay at your place tonight? I spend most of the night watching QVC anyway. This way you can still get some sleep, and if Lou turns up, I'll be there waiting."

I stand up and take my keys and Grandma Lou's coat

from the table. "No. No, I have to find her. I can't just—how do you even expect me to sleep?"

"Faith, you can't just roam the streets at night."

"Why not? That's probably what Grandma Lou's doing." I shake her jacket in my fist. "And she's probably freezing too. You stay at my house if she comes back. Please."

Miss Ella crosses her arms. "You just be safe out there, Faith. Your grandmother would kill me if I ever let anything happen to you."

Behind the wheel of the car, I sit at the stop sign at the end of our street for a minute. I don't even know where to start. My first thought is that I should call someone. Matt or Ches. Maybe even Dakota. I'd be gutted if any of them had to deal with something like this on their own, but Ches was in such a hurry to leave today, and I already ditched Matt. And Dakota's shooting overnight. I haven't even told Matt or Ches that something's up with Grandma Lou.

I tell myself all the things we tell lost pet owners at the shelter. Most lost pets don't go far. Look for food sources. Water sources. Warm places. Except Grandma Lou isn't a pet.

I head for the elementary school playground down the street. The only thing of interest I find is two teens hooking up in the tunnel slide and a burned-out joint in the parking lot. The schoolyard is pretty eerie. I peek through every window just in case and check around the dumpsters too.

Back in the car, I give in and call Matt, but I'm sent straight to voice mail. "Matt?" My voice cracks on his name. "Call me back when you can."

As I'm hanging up, my phone vibrates with a text.

MATT: Hey. Sorry. At a movie with that barista. Call you later.

Great.

I begin to type a response, explaining that I think Grandma Lou is missing, but immediately hit the backspace button. Maybe this is nothing. Maybe she's totally fine and this is all just some kind of weird misunderstanding. He'll call me after, and if we still haven't found Grandma Lou, I'm sure he and Ches will come over ASAP.

I glance around the school property. Suddenly Glenwood feels too big. For all I know, now that I'm at the school, she could be at the playground.

That's when I know what I have to do.

I park my car on the back side of the elementary school and pace for a minute. What's the point of being able to fly if you're not going to actually fly, right? And I've never tried flying longer distances, but now's the time.

I've given myself a million reasons not to stretch my flying muscles. I don't know what I'm doing. I don't want to get caught. But the truth is that I'm scared. No matter what I know to be true about superheroes from every comic or movie I've ever consumed, none of it prepared me for the reality of being one myself. I know how all this should work—secret identities, ruthless villains, and badass superpowers—but this isn't a comic book or a movie. If I'm going to do this, it's going to be on my own terms.

Just like how I concentrated so hard on landing in the corn maze, I span my arms out and let the wind take me, and I'm soaring through the air. For a moment I feel graceful. I feel in control of my body in a way I never have before. In that moment, for just an instant, I've found my purpose. Floating higher and higher, I can't help but grin from ear to ear. Even though Grandma Lou is missing, I'm flying and I'm doing it with absolute precision. Holy—

An earsplitting caw rings in my ear, accompanied by the flapping of wings. I open my eyes just in time to see a bird whiz straight past my head.

"Hey!" I shout at it, spinning around in midair. "You could have taken my head off!"

Add bird flight patterns to the list of things I need to research.

I look down and— "Holy crap. Oh my God. Oh my God." Am I scared of heights? I don't even know. Should I be scared of heights? Um, yes. Probably. Wow. Am I ever going to get used to this?

I'm not as high up as a plane, but I'm definitely not skimming rooftops either. The fear dissolves as I realize how mother-freaking cool this is.

"Woo-hoo!" I shout, zipping in a circle. My voice is swallowed up by wind, and all the people of Glenwood who live their very normal, very average lives have no idea that Faith, the bubbly fat blond girl who's a walking Wikipedia page for all her favorite fandoms, is flying high above them.

I'll never forget swimming with my mom at our apartment complex's pool. Mom wasn't a small person either, and she and I floated all over the pool—me in my swimmies—as she talked all about how feeling weightless was her favorite thing in the world. That's how I feel in this moment—totally weightless—and the best part is that the joke's on everyone who's ever made fun of me or whispered about me, because in the end, I'm the one who's lightest on her feet.

This is a whole new view of Glenwood. I can even see the Minneapolis and Saint Paul skylines from here. I want to see how far I can go, where my flight can take me.

But tonight I'm on a mission. I have to find Grandma Lou.

Meticulously, I weave up and down every neighborhood, scanning alleyways and backyards. I'm thankful for the cover of night, but this would be so much easier with some daylight.

I even do a low flyover of the old factory where Grandma Lou used to work, baking and packaging snack cakes, but there's no sign of her.

My cheeks and fingers are numb with the cold. I've got

to really think about some kind of weather-appropriate attire if I'm planning on flying through Minnesota nights. After a while, I find myself on Ches's side of town, and I hover over her street. I know Matt's not there and that he's out with his barista, but still my heart is in my throat as I check just to be sure that his car isn't at her house.

It's not. Matt's car is nowhere to be seen, but just as I'm about to soar off a little higher, I notice someone walking out of Ches's front door.

Grant Vincent, slimeball extraordinaire.

"See you later, Ches Pie," he calls as the door shuts behind him.

I watch as he walks out to his Jeep and then takes off down the street.

Ches hates Grant just about as much as she hates organized religion and the patriarchy. What could he be doing at her house? And calling her pet names! There's no way she's hooking up with him. Ches would never. She can't stand guys like him.

I wish I could just swoop down there right now and ask her. *Hey, uh, I was just taking a quick nighttime fly because my grandmother is missing. Oh yeah, and my grandmother is kind of falling apart and I basically have no guardian right now, but could you please explain why the hell the sleaziest guy in school just left your house and called you Ches Pie? Which, by the way, is a pretty cute nickname. Why didn't I think of that?*

Yeah, I don't see that going over very well. And besides, I've got bigger issues tonight.

If Grandma Lou weren't missing, I'd be able to enjoy the freedom I've found in flying tonight, but no matter how hard I search, I don't find any sign of her.

After what feels like hours, I make my way back to the school, where I left Grandma Lou's car. I check my phone to find no missed calls or text messages.

At home, Miss Ella is sitting on the couch, watching QVC just like she said she would be.

"Anything?" I ask.

She shakes her head and hops right up, shuffling into the kitchen. "You look like you've just taken a stroll with a tornado. Let's get you something warm to drink. Come on."

I take my coat off and leave it on the hooks by the front door, where I also leave Grandma Lou's coat. Yanking one of the fleece throws off the back of the couch, I wrap it around my shoulders and cozy myself into the couch.

Miss Ella returns a minute later with some hot chocolate and a few of the little biscuit cookies Grandma Lou eats with her late afternoon coffee.

The hot chocolate burns as it goes down, but it feels too good, so I ignore the tingling on my tongue as it singes my taste buds. After I finish, I kick my legs up underneath me and force my eyes open, fighting off drowsiness. I need to be awake to hear my phone or the doorbell.

My thoughts begin to slow, and the television feels farther and farther away until I'm flying in loops all over the
city, searching and searching. Days pass and I watch as my
friends and everyone I've ever met live their lives below me.
I'm destined to watch them from above, but I can never quite
land. Even Mom and Dad are there, ducking in and out of
coffee shops and comic book stores. I'm just a spectator. Forever on the outskirts.

My head begins to pound until I nearly scream. It's like
I'm being activated all over—

"Faith! Faith! Wake up." Miss Ella shakes my shoulder as
she hustles past me to the door.

The door! I jump up, shedding my blanket, and push
past Miss Ella to answer the door.

And there she is. Grandma Lou in her housecoat and
slippers, flanked by two officers, a man and a woman, with
sympathetic expressions on their faces.

"Faith?" Grandma Lou says.

She knows me. I don't know what version of me she sees,
but it doesn't matter. The officers guide her inside and I pull
her close to me, squeezing her as I realize for the first time
how petite she is compared to me. In my arms, she feels so
frail and small.

"Is this your grandmother?" asks the female officer,
whose hair is slicked back into a low ponytail.

I pull back from Grandma Lou and Miss Ella guides her

to the kitchen, wrapping her in a blanket.

"Yes," I tell her. "Yes, she is."

The other officer nods toward the kitchen. "Is this the first time something like this has happened to her?"

I swallow, but my throat's too dry. Something about admitting this to two police officers makes it too real. "She's been more and more forgetful lately. Just not really herself."

Officer Ponytail motions to the living room. "Mind if we sit down for a moment?"

"Not at all," I tell them, offering them the couch while I take Grandma Lou's recliner.

"I'm Officer Grundy and this is Officer Florez," says the woman.

"My name is Faith."

"Faith," says Officer Grundy, "we got a call about a woman at Parkway Grocery on Eighth."

"That's m-miles from here," I stutter, thinking about her flimsy little slippers and housecoat.

"They were getting ready to close up and there was a woman pacing the baking aisle, looking for some kind of mix. She couldn't tell them what it was. So finally they called us and she didn't have any kind of ID on her, so we took her down to the station. We heard someone mention a potentially missing elderly woman matching her description," Officer Florez explains.

"Why didn't you call?" I manage to ask.

"We did."

"I—I must have fallen asleep."

"It's okay," Officer Grundy tells me. "But when she's had some rest, someone needs to talk to your grandmother about going to see someone about all this. We'll need to send senior services out for a welfare check."

Miss Ella hovers in the doorframe. "We'll take care of her, officers."

"And you are?" asks Officer Grundy.

She hikes her thumb back toward the kitchen. "That woman's neighbor of forty years. We've survived children, husbands, and a dozen deaths together."

"Faith," Officer Grundy says, "I'm going to give you my card in case you need to talk to anyone else about this. I went through something similar with my mother this year."

She stands, but Officer Florez isn't so quick to move. "I'm assuming you're a minor, Faith," he says.

"Well, just barely," I tell them. "I'm a senior. In high school."

Miss Ella comes to stand beside me as though she can sense where the conversation is headed. "I told ya both we'd take her to the doctor. The woman just got a little confused, is all. Maybe if they wouldn't keep reorganizing the damn grocery store, she could've found what she was looking for."

And with that, Officer Grundy and Officer Florez stand to leave. They each hand me a card on their way out.

Miss Ella helps me guide Grandma Lou upstairs. She is aware of us, but still foggy.

"I wouldn't normally condone such a thing," says Miss Ella before she opens the front door to leave. "But I think it might be best if you thought about staying home from school tomorrow. I can come over in the morning and we can talk to Lou together."

I nod. "Thanks for everything tonight." Miss Ella isn't really a person I get along with very well, but she's definitely the kind of person who doesn't run away from the hard stuff. I can see why she and Grandma Lou have been friends for all these years despite their differences.

"You did good tonight, girl."

With all the doors locked and the heat turned up a little higher than normal, I lie in bed with my eyes wide open. This whole time I've thought I was some kind of superhero-in-waiting and that if I just tried hard enough, I could save everyone. The animals, the homeless, Gretchen, Colleen. But whatever's wrong with Grandma Lou . . . that's not anything I can save her from. No amount of sleuthing or flying or useless blog posts will fix this. Whatever's happening to Grandma Lou is an evil I can't defeat and I'm foolish for even trying.

20

I stay home from school the next morning, and the only thing that wakes me up is the incessant ringing of my phone.

I throw my hand over the phone on my nightstand, dragging it to my ear, and I swear it feels as heavy as a brick.

"Hello?" I say, my voice muffled by my pillow and blankets.

"She's alive!" Matt says.

Annoyance riles up inside of me. Where was he when I needed him? He didn't even try calling me after his movie.

"Where are you?" Matt asks. "It sounds like you're under water. And you're missing school. I didn't even know you could physically bring yourself to miss school."

"I'm home," I tell him, searching for a way to pluck the details of my memory of last night and put them into a nice, bite-size sentence that won't make him totally freak out.

And then, as every detail of last night rushes back, a slow

panic balloons in my chest, because today is the really hard part. Today I have to talk to Grandma Lou.

"And OH MY GOD. I swear, barista boy and I saw a UFO as we were walking out of the movie theater. He's really sweet, by the way, and is a freshman at the community college. But like this UFO thing was WAY too big to be a plane. Or maybe it was, like, Mothman. Do you remember that movie about Mothman that Ches made us watch?"

My head is spinning and I can't bring myself to compute whatever he's just said into anything meaningful. "Is Ches with you?"

"I'm here!" Ches says.

I nearly ask Ches what she was doing with Grant, but it doesn't really seem like the time. I lower my voice so Grandma Lou can't hear me. "Grandma Lou went missing last night."

"Oh my God!" Matt says.

"Is she okay?" asks Ches. "Did you find her?"

"Why didn't you call us?" asks Matt.

"I did," I say quietly. "You were at a movie—"

"Faith," Ches says, "that's like a 911-leave-the-movie-early kind of situation. And you didn't even try—wait, is she okay? You never said."

I sigh into the phone. "She's fine. Mostly. She's been forgetful lately, and it sounds like she was just really disoriented."

The floorboards outside my bedroom creak. "Listen, I've got to go, but I'll tell you both more later."

"We're so sorry, Faith," Matt says.

"Thanks," I say. "More later."

By the time I brush my teeth and loop my hair into a ponytail, I find Grandma Lou and Miss Ella already sitting at the kitchen table.

Grandma Lou stands up. "Let's get you some breakfast and—"

But I hold her in a tight hug, because I'm so thankful to see her as the version of her that I know and recognize. She sinks into me and I can feel her tears absorbing into my T-shirt. Grandma Lou doesn't cry much. Even when Mom and Dad died, she didn't let herself get too emotional in front of me, but right now she can't keep it together and act like everything is normal.

She squeezes me to her and then takes a step back, quickly drying her tears. "You sit down. I'll get you some eggs and toast." She clears her throat as she turns her back to us, and I sit down beside Miss Ella. "Now," she continues. "I spoke with Ella and I think it's best that you keep taking the car to school and work. I'm going to give Dr. Hufford a call and let him know that I've been . . . missing time and just not remembering things like I used to. Ella was kind enough to volunteer to take me."

"I—I can take you," I tell her.

"Don't be silly," Miss Ella chimes in. "No use in you wasting school days. This is your senior year, after all."

Grandma Lou sniffles as she cracks an egg over a frying pan. "That's right. Speaking of, you and I need to sit down and put our heads together as we start thinking about your plans after high school."

"I'll stay here," I tell her. "I could go to the community college. Besides, there's no use in me wasting all that money on freshman-level classes. And I would just feel better if I could be here with you and take care of you."

She doesn't even turn away from the stove as she says, "You will do no such thing."

Grandma Lou doesn't know the half of it. She has no idea that her perfectly well-behaved Faith lied about the whole summer and was inducted into a cabal of freaks with superpowers.

"Let's just deal with one thing at a time," I finally say.

The only reason I leave the house that whole weekend is to work my after-school shift on Friday at All Paws on Deck. Even then, I nearly call in sick until Grandma Lou agrees to have Miss Ella over at the house. I know Grandma Lou is getting irritated with all my hovering and fussing, but she doesn't say anything. She knows I've already lost so much.

Every few hours, I feel myself settling into this new normal, and even though we don't actually know what's wrong with Grandma Lou yet, my brain keeps writing different scenarios of what the next few days, months, and even years might look like. Then the freshness of it hits me all over again, and I'm faced with a whole new rash of fear and anxiety as I realize that this could be the beginning of the end for Grandma Lou. After that, I remind myself that she hasn't even gone in to see her doctor yet, and the cycle starts all over again.

On Sunday morning, I wake to a few texts from Dakota.

DAKOTA: Hey!

DAKOTA: Haven't heard from you since Thursday night. I got so caught up with work that I didn't even ask if you made it home okay.

DAKOTA: Today's bath day for Bumble. Could use some backup if you're bored. Or maybe just some pointers. lolololol

DAKOTA: You've been the hottest gossip on set for the last few days! No one can believe that you actually tied Marge in trivia. Even Marge herself was talking about how great you are.

DAKOTA: Ahhh sorry to bombard you with texts!

Not even the thought of talking to Dakota can lift my spirits. So I don't. I don't talk to anyone, because in the end it's me and Grandma Lou. That's it.

On Sunday night, when I'm sure Grandma Lou is in a deep, deep sleep, I slip out the back door and stand in my backyard with my arms spread wide as I visualize myself flying. My feet hover in the air for a few seconds, before reality drags me back down. I'm no superhero. I'm no flying wonder.

I'm just a girl stuck in a rinky-dink suburb, slowly losing whatever family she has left. Flying, no matter how high I go, will never solve the problems waiting for me on the ground, because the problem with flying is that eventually you have to land.

 **21**

On Monday morning, Miss Ella is camped out at the kitchen table and Grandma Lou has even made me lunch to take to school, something she hasn't done since I was in middle school. From what I remember, Grandma Lou's brown-bag lunches are pretty grim, but I'll happily eat every last bite.

"What time is your appointment?" I ask as she's shuffling me out the front door, like this is all some kind of quiz.

"Two o'clock," says Grandma Lou through the screen door.

"And I'm taking her!" says Miss Ella. "Right after we hit up water aerobics."

Grandma Lou rolls her eyes. Giving up her freedom and attending all of Miss Ella's many activities just so I can go to school with peace of mind is turning out to be quite the sacrifice.

"You'll love it," I whisper to her. "Don't forget your swimming cap."

She snorts and slams the door.

"Love you!" I call.

"Love you!" she hollers back.

By the time I texted Matt to remind him I'd be driving myself to school, I'm guessing he'd figured out that I was sort of ignoring him, because all I got in response was a brief k.

I expect for school to feel somehow different, like everyone might know that my life has been altered in a major way, but everyone is still consumed with Colleen and Gretchen, who was recently put into a medically induced coma.

I call Grandma Lou the moment school lets out.

"Well? What did he say?" I pant into the phone after practically running to my car for some privacy.

"He did a few tests and referred me to a specialist for next week."

"Next week?" That's so far from now. "Can't they see that this is urgent?"

Grandma Lou sighs into the phone. "Faith, this might not all unfold as fast as you'd like."

I let out a deep groan.

"And we've got to talk about this Miss Ella thing. I've got my limits," she whispers, and I can hear a door shut behind her. "I want you to feel comfortable leaving the house. I do. But darling, I need my freedom."

"But—but . . ." I try to imagine what I'd do if someone told me I had to be babysat every waking minute. "Can she at least check in on you a few times a day? Maybe we can come up with some kind of compromise."

Grandma Lou sighs. "I guess we can consider a compromise." She covers the speaker with her hand. "Just a minute! No! Do not cancel my recording of *Ellen*!"

"Thank you," I tell her.

"We'll make a plan when you get home. Fair?"

"Fair."

The week passes in a blur. I eat lunch with Matt mostly. Sometimes Ches shows up, but she usually texts us to say she's studying or going to tutoring or some other school-related thing ending in *-ing*.

After a round of MRIs and a few other tests, Grandma Lou's doctors suspect she's experiencing dementia. I spend most nights falling asleep with my phone to my chest, mid-scroll on some article about potential cures or the reality of living with someone with dementia.

I pull back from the newspaper and forget to pay close attention to anything new that might be going on with Colleen or Gretchen. At work, I coast through the motions. Dakota texts and I always reply, but I never give an actual answer or set a date when she asks to hang out or see me. Same for Johnny. All I can bring myself to concentrate on is what's in front of my face at any given moment and Grandma Lou.

On the second Friday of November, we see our first snow. Dad always loved the first snow, before the sludge has piled up along the side of the road and everything is so wet and cold, it never gets a chance to properly dry. There's an electric energy in the air and everyone at school is a little bit more distracted, a little bit rowdier. In response, some teachers are desperate to keep our attention and others are just as ready for an excuse to mentally check out.

As I'm digging through my backpack, looking for a highlighter for world lit, my phone lights up. I hold it inside my backpack, because Mr. Ramirez has a history of confiscating phones, and check my messages.

DAKOTA: Is it as easy to skip school as it is on TV?

I grin and type back: I've never tested this theory.

DAKOTA: I don't mean to be pushy, but I feel like you
might be avoiding me, so I might actually be
outside your school.

I lean forward at my desk and squint in the direction of the parking lot. Through the slowly drifting snow, I see two headlights flash three times in quick succession.

DAKOTA: Flashing you.

DAKOTA: Get your head out of the gutter.

I've never skipped school, I type.

DAKOTA: Never?

ME: I wouldn't even know how.

DAKOTA: People are always asking for a hall pass in the
movies. You could start there?

I guess it's worth a shot. I raise my hand.

After a minute, Mr. Ramirez turns his back to the white-board, where he's been writing vocabulary words. "Yes, Miss Herbert?"

"Can I use the restroom?"

"I don't know, Miss Herbert. *Can* you?" When his tired teacher joke doesn't get a response, he rolls his eyes and motions for me to go.

With his back to the classroom again, I quietly slide the contents of my desk into my backpack and slip out the door. Most teachers don't say anything to students who take their backpacks to the bathroom, because no one wants to be the teacher who makes a student fess up to needing to take whatever menstrual products are in their bag into the restroom. But Mr. Ramirez is totally not that considerate, so I tread lightly as I make my way out the door.

Once I'm in the hallway, though, sneaking out to the nearest exit is actually as easy as it is on TV. Dakota is waiting for me with the car door open just past the fountain (which is never actually turned on) in front of the school. I can practically feel the eyes of every student and distracted faculty member as I make my great escape.

The moment the door shuts, Dakota's hand closes over mine as she pulls me close for a hug. "I missed you!"

"Go, go, go!" I say, the adrenaline racing through me as I let out a squeal. If I weren't so scared of getting caught, I might have savored that hug for just a moment more.

Her tires spin for a moment before we take off, out of the parking lot. For the first time in a while, I let myself feel like someone could rescue me.

I don't ask where Dakota is driving or what her plans are. I just watch the snow cascade over us through the glass of her sunroof until finally, she pulls up to the diner a few blocks from my house. It's a place that's been around forever and whose sign simply reads *Diner*.

"You hungry?" asks Dakota.

I think about my forgotten bagged lunch still sitting in my backpack. Today with the snow, our usual spot outside wasn't available, so I didn't even bother searching out Matt and Ches and instead holed up in the journalism room, digging through more search pages, looking for anything that might hint at some kind of cure or treatment for dementia. I'd gone so far as to use a translating website to read an article published in a Latin American medical journal.

"Definitely," I say.

Inside, Dakota orders a hot chocolate and I order a coffee. She shrugs out of her black puffy jacket and rubs her hands together before sitting on them. Her shirt is a plain white undershirt, threadbare from countless washes, and I can see her black bra underneath. A few stray snowflakes melt into her hair as she peruses the menu.

"So I guess you're going home soon for the holidays, right?" I ask.

"This is home," she says with a shrug. "Wherever I am is home."

"Oh, I just mean that I thought you'd be going back to LA, maybe?"

She shakes her head. "Some people will probably make a short trip back for Thanksgiving, but a few of us stragglers without family to go home to will probably stick around."

I nod, unsure of what to say. Before the last two weeks, I would have invited her and any other crew in need of a place to go over the holidays. But there's no telling what state Grandma Lou will be in over the next two weeks.

We place our order: blueberry pancakes to share, chicken-fried steak for me, and a veggie omelet for Dakota.

Dakota rocks back and forth in the booth for a moment before saying, "So I feel like I did something? Like I said something? And now you've been distant."

I shake my head, but the words aren't there. Every time I try to open my mouth to speak, tears begin to well.

Dakota reaches across the table and takes my hand. "You can tell me, Faith. If I did something, you can tell me."

I nod, mostly to myself. It's not that I don't want Dakota to know, but saying this out loud is something I can't take back. There's a permanence to it. Some kind of finality. And even though I know there's no cure for dementia and Grandma Lou will likely not live to see one be discovered, saying she has dementia, telling someone else, makes me feel like in some way I've given up on the idea that things could ever go back to the way they were. I clear my throat, forcing back every tear. "Grandma Lou has been diagnosed with dementia."

For a moment, something that looks like relief passes over her face, but it's immediately replaced by a deep sympathy. "Oh, Faith. I'm so sorry. God, I'm such an asshole. I can't believe I made this about me. Of course you have a whole life outside of me and . . . is there anything I can do?"

I shrug and a tear slips down my cheek. "That's the million-dollar question, isn't it?"

"Is she getting good care? Is that something . . . can she afford that?"

My pride bristles, but a fresh tear rolls down my cheek and I quickly wipe it away. "We're fine, I think." I pause. "When I got home from visiting the set that one night, she was gone. I couldn't find her anywhere. And she was just gone. It wasn't like she'd run out for an errand. She left her phone, coat, and wallet."

My phone rings. Matt. I quickly silence it. He's probably just wondering why I'm not at school. I think he'll actually take a little too much joy in the fact that I'm skipping school for the first time.

"Why didn't you call me? I could've helped you look for her. Or at least been with you."

I think about the feeling I had when my call to Matt went

straight to voice mail and how he texted, promising to call me after his movie. I'm sure Dakota would have answered, but she was busy. She has an actual job.

"When the police finally found her, she was in her housecoat and slippers. She was so disoriented, like that one episode of *The Grove* a few years back when Henrietta woke up in a different timeline.

"I knew that Grandma Lou was right there in front of me, but her whole body felt like a shell. People kept saying stuff like that to me when my parents died, that their souls had left their bodies. I was so mad that they wanted to be cremated. Now I get it, but at the time, I couldn't stomach the thought of their bodies no longer existing. That night, though, when the cops brought Grandma Lou back home, I finally understood. She was right there, but she wasn't in her body. She was gone. The Grandma Lou I knew was still gone."

Dakota unwraps her silverware and hands me her napkin. I realize now that I've been crying this whole time. Never-ending tears roll down my cheeks, pink with warmth.

"Let's have Thanksgiving together," Dakota says.

"I—I don't think we'll be doing much of a big thing this year. Honestly, it's just normally the two of us and sometimes Miss Ella. We don't really go all out."

"It'll be good," Dakota promises. "I can invite some people from the crew. We can do it at my place if you don't want to do it at your place."

"But what about Grandma Lou? What if it's a . . . bad day?"

"Then we'll cancel," she says simply. "I'll come over with pizza and a movie to keep you company. That'll be that."

I let out a *hmmm* sound. A white girl with a body like mine, but shorter and more shapely, walks past us. Her jeans are low-slung on her hips, and despite the weather outside, all she wears is a black sweatshirt with the hood covering her head, blond curls tucked inside. She studies me and then Dakota, her eyes darting between us. I feel a little exasperated and almost find myself just saying, *Yes, she's who you think she is*, but I don't want to cause a scene or bring Dakota any unwanted attention.

"Friendsgiving," she says, pulling my attention back. "Maybe Matt and Ches can even come over after their family dinners."

Matt is always desperate to get out on Thanksgiving. His family eats their turkey so early it might as well be brunch. And Ches hates Thanksgiving on principle and usually spends the whole day lecturing her mother and brothers on how it's a holiday rooted in racism and colonialism. (It's a whole spiel.)

"I'll order a turkey," Dakota says. "And a tofurkey. We can go out and buy decorations. It'll be fun. I think you need fun, Faith Herbert."

"Friendsgiving." I test out the word. "I know Grandma Lou would love it. Mainly because she loves you."

The waitress comes back with our food, and we eat in contented silence for the most part. Dakota cuts the pancake like a pizza, which she swears she's done since she was a kid. We talk a little more about memories from our pasts. The kind of memories that would make most people sad, but they're memories that Dakota and I cling to. The way her mom only bought groceries from gas stations and how my parents would let me go to midnight movie showings of their favorite franchises or the way her mom would play with her hair as she fell asleep or how the thing that scared me most used to be my parents fighting, but now I panic every time I realize it's harder and harder for me to remember the sound of their shouting voices as I would lie quietly in bed, begging for everything to be all right.

Dakota never had an easy life, and I do feel bad for her at times, but I also know what a strange pain it is for people to feel sorry for you. So I brush any sympathy for Dakota away, and I don't cringe when she tells me details of her stories that are huge red flags of a shitty parent. Instead, I let her enjoy the good and hold on to it, and she does the same for me.

Dakota insists on buying. "You can't tell me your grandma's sick and not let me buy you some pity pancakes. That's not how that works."

"I'm going to remember this," I tell her. "Pity pancakes. Someday it'll be me buying and you who needs the pity."

She laughs. "Fair enough."

Our whole table shakes, plates and glasses clattering as someone smacks their hand down on the table.

I look up to find the girl with the curls and the sweatshirt.

"Is something wrong?" I ask.

"Whitney," Dakota says.

The girl lifts her hand, and there on the table is a tiny little tablet. A+.

"I told you I'd find you," the girl says through gritted teeth. Her eyes are bloodshot and the color is gone from her cheeks. "But you underestimated me."

"Whitney." Dakota touches her hand. "Maybe we could talk about this outside. You're making a scene. You don't want to do this."

Whitney turns to me, a demented smile playing at her lips. "She has a type, you know."

I shrink back in the booth.

Dakota's grip on her hand tightens. "Don't you dare talk to her, Whitney. Don't make me call the cops. You're not supposed to be here." Dakota takes the A+ and drops it in her glass of water; it slowly begins to dissolve.

Dakota stands and motions for me to do the same. "Let's go. Whitney, I'm serious. If you violate your restraining order again, I won't be so forgiving."

Restraining order? That kicks my heart rate up. Is this Whitney girl violent? I lead the way to Dakota's car and Whitney silently follows, close on our heels.

"Get in the car," Dakota says under her breath.

Even as our doors shut behind us, still Whitney is there, standing right in front of the hood of the car. Luckily, when Dakota pulled through this spot, no one else parked behind us, so we can still back up without confronting Whitney. She smacks both hands down on the hood of the car, startling me, but Dakota is unshaken. I can't even begin to imagine all the crazed fans she's had to deal with. I am sufficiently freaked out.

Whitney continues to hit the hood of the car as Dakota slowly backs out. I don't know how she's keeping her cool. Dakota backs up straight into the street as soon as the traffic is clear, and the moment she's sure there are no pedestrians, she speeds off.

After a moment of weighted silence, I finally say, "Who. Was. That."

She shakes her head. "Someone from a past life. No one you need to worry about."

"No," I tell her, a firmness in my voice I barely recognize. Something about the way Whitney said Dakota had a type and the A+ she smacked down on the table; none of it sits well with me. "I just spilled my guts to you. Your turn."

After considering this for a moment, Dakota pulls over into an alleyway not far from my house.

Snow continues to slowly drift down around us, and Dakota shifts into park and takes off her seat belt. I wait for her to say something, but instead she leans forward as she twists her hands around the steering wheel. I can't imagine anything she could possibly say that would make her whole body react in such a way. It's easy to feel like I know Dakota so well. The details of her life are all over the internet, rehashed over and over again. But in all reality, we've only hung out a handful of times, and everyone has secrets—even me.

"You can tell me anything," I promise her. "You don't owe me an explanation, but I am really freaked out right now. For myself, yeah, but really for you. Are you okay? Are you in danger?"

Her shoulders soften at my concern as she leans back and turns to face me. "Whitney was a fan." She pauses, perhaps thinking very carefully about her next words. "A really big fan. Who I also happened to think was a great person."

"So what happened?"

"Well, we met about a year ago when the show was filming in Illinois."

"Like how we met?" I ask. Something in my stomach turns.

"Not exactly," she says. "But kind of." She tilts her head back, watching the snow through the glass of her retractable roof. "We got along. She was funny and sweet . . . and beautiful. But suddenly, she was partying more and more with the cast. Well, the ones who party."

"With Swan?"

She nods. "Yeah, Whitney had basically turned into Swan's little pet. They'd party all night, and then Whitney would show up at my place drunk and high. She was kind of just throwing her whole life away. And then one day, Swan decided she was done with Whitney. Maybe she didn't find her entertaining anymore or maybe Swan just kept her around solely for the sake of chaos."

That makes me fidget in my seat. "Swan sounds kind of awful." I can't help but remember what Swan said to me that night on the roof about Dakota. *She's got a thing for strays.* Is that what I am? A stray?

"You're not wrong. And that's when things went really bad. Whitney was showing up to the set while I was working or at my house, banging on my windows. One night she even broke into my house. That's when . . . that's when Margaret stepped in. She got the network's lawyers to get a restraining order against Whitney, and then she moved the show to Glenwood."

"Wait, wait, wait." I shake my head in disbelief. "You're telling me Margaret Toliver moved an entire show across state lines because of Whitney? I'm not saying what she did wasn't awful . . . but that seems extreme. And expensive!"

Dakota nods. "The network fought Marge on it, but that's why she's great. She doesn't mess around when it comes to the people she cares about."

"Wow." It comes out like a sigh. "Should we, like, call someone about Whitney? The police? Your lawyers?"

Dakota shakes her head. "I don't think she's going to be a problem."

The image of her pounding her fists on the hood of the car rings in my mind on a loop. "Were you . . ." My cheeks flush before I even ask the question. "Were you more than friends?"

She holds my gaze without looking away once. "Sometimes."

I clear my throat, heat swelling my cheeks all the way to my ears. "So you had feelings for her?"

"For a time."

"And when she said that I was your type?" Something about the word *type* doesn't sit well with me. What does that even mean?

"Well, that's not untrue," she says.

"What do you mean?"

She looks down at her hands in her lap and then back at me. "I like optimists. I like people with blond hair. I like girls with generous curves. I like people who like the same things I do and share my values. And I like people who challenge me. I like you, Faith."

Generous curves. The words hang there for a moment, dangling in front of me. I've never blinked, not even once, when someone said they had a type. Brunettes, tall and lanky, compact and curvy, curly hair or straight. All those things are fine. But I'm more than curvy. I'm fat. And I've never heard someone say that my body type was just their flavor. Something about it makes me feel almost dirty, but how is it any different than when people like a feature in someone else? It's not all Dakota likes about me. She said so herself. And then it hits me: DAKOTA ASH LIKES ME.

"You l-like me?" I finally manage to stutter.

Dakota blushes. Dakota Ash blushes because of something I've said. "I don't even know if you like girls. And it's okay if you don't. It's okay if you just want to be friends. And it's okay if you don't. Especially after what just happened. And I'll be totally honest: I don't know what I can be for you right now. I have a lot happening in my world. Things you don't know about. And if you want to be more than—"

I lean over the center console and press my lips against Dakota's lips mid-word. I gasp and immediately pull away. It's such a brief kiss that it could almost be platonic, but it wasn't, and my cheeks are on fire. "Oh my gosh, I'm so sorry. That was totally—"

Dakota shifts toward me, her whole body invading my space as she cradles my jaw, her other hand lacing up the nape of my neck and through my curls. Her lips aren't forceful, but they're assured and delicate at the same time. I move in harmony with her, and some instinct I wasn't even aware I had guides me as she deepens the kiss.

She pulls back for a moment and traces my lips with the

pad of her thumb before kissing along the line of my jaw. "Beautiful," she whispers.

This is the moment when my biggest celebrity crush also becomes my first kiss, and of course I would never share this with the readers of *Faithfully Yours*, but honestly, they wouldn't believe me anyway. I wouldn't believe me. This is as good as flying. No, better.

Dakota spreads her fingers through my hair, looping them behind my ear and pulling me closer to her. "Is this okay?" she whispers into my lips.

I nod feverishly as I trace my hands up her arms, her lips parting mine, our tongues finding one another. My phone rings again, and we both chuckle into one another as I toss it in the back seat. I wish I could leave my body and hover above this moment like I did over all of Glenwood. I bet we look like a snow globe here in her car, the two of us sharing a kiss so tender, so hungry that I can't imagine how I lived up until this moment without her lips on mine.

A blaring honk startles us apart. I look over my shoulder and Dakota checks her rearview mirror, both of our lips swollen and our chests shuddering. Behind us, a truck honks again and without a word, Dakota waves to the driver behind her and begins to drive, exiting the alley on the other side.

In the snowy silence, the sky darkening much earlier than it should all around us, I reach over and take her hand in mine. I've flown off buildings and soared over my entire town, but this feels like the bravest thing I've ever done.

As we pull up in front of my house, I check my messages to find that Dr. Bryner is closing up the shelter early. The weather isn't severe by any means, but I'm guessing she just wants to go home and snuggle with her wife.

I invite Dakota inside and we watch television with Grandma Lou until dinnertime, when we all decide to order Chinese food. Dakota runs out to pick up the food and goes home to get Bumble, who has a newfound passion for orange chicken. After dinner, Grandma Lou goes upstairs to read in bed, and Dakota and I spread out on the couch with Bumble draped over us.

We sit there, watching a movie about some kind of superhero sacrificing themselves to save the world from a fiery apocalypse. Our hands are splayed out over the middle cushion, and over the course of the movie, our fingers inch closer and closer together, Bumble's ears twitching every time. It starts with a pinky and then slowly, one finger at a time, our hands become intertwined. It's almost as though just hours ago, we weren't sharing a frenetic kiss in a snowy alleyway. Almost as though this is our first time holding hands. But everything feels new all of a sudden with this fresh piece of information: I like Dakota Ash. She likes me. For a moment, I think about Johnny, but then Dakota is sliding across the couch, her head half in my lap. For the first time in weeks,

I'm not racking my brain, trying to imagine how I can keep things with Grandma Lou as normal as possible and somehow slow down the clock.

Tonight I'm just a teenage girl, cuddling with her crush on a couch, one very large dog sandwiched between them.

22

Dakota and I spend the whole weekend in our own private bubble. We take Bumble to the dog park. We go see a midnight movie downtown on Saturday. We even go grocery shopping, and I show Dakota how to make homemade dog biscuits. I don't fly. I don't find myself between Matt and Ches and whatever drama they're currently embroiled in. I don't worry about Grandma Lou's dementia. It is possibly the happiest I've been in a very long time. In fact, it's taken spending this weekend with Dakota to realize how deeply I'd spiraled downward. It took being happy to realize how sad I'd become.

On Sunday night, Dakota walks me to my front door, Bumble in her back seat, her tail slapping against the window. "Don't forget to invite your friends to Thanksgiving," she tells me.

"Friendsgiving," I confirm, loving the sound of the word.

The next morning at school, I text Matt and Ches, asking

them both to meet me at lunch. Neither of them are in physics class, and I sit waiting for them at lunch, but the only person who even acknowledges me is Johnny, from across the cafeteria. I feel a twinge of guilt as I realize that whatever was going on between us has drastically changed, except he has no idea.

Still, there's a pep in my step I haven't felt in weeks, and when, at the end of the day, I finally get a text back from Matt telling me that he stayed home from school, I decide to stop by and see him on my way to the shelter. I even stop at a drive-through and get him a latte with extra caramel and whipped cream.

I have to ring the doorbell twice before Matt answers, his face ashen, a frown creasing his expression. He wears flannel pants and a World's Best Mom T-shirt.

"Are you okay?" I ask. "I brought you a latte. Extra of the good stuff."

He takes the latte from me and sets it on his mom's fancy console table. I bite my tongue to restrain myself from asking if he's going to drink it.

All the snow from Friday has melted except for a few shadowy corners near his front door. A gust of wind whips down the street, and still he doesn't ask me to come in.

He crosses his arms over his chest. "Where were you this weekend? Where have you even been for the last few weeks, Faith?"

"I'm—I'm . . . I was with Dakota this weekend."

He throws his hands up. "Of course. Of course you were with Dakota."

A familiar annoyance inside me raises its hackles. "You keep doing this," I say. "You can't just let me be happy." I shake my head. "I get it, okay? You and Ches have known each other since you were in diapers. I *love* you both. But for you two, it'll always be Matt and Ches first, so sue me for having a crush and really falling hard for someone and for wanting them all to myself. But you want to know what? It felt good. It felt good to be someone's first pick."

Matt's nostrils flare, and he opens his mouth to speak, but I'm faster.

"All I was coming here to do today was to invite you to my house on Thanksgiving. You and Ches both. Dakota was going to bring over some people from the show, and Grandma Lou would be there and probably Miss Ella too."

Matt begins to laugh, quietly at first and then hysterically. "You have no idea. You have no clue, do you? Have you even been paying attention for the last few weeks, Faith?"

"What are you talking about? Paying attention to what?"

His eyes are bright with tears. "Ches. Our Ches!"

"She's been stressed," I say. "I know it's a tough year for her right now."

He laughs again, and nothing about it is sweet or light-hearted. "Ches was arrested, Faith. On Friday night. She was in jail all weekend and finally saw a judge this morning. Her mom can't afford bail and the judge wasn't interested in cutting her a break."

"Why would . . . what would she have been arrested for? Ches would never do anything to—"

"A+. She was with Grant—that cretin—when some kind of deal was going down, and Grant pulled out his daddy's gun and *shot* the other dealer. They were both arrested. Ches's mom says it doesn't look good for either of them."

"What? Grant had a gun? What was Ches even doing with him? I'm going to kill him."

"If he ever gets out of prison," Matt says. "The guy is in ICU and it doesn't look good."

I gasp. "But—that—"

"Makes Ches an accessory to assault at best and murder at worst," he finishes. "She swears she was in the wrong place at the wrong time."

I can trace the dots in my head and piece together reasons why Ches might need to take A+ and even why she would sell it, but the idea of her actually getting tangled up in a drug deal seems impossible, and Grant is awful, but I can't imagine he would actually shoot someone. Though I don't even know Grant. Maybe he was just carrying the gun for intimidation and things got out of hand.

And then the guilt hits me as I'm reminded of every moment I wasn't there for Ches in the last few months. All that time spent studying. That night right here at Matt's house in his backyard, when she let herself be fragile with me.

I cover my mouth with a shaking hand as I begin to cry. "Where is she now?" I finally manage to ask.

"Her mom says the district attorney wants to move fast on this and her lawyer's trying to get her a plea bargain so they can just get some info on A+ and how it's circulating and who's behind it, since it's, like, suddenly everywhere. Looks like she'll tell them what she knows and go to some juvie rehab center for a few months."

"But her senior year . . ."

He nods. "Her mom says she'll still be going to school in rehab, but I think her chances of getting any kind of academic scholarship are basically shot. Honestly, she probably won't even be able to graduate this year." He looks at me and for a moment, I can see that the pain I'm feeling is also his pain, but then his whole body changes as he remembers how distant I've been.

Matt's mom pulls into the driveway and sees me standing there. She rolls down her window and calls to me. "Oh, Faith! Honey, I just got back from the grocery store. You ought to stay for dinner or come back by if you're at the shelter this afternoon."

"Faith has plans," Matt says before I can even answer for myself, reminding me that he is definitely not happy with me.

I nod, even though there's nothing I'd love more than

for Matt to just get over his beef with me and let me in. I don't want to confront all this alone. "Yeah, Grandma Lou's expecting me."

"You tell Lou I said hi," she says. "Matt, come help me with these groceries."

Matt shuts the door behind him and we walk down the walkway. Before I head to my car parked on the street, I turn to him, unsure exactly what I can or should say in front of his mom. "You'll call me? If you hear anything?"

He looks at me for a long moment. "Are you going to answer?"

I nearly toss back an equally catty remark, but I'm not as quick on my feet as Matt and I'm too angry to even think straight, so I storm off.

 **23**

Work is too quiet. Our kennels are more empty than full, and the most pressing issue for me to deal with is organizing the missing pets board, which unfortunately leaves me to nothing but my own thoughts.

I try over and over to understand how it is that I could have missed something huge. Either I never knew Ches at all or she became someone else without me ever even noticing. I can't decide which is worse.

But then I consider my own secrets. If Ches and Matt knew the real me, they might not recognize the Faith they thought they knew.

"Faith?" Dr. Bryner asks.

I shake my head, loosening my thoughts as I realize she's probably called my name more than once. I blink. "Sorry."

She plops down in my office chair, spinning in a circle to face me. "You been okay lately?"

Dr. Bryner isn't insensitive, but for her to notice something is up means that I haven't done a very good job of keeping it together.

"You know, Faith, you remind me of Kit."

"Is that good?" I ask.

She laughs. "Well, I did marry her, so yeah, I would say so. But it's not just that. You both brood in the same way, which is to say you're not very good at brooding."

I let out a huffing sigh and cross my arms.

She laughs again, and then coos a bit as she realizes my pride is a little wounded. "It's not a bad thing, I swear it's not. I just . . . I think we all spend a lot of time glorifying people who know how to sweep their feelings under the carpet or people who are tough. But there's not just one right way to be strong. You know that, right?"

I know she doesn't know about me and my newly discovered abilities, but I feel like she can see straight through me. I can't help but wonder if my abilities are wasted on me, especially now, when everyone I know and love is falling apart and I can't save them. What's the point of having superpower abilities if you're incapable of rescuing anyone?

"My Kit . . . she's so full of emotion and feelings. She's brimming with them, and when we were kids, she spent so much time hiding that part of herself, but—and I might be way out of touch here with whatever you're dealing with— maybe it's okay to let your feelings take the front seat. Maybe that's just what you need. Maybe your ability to feel so deeply is what makes you so special to begin with."

Wouldn't that be something? If my feelings made me more of myself and not only that, but if they were the reason why my powers were so . . . super. It sounds good. It sounds wonderful. But is it even possible?

"Thanks, Dr. B.," I say. Even if I don't know what to do with what she's telling me, the fact that she's even taking the time to talk to me like this feels special.

"You can call me Suzanne." She stands and reaches for her jacket on the hook.

The familiarity of it warms me, but I shake my head. "You worked way too hard to tack that doctor title to the front of your name for me not to use it."

"My student loans would agree with you," she says. "I'm going to head out early today. You okay with locking up? You know the code for the front door, right?"

I nod. "Yeah, I've got it."

After she leaves, I gather all the trash and recycling, since tomorrow is our pickup day. Normally this is a two-person job, because our alleyway door locks from the inside, but I just wedge a rock between the door and frame and cart all the bags and recycling down the alleyway. Even though the sun is still setting, it might as well already be nighttime between these two buildings. Dr. Bryner told me she was out here by herself one time when someone tried scaring her by jumping out of the dumpster while their accomplice broke into the shelter and stole tons of medical supplies.

A gray-and-white cat tail swings around the edge of the dumpster, putting my imagination to a halt before I scare myself, and I carefully set everything I'm carrying on the ground so I don't startle the cat. "Kitty," I call. "Baby kitty!"

We've found dogs and cats back here. Sometimes pregnant mamas searching for safe places to have their litter and sometimes jerks dumping pets they never truly wanted.

I turn the corner around the side of the building, but the cat is nowhere to be seen. Cats are tough. There are lots of ways to catch them using traps, but I hate seeing them so stressed out when it happens. Last spring it took me six months to catch a black kitten who frequented our alleyway, but by the time I coaxed him inside, all he wanted to do was curl up beside me at my desk.

After having no luck with the cat, I throw the trash in the dumpster and put the recycling in our bins. The back door, though, is shut tight. No rock in sight. "What the hell?" I mutter, and yank on the door. "Ugh."

With my arms crossed tight around my chest, I trudge around the whole building, wind whipping me in the face. Inside, I gather up my things, and by the time I zip my coat, the clock strikes six and it's time to go. I do a once-over to make sure everything is just where it should be. Dr. Bryner's left me to lock up only once more on my own, and I'm not going to mess it up. And that's when I see it.

Written over my perfectly organized missing pets board in bright red marker are the words *SHE ISN'T WHO YOU THINK SHE IS*. Each letter has been traced over and over again, making it all look that much more manic. *She isn't who you think she is.*

I can barely breathe. Someone could be in here with me right now. And then I know it. I'm not alone. Or I wasn't alone. I don't even know. Whitney. It had to be Whitney. This has to be about Dakota. But how could she know that I work here?

I tear the papers down and shove them in the trash, not bothering with shredding or recycling. I check on the animals in their kennels once more, knowing I could never live with myself if something happened to them. The second they're all accounted for, I grab my keys and burst through the back door before locking up as quickly as I can and then racing to my car.

I have to go home. I have to check on Grandma Lou. I have to find Dakota. But I can't go home. What if Whitney follows me? But if she knows where I work, it can't be that hard to find out where I live.

I run over the speed bumps leading out of the parking lot much too fast, causing the car's undercarriage to rattle beneath me.

"Call Dakota!" I shout at my phone. The line rings over and over until I hear her voice mail. I try again and again until I falter at a stop sign. In one direction is Grandma Lou and home. In the other are the production offices and Dakota. The car behind me honks, and I turn, hurling myself to the heart of *The Grove*. I dare Whitney to follow me. I dare her.

I park outside the massive warehouse. There are a few cars, but not enough for them to be filming. I don't see Dakota's car, but if I could just find Margaret or even one of those security guards I've seen hovering around before, maybe they could point me to her.

With the settling darkness, the temperature has dropped enough now that I can feel the chill in my bones when I get out of my car. The doors to the production office are locked, so I duck under one of the partially open freight doors. The sets are completely dark except for a few security lights. It's warmer in here, but only because I'm protected from the wind. For a moment, I'm distracted by a table of props. A gun, a half-smoked pack of cigarettes, and an envelope full of documents that reads *EMANCIPATION* at the top. I can't even begin to imagine what all those props mean for next season, but—actually, I can imagine, and I have to actively remind myself that I'm on a mission right now, and not only that but some unhinged stalker girl could be literally on my tail at this very moment.

Okay, Faith. Concentrate. I check my phone, but nothing from Dakota.

In the far corner of the warehouse is a set of stairs leading to another floor with a door and windows covered in blinds. I remember noticing the room when I first visited the warehouse and had assumed it was probably an old supervisor's office. Then the lights were on up there, glowing from behind the blinds, but now it's just a vacuum of darkness hovering above the warehouse. In fact, if I hadn't seen it the first time, I might not even have noticed it now.

After searching around once more for anyone who could possibly point me to Margaret or Dakota, I walk up the metal staircase. Yanking on the door does nothing. The knob jiggles in my hand. It's not locked. It's just stuck. I try the door again and this time I lift up, which seems to do the trick. I fumble for a moment for the light switch on the wall. Above me, the lights buzz and flicker before turning on completely.

My eyes strain as they adjust to the harsh lighting. All the desks once occupying this room are pushed to one corner, precariously stacked on top of one another. But right in front of me, nearest to the door, is a hospital bed with monitors buzzing and beeping and a bag of fluids hooked up to an IV, which is connected to the arm of the girl in the bed.

The girl lying in the bed. A girl in the bed. Girl. The words loop in my head over and over again. *It's just another set*, I tell myself. *This isn't real.*

But it is. And I know that girl. I barely recognize her ashen complexion and her hair slicked back and away from her face.

Colleen Bristow.

I've really got to quit stumbling upon nearly dead girls. It's turning into a habit.

I rush to her side and try to shake her awake. "Colleen, Colleen, Colleen, Colleen, Colleen." I whisper her name over and over again, but she's not waking up. According to the monitors, her heart rate seems normal—at least from what I know about monitors like these from television shows—but she's unresponsive. Like Gretchen. Except Colleen seems like she's just sleeping. Gretchen was definitely awake, even if she was only a shell.

"Colleen, wake up," I beg her. "Please, wake up."

I pace at the foot of her bed. I can't leave her. But what is she even doing here in the first place? Who brought her here? What did they do to her? Is it the same thing that happened to Gretchen?

Footsteps pound up the metal staircase. I quickly scan the room for exits, but there's only one way in and one way out.

You can't fly if there's nowhere to go.

24

I duck down and roll under Colleen's bed. It's the only place I can think to hide. I watch as two sets of feet in black boots walk in, followed by two feet in red flats.

"Did someone leave the light on in here?" asks one voice. I don't want it to be true, but I quickly recognize the voice to be Margaret's.

I hold my breath, waiting for the other voice. *Please don't be Dakota. Please don't be Dakota.*

"I'll check the tapes," a deep, husky voice responds. "Maybe whoever brought her here after the procedure. We've just got her in here for temporary monitoring anyway."

I hold a hand over my mouth, silencing my sigh. Definitely not Dakota. My heart thuds in my chest so loudly that surely everyone in this room can hear it, even Colleen.

"How much longer do we give her before pulling the plug?" the voice asks.

One set of boots approaches the bed so closely I could tie the shoelaces together.

"The A+ identified her as a psiot," says Margaret. "She was a success! A true success! There's no pulling the plug on her or this project."

"I don't know that we can actually say that she was identified via the strain we injected her with. At least not with assured confidence, ma'am," says a third, mousier voice.

I nearly choke. A psiot? Did Margaret Toliver just use the word *psiot*? And could she really be talking about Colleen Bristow? Colleen isn't a psiot. She couldn't be. She's just plain old Colleen. But then I was just plain old Faith before Peter activated me.

And A+ . . . the same drug Ches was caught—

My phone rings and I fumble to pull it out of my pocket only to find Dakota's face flashing on my screen. I don't have time to think about how stupid I am and how no one teaches you how to be a psiot or a superhero or whatever but if they did, the first lesson would be to put your stupid phone on silent.

"Is that you?" Margaret asks.

And before either voice can answer, I roll out from under the bed and make a run for it, dashing to the door.

"Stop her!" screams Margaret from the other side of the bed.

I yank the door up and out as hard as I can and slam it

behind me, praying the door jams to buy me just a bit of time.

On the landing, an instinct I feel like I've been searching months for takes over, and I shoot off from my feet, soaring over the handrail. "Whoa!" I gasp, realizing just how close I am to the ceiling before leveling out and just holding my position there in midair.

Behind me the door flings open and a balding man with a scar darting through his left brow crowds the doorframe. Nigel. I recognize him from the club that one night. He stands, slack-jawed, with Margaret behind him, her face mirroring his. I guess it's not every day you see an unexpected fangirl floating forty or fifty feet off the ground.

Adrenaline and self-assurance more potent than anything I've ever felt pulse through my veins, and suddenly Nigel begins floating. At first a few inches, and then inches turn into feet.

Nigel lets out a panicked yelp.

I look down at my hands, expecting to find lightning pulsing out of my fingertips or lasers shooting from my eyes. Did I do that? How? And if I did actually do that, how do I do it again?

Nigel drops back down to the landing on all fours, his chest heaving.

I don't know what the hell that was all about, and I don't think I have time to figure it out right now.

On the other side of the warehouse, Dakota walks in

through the loading dock, her phone pressed to her ear as she leaves a voice mail—presumably for me. "Hey, just calling you back and was thinking—" Her whole body freezes as she sees me flying toward her until my toes skim the concrete floor.

But it's not surprise I see written across her face. She glances past me to Margaret, where she still stands on the landing of the stairs, and then back to me. Dakota's expression isn't full of marvel at the sight of me flying. Instead, her face is taut and concerned, like a kid who's been caught red-handed.

I don't have to ask. I already know. Dakota's in on whatever secret Margaret is keeping.

My whole body crashes as I'm tackled to the ground by a tall bald guy—Nigel. Pounding my fists against his chest, I do everything I can to squirm out from under him. I really need to pick up some self-defense skills. A swift kick to the groin buys me just enough time to fly back to my feet. Flying in closed quarters is pretty sticky, so I take a gamble and sprint toward the exit on foot. Toward Dakota.

"Stop her!" screeches Margaret.

Dakota's eyes narrow on me. Would she? Would she really try to stop me?

I don't want to find out.

Pure power strums through my veins as I push off from the ground and soar up just high enough to glide right over her before tumbling to the ground and rolling under the freight door. Somehow the act of getting into my car is the most challenging thing I've done in the last two minutes. My hands shake as I search for my car keys and stab them into the ignition.

A loud pop shoots off behind me, and there's Dakota racing toward me with a—with a gun! In her hand! An actual gun!

Oh hell no. I hit the gas, my tires spinning for a moment before I take off just in time to hear another pop echo behind me. She's shooting at me! Dakota—the girl I kissed just yesterday—is now shooting at me.

I get one last glimpse of Dakota as she chases after my car, dirt flying up around her and a black pistol dangling from her fingertips as I speed away.

**25**

For what feels like hours, I drive in circles. I can't go home. They know where I live. And not only that, they know what I can do. I wish I could talk to Ches. Maybe she'd have some kind of answers for me.

Guilt and anger assault me in waves. Ches. I should visit Ches.

I'm almost out of gas and I have to go home eventually. I can't leave Grandma Lou alone for that much longer.

When I finally pull into the driveway, the porch light is on. "Grandma Lou?" I call, walking through the front door and past the living room, where the TV plays through her shows. "Grandma Lou?"

"We're in here," she calls from the kitchen.

My whole body tenses. Sitting there at my kitchen table is Dakota, flanked by two hulking men in black T-shirts and jeans. All these bodyguards look the same time. Beefcake meatheads. I guess Nigel was still a little shaken up from his quick little flight, which I still don't understand at all.

"Dakota was just introducing me to her friends, Remi and Carl," she says, pointing to each of them before spooning some casserole into a dish for me. "I told her you must have gotten held up at the shelter."

I nod, barely able to keep my cool. I wish I could send some kind of signal to Grandma Lou by simply raising my eyebrows. "Yeah. The shelter."

Grandma Lou looks from me to Dakota and back again. "I'll, uh, give you and your friends a moment." She points to Carl again. "You don't leave before I can get you my casserole recipe."

Carl nods. "Yes, ma'am."

I don't know if that totally freaks me out or at least gives me some sense of relief that they didn't do anything to Grandma Lou, but I'm angry at just the thought of it. How dare Dakota come into my home with my grandmother? Especially when she knows everything that's going on with Grandma Lou. Surely she wouldn't use that against me. But who knows? I don't think I even know her anymore.

I try to see if there are knives left in the knife block or anything else on the kitchen counters that might help me defend myself.

"We're not here to hurt you," says Dakota, catching my gaze as I size up the utensils drying by the sink.

I turn to her, my voice venomous. "Is that what you say to all the girls you chase after with a gun?"

She shrugs. "I was only trying to slow you down. Hit a tire, maybe."

"That's supposed to make me feel better?" I say a little too loudly.

Dakota pulls out a chair for me to sit, and between Remi and Carl, I don't think I have much of a choice.

I set down the plate Grandma Lou left for me on the table and push it away. I have no intention of eating right now.

Carl pulls the plate in front of him. "You mind?" he asks.

I shrug. "You probably left a bruise, by the way."

He grunts before digging in. "If that's all you walk away with, consider yourself lucky," he says with a mouthful of casserole.

A chill crawls up my spine. "What do you want?" I ask Dakota, trying so hard to see her for what she is and not what I wish she were.

"I want to talk to you about what you saw."

"Oh, you mean the unconscious girl hooked up to an IV and monitors in the middle of a warehouse where your TV show films? And how the A+ is coming from you all too?"

That last part I don't know to be totally true, but maybe she can confirm that for me.

Remi cracks his knuckles before crossing his arms over his chest.

How is this even my life right now?

"Listen," says Dakota, leaning toward me. "This is all part of something bigger. It's more than a few missing people and animals and a harmless upper circulating around high schools."

"You knew I was looking for Colleen," I tell her. "And what about Gretchen? She's still not responding to anyone! And what kind of person abducts animals?" I feel absolutely sick with myself that I fell so hard for her and that even now it's difficult to parse out my feelings for her.

Remi grunts and Carl takes one last bite of casserole before mirroring Remi's posture.

"Faith, you can be a part of something big. But if you want no part of this . . . or me, then you at least have to promise me your silence."

"Why would I ever do that? Did you know Ches got caught selling that A+ garbage? Actually, not even selling it. Just in the wrong place at the wrong time, and her life is basically ruined now. And what about Whitney? Was she even a stalker, or was she just some other person whose life you ruined?"

Anger flares in her nostrils. She stands, and Carl and Remi follow her lead. "I don't want bad things to happen to you, Faith. I don't want bad things to happen to Grandma Lou or Matt or Ches or anyone else you love. But that's up to you. All you have to do is keep a low profile like you always have. Besides, that shouldn't be too much of a challenge for someone like you. You're unnoticeable, Faith. Unremarkable. Do yourself and everyone you love a favor and stay that way."

I pull my body back as far away from her as it will go. Unnoticeable. Unremarkable. How could she say that? I nearly hiss from the sting of it, but it takes just a second longer to really understand exactly what it is she's trying to say to me. "Are you—are you threatening me?"

Dakota nods. "Yes, Faith. I am. And don't for a minute think I won't follow through."

26

The moment Dakota and her two meatheads are gone, I check every door and window. After doing the dishes and mentally searching the last few months for some kind of clue, I sit down in the living room with Grandma Lou while she watches the news.

"Everything okay with you and Dakota?" she asks. "I didn't realize she had bodyguards, but I guess when you're as famous as she is, you can never be too careful."

"We're fine," I tell her, pulling a quilt around my shoulders and lying down on my side as the blue glow of the television washes over us.

"You know you can be honest with me, right?"

I nod. "Yeah, Grandma Lou."

"And you know I wouldn't think anything of it if you and Dakota were . . . more than friends, right?"

My lower lip quivers. Of course Grandma Lou would

see what was right there in front of her. I never even thought twice about what she might think about me liking other girls. More than anything, though, I hate that Dakota stole this perfect moment from me. "Thanks," I tell her. "I think whatever was happening with me and Dakota is over . . . but I have a feeling it won't be the last time I have feelings for a girl. Or boy."

She chuckles. "We used to call that switch-hitting back in my day."

I laugh and cringe a little too. "I think the word these days is bisexual. Or pansexual," I offer.

"Well, whatever you want to be called is up to you, and I'm sorry to hear about you and Dakota. I liked her quite a bit, but if she doesn't make my Faith happy, then she doesn't make me happy."

This is a moment I want to treasure and remember forever, because I know my days with Grandma Lou are numbered, but all I can think of is Colleen in that bed, and her sister, still searching for her.

I don't know if I can save Colleen. Or anyone else who might be there, but I have to try. I have to talk to Ches. If she's embroiled in A+, maybe she knows something that will help me, or at the very least I can warn her that this situation is much bigger and scarier than she knows.

After Grandma Lou goes to bed, I open my bedroom door and climb out onto the roof. What's the point of flying if you can't sneak out of your room to do it at least once? At least that's what I tell my brimming uncertainty. After zipping up my jacket, I make a running leap off the roof and begin to fly toward the jail, ignoring the tension coiling in my chest. I've never actually visited someone in jail before, but there's a first time for everything.

I decide to land a block from the police station, since they probably have security cameras in the parking lot. Inside the police station, a younger white officer with her auburn hair wrapped in a low bun at the nape of her neck sits with a pen in hand, jotting something down, a phone cradled in the crook of her neck. "Yeah. Uh-huh. Yes, ma'am. Well, this is a nonemergency number, but even then, ducks in your hot tub is more of an animal control issue, but I'm sure if you just leave the ducks—" She holds a finger up for me to wait just a moment. "Hello? Ma'am?" She pulls the phone back and stares at it.

I stand there for a few moments as she jots down a few notes and signs off on some kind of form. Finally, she looks up and, with a sigh, asks, "Are you here to report a crime?"

I shake my head. "No, I'm here to see an inmate."

"Unless you're the youngest lawyer in the state, you'll have to wait for the inmate to get transferred to county."

This would be so much easier if Ches didn't have an early birthday and hadn't turned eighteen in August. If she was still a minor, I bet she would've already been released to her mom or something.

This cop seems pretty tough, but I'm not budging until I see Ches. I look at her badge. "Officer Taylor? Can you at least tell me if my friend is here? Her name is Francesca Palmer. She was arrested a few days ago and she's waiting to see the judge again."

"I said it once, but I'll say it again. Unless you're her lawyer—"

"Faith?" asks a voice I recognize from behind Officer Taylor. "Faith? Is everything all right?"

Detective Wallace sidles up beside Officer Taylor. I haven't seen or spoken with her since the night at the corn maze, which makes me wonder if she's gotten any further on what happened to Gretchen.

"I'm trying to visit my friend. Her name is Francesca Palmer."

She nods and leans in closer to me. "That girl's your friend?" She lets out a low whistle. "DA is coming down hard on anything that has a whiff of that A+ stuff. If your friend knows anything, she should talk and get herself a deal."

"I have to see her," I say with absolute desperation.

Detective Wallace looks to Officer Taylor, who shrugs and says, "Your funeral."

Detective Wallace opens a swinging gate for me to walk through. "I can give you five minutes. Follow me."

It takes everything I have not to squeal and hug Detective Wallace, but I suck in a deep breath and gather myself.

Detective Wallace doesn't strike me as a hugger. And Officer Taylor is definitely not a hugger.

I follow Detective Wallace through a maze of desks, some of which are occupied, but mostly ten o'clock on a Monday night in Glenwood seems like a pretty quiet time at the police station.

Down a hallway and a few turns later, Detective Wallace takes me to a desk, where she waves to the officer behind the counter and signs me in. She flashes her card at a panel above the door handle before leading me into one of those rooms, just like I've seen in countless movies, that's divided in half by Plexiglas with tables, chairs, and phones on either side. It's actually kind of cool to even see one of these rooms in real life, and if this weren't such an awful situation, it might actually be sort of fun.

Detective Wallace has me wait at the second chair. "I'll be right outside. You've got five minutes."

I nod. "Thank you. Thank you so much."

"Maybe you can talk some sense into her."

I wait in silence for about ten minutes before the door on the other side of the glass swings open and Ches shuffles in with an officer close behind her. I expect her to be cuffed, but she's not. Her hair is shiny with grease and pulled back into a floppy ponytail. I barely recognize her without her perfectly smudged eyeliner. The most shocking thing, however, are the bright orange scrubs they've given her to wear. Definitely not Ches's aesthetic.

The moment she lays eyes on me, her chin begins to quiver.

Instinctively, I stand, like I might somehow be able to press my body through the glass and hug her. "Hey, it's okay," I coo.

She sinks into her chair and picks up the phone, and I do the same.

"I'm so embarrassed," she blurts.

"No, no, no," I tell her. "Don't be embarrassed. It's just a waste of time and energy. You made one mistake that turned into something way bigger and got blown out of proportion."

Tears spill down her cheeks as she hiccups back a sob. "I just needed a little extra help to stay awake. I swear. And then Grant—stupid Grant—asked me to meet him the other night and then bam! Here I am. It was so scary, Faith. There was so much blood. And what if this is on my record forever? What if—"

"Ches, listen, I know you're probably really freaked out, okay?" I look up at the clock on the wall above her head. "But I need you to be very careful." I clear my throat before whispering, "These people are dangerous. This is much bigger than Grant or a stupid little drug to keep you up at night, and probably even bigger than this injured drug dealer. Do you have a lawyer? Doesn't the court appoint one for you or something?"

"No," she says. "That's what's so weird. My mom said a lawyer contacted her and that they were hired by the people Grant worked for."

"Well, what did she say?"

"What was she supposed to say? We can't afford a lawyer, and Mom thinks this one is probably at least better than whoever the court appoints."

I remember what Detective Wallace said about Ches getting a deal. "Ches, is there anything you know about the people who are behind all this? Anything you can share with the police to get you out of here?"

She huffs. "Everyone thinks I know stuff. It's all stupid Grant's fault. That kid doesn't know shit, but he's talking a big game, like he's some kind of kingpin, so now they think we know way more than we do. I've said it a million times, Faith. Wrong place. Wrong time."

"I believe you," I promise her.

"Will you get my homework for me?" she asks with a sob.

"Of course," I say with a sad nod, even though her problems are much bigger than late homework.

"And—and Grandma Lou . . . is she doing okay?"

My heart contorts in my chest. "Oh, Ches . . . yes, she's okay for now."

So many things are racing through my head. I don't have any proof or evidence to offer the police to get Ches out of here. I could tell them about Colleen. I mean, I *should* tell them about Colleen. And I will, but I just need to buy myself a little more time to figure out a few more things. If the police just walk right into that place with a warrant, I might never find out what Margaret knows about psiots—or maybe Margaret is a psiot! A small hopeful part of me thinks that maybe this is all a misunderstanding and that no one's actually been hurt and that this is for some kind of greater good. Because no matter how hard I try to convince myself otherwise, I can't shake Margaret from the pedestal she's on in my head.

"All right," says the officer in the corner of the room. "Time's up."

"Ches, listen to me. Everything is going to be fine. I'm going to get your homework. You'll see the judge again and they'll see that this is all Grant's fault."

"Move it," the officer says.

"I'd never even seen a gun in real life until he pulled it out." Ches stands and I press my palm against the glass, wishing I had the ability to dissolve it by just the touch of my skin, so that I could take her hand in my hand and tell her that it will be okay. I want to tell her exactly what to do, but I don't even know what the hell to do myself. "I love you, Ches. I'll come and see you again as soon as I can."

She presses her palm against the glass too. "I think they're moving me in the morning," she says in a hurry as the officer grips her upper arm.

"I'll call your mom," I promise her. "And I'll bring Matt next time."

She sniffs. "I love you too, Faith."

27

The next morning, I barely make it to school on time. After I park the car, I notice Matt walking inside, his backpack slung over one shoulder. "Matt!" I call.

He glances over his shoulder and then keeps walking.

"I know you saw me," I mutter. I'll catch up with him at lunch and tell him I saw Ches. Maybe she'll have seen the judge again.

For first period, I head over to journalism and the hallways are swirling with energy.

Johnny sits at my desk, waiting for me. "Oh my God, there you are." He hoists his phone out in front of me, hands it to me, and hits play on a video.

"Yes, Sue," says a man in a black zip-up jacket with the Channel Five logo embroidered to the chest. "This is as close as police will allow us to the scene, but it appears that the vehicle delivering the two suspects from the jail to the courthouse this morning was struck by an armored vehicle. One suspect was killed during the collision and the other was taken by the drivers of the armored vehicle. We have yet to confirm which of the two suspects was killed on impact." The screen cuts to a picture of Ches and one of Grant, both last year's school photos. "One of the suspects is confirmed to be Francesca Palmer, and while the other is a minor, it's believed that he is Grant Vincent, the son of Paul Vincent, the CEO and cofounder of Vincent and Walt Lending."

The phone drops from my hands and the air is sucked out of my lungs as I realize there's exactly a fifty-fifty chance that Ches is dead.

The journalism door swings open and it's Matt, barreling toward me. "Faith." My name is the only word he manages to get out before he's sobbing.

I hold him in a hug and we're both crying into each other's shoulders.

"We should have been there for her," he says. "This is my fault."

I want to tell him that no, it isn't. This isn't the kind of thing that's so easily clear-cut, but the truth is that I don't know. Maybe this is our fault.

I pull back from Matt. "I have to go," I tell him.

"What? Are you serious? I'm coming with you."

I'm not quite sure how to let him in on my psiot abilities. I don't know if he can handle the possibility of one best friend being dead and the other harboring the superhuman skill of flight in the same day. "I can't take you with me right now."

His expression hardens. I'll figure out how to tell him, how to explain all this. Just not today.

I hug him once more and give him a kiss on the cheek. "I'm sorry. I love you." And then I have to choke back a sob as I remember the last time I told Ches I loved her, with our palms pressed against the Plexiglas at the jail.

I double back for my bag and Johnny catches my wrist. "Where are you going?"

I only shake my head at him as I squeeze past Mrs. Raburn before the final first-period bell rings. Secrets suck.

Thankfully, Grandma Lou is out with Miss Ella, so I don't have to worry about either of them pestering me about skipping school. At home, I race up to my room and lift my mattress, revealing a small pile of mementos from my time at the Harbinger Foundation. The hospital gown I escaped in, my intake bracelet, and a napkin with Peter Stanchek's phone number on it.

I promised myself I'd never call this number. It doesn't even take closing my eyes to remember the moment Peter handed me this napkin. *In case of emergency*, he wrote above the phone number.

That night when Peter broke me out of the Harbinger Foundation, after I dove off the roof, I waited for him on the ground as I paced back and forth. The moment I hit the ground I felt immediately guilty for leaving him up there to fend for himself. Surely, though, he was capable of escaping that kind of dilemma. For all I knew, Peter was the bad guy and the Harbinger Foundation and Mr. Harada were trying to contain him.

I shook my head. Nope. Something didn't feel right. With both my fists curled into balls, I pushed off from the ground as hard as I could. I'd just fly right up there and see what was going on myself.

About halfway up the building, I heard a guttural scream as a body was flung over the edge.

Wait. I knew that Cubs T-shirt. Clumsily, I changed course and flew straight for him. I was about as good at flying as I was navigating bumper cars, which wasn't very good at all, but I tried with every ounce of energy I had.

Swooping down, I threw my arms out and prayed this would work. A gust of wind rushed past me, making it hard to breathe.

I grunted as Peter's body collided with mine. He was falling so quickly and with such force that it took everything in me to slow our momentum.

Below us, I spied a full dumpster. Our chances were slightly better if we hit that instead of the concrete.

Thud! Our bodies hit the bags of trash and the two of us lay in the dumpster spread out like starfish.

"Whoa," Peter said.

Overhead, people peered over the edge, but it was too dark down here for them to see us.

Peter's phone vibrated. "Hello? Yeah, meet us on the south side— Faith, we gotta move it before those guys figure out we're not dead."

"My whole body hurts from that landing."

Peter laughed. "My face even hurts."

Both of us moaned as we swung ourselves over and out of the dumpster, and in seconds, a small red Toyota Prius squealed to a stop at the end of the alleyway.

"Where are we going?" I asked as we jogged toward the car.

"Well, you have two choices. You can stick with me or you can go home."

"Faith!" I heard a voice call through a gust of wind.

"Did you hear that?" I asked Peter.

"Hear what?" he asked as he slid into the front seat.

I shook my head and got into the back. I was so desperate to hear my own name again that I could even hear it in the wind.

A white girl a little older than me with her black hair chopped into a pixie cut raised a perfectly manicured and pierced eyebrow at me from the rearview mirror. "Who's this?"

"I'm Faith," I told her. "Thanks for the ride."

"Kris," she said, and turned to Peter. "You want to tell me what the hell is going on?"

As Kris drove us out of town, Peter told both of us everything. The Harbinger Foundation wasn't as benevolent as they'd made themselves out to be. Toyo Harada was building an army of psiots and wanted Peter to activate them at his command. This left Peter with no choice, since he was the only psiot with his particular skill set.

He turned back to me. "Activation is like those old witch tests from back in the day, when they'd throw suspected witches in a lake with boulders weighing them down. Escape and you're a witch. Sink and congrats! At least you were human. Activation is a fifty-fifty chance of survival at best. But because of whatever messed-up stuff I have going on in my head, I can attempt activation without harming the subject, so my options were stick around and watch Harada's lackeys attempt activation on innocent people and possibly kill them or help Harada build his army of psiots, which I'm pretty sure he doesn't plan on using for good."

"That's, like, straight out of a comic book," I said. "Do you have, like, a secret identity or something?"

Kris laughed. "I like her."

"So I don't know what's next, but I know it includes taking down Harada," Peter said.

"What about the other kids I was brought in with?" I

asked, remembering that girl on the bus with freckles peppering the bridge of her nose.

He shrugged. "A few were successfully activated, but some are probably dead."

The thought made me sick with guilt.

"Listen," Peter said. "I'm haunted by plenty of things. Trust me. Don't let this destroy you."

In the rearview mirror, Kris gave me an encouraging smile. "You're alive. You saved Peter. That counts for a whole hell of a lot."

Their words helped, but I still thought about not only the others who had died, but the ones who had been activated and would be Harada's pawns. They were trapped, and I hadn't even tried to go back and free them.

"Peter," I said, "why did you even bring me here to begin with if you were just going to ditch this place anyway?"

He shook his head. "I guess I still had faith." He chuckled. "I thought maybe Harada wasn't all bad and that I don't know . . . but I was wrong. That's for sure."

The three of us sat there in silence for a moment, allowing the weight of that to sink in.

"So, Faith," Peter said, interrupting our guilt fest. "We can take you home or you can stick with us if home isn't a good option . . . or if home doesn't even exist."

The way he said it sounded like he spoke from experience

and that home wasn't a concept Peter had much practice with. I was lucky, though. I had a home. I had friends. I had Grandma Lou. But this could be an adventure. My greatest adventure. I could kick ass and maybe even save the day. It all came back to Grandma Lou, though. We only had each other. If I was going to leave, it couldn't be without a goodbye. "Home," I finally said.

Peter studied me for a moment before nodding.

I liked Peter and Kris. I liked how familiar they were with each other and all the ways they reminded me of Ches and Matt . . . if Ches and Matt also had raging crushes on each other. The three of us took turns driving, and Kris even ran into a truck stop and bought me some sweatpants and a T-shirt.

It was early morning when Kris crossed the town line for Glenwood, the splintered welcome sign greeting us. "Home sweet home," she chirped.

"You sure you can't stay with us?" Peter asked as we stood in front of my house. Grandma Lou would be awake at any moment. Miss Ella was probably already snooping from her bedroom window.

"This was a mistake," I told him. "These last few weeks were a huge mistake." But the truth was that part of me wanted to stick around with Peter and Kris. After Ches and Matt ditched me to go to Georgia for the summer, it was hard to feel like I even had anything to go back to.

"Didn't seem like a mistake when you saved my life."

I laughed. "Someone would have caught you."

He shrugged. "I'd rather you stick around so I don't have to take my chances."

"Peter," I said. "Thank you for saving me. In the lab. And then freeing me. I would've . . . who knows what would've happened to me?"

"Guess that makes us even then," he said.

"Guess so."

"Besides, you need to graduate high school. Do all that normal teenage bullshit I missed out on."

Kris rolled her eyes. "Psiot or not, normal teenage shit never stood a chance against you, Peter."

That morning when Grandma Lou woke up to find me back home, she let out a delighted squeal and immediately made plans for some kind of Spam-based dinner that night. She couldn't believe I was home a few days early and that the camp bus had dropped me off at my house.

"Now, that's what I call service," she said.

She berated me a bit for never responding to her calls or postcards—none of which I ever received. I spent the next few days breathless over the fact that I'd come home so simply, reinserting myself into normal life like nothing had changed. Like I hadn't been part of some dangerous experiment I'd only barely survived and as if I hadn't woken up with a superhuman ability to soar through the sky.

Now, with the memories of a summer I wish I could forget spread out in front of me, I tap Peter's number into my phone. For a quick moment, I wonder if this was the kind of emergency he meant, but truthfully, I don't have time to second-guess myself. I can only act.

The line rings over and over again so many times that I almost just hang up, but then Peter's voice says, "If you've got this number, you know who this is. If you don't know who this is, lose this number. If you're still on the line, leave a message after the beep."

"Peter. It's Faith. I've gotten myself into—something's going on in Glenwood. I need you to call me back." And because I don't want there to be any mistake, I add, "This is an emergency."

I try calling again but get the voice mail again. With little else to do, I put everything back under my mattress, and then I lie on my bed and call Peter once more. This problem is much bigger than me.

I lie there for a while with my phone clutched to my chest until drowsiness begins to sink around me like a fog. I should turn the news on. Maybe there's an update on the crash. Maybe they've released the name of the deceased. I don't want to hope that it's Grant . . . but I do hope that it's Grant. I just hope . . .

My phone rings again and again and again and it won't stop. It won't stop. My fingers fumble over the screen and I hold it to my ear. "Peter?" I ask, my voice thick with sleep. "Finally."

"Faith." But it's not Peter who speaks my name. "Faith. Can you hear me?"

For a moment, it's easy to forget that the last twenty-four hours even happened. It's easy to imagine that this Dakota is the same Dakota who just two days ago kissed me, but then I quickly remember that just yesterday that same Dakota shot at me.

"Faith?"

I sit up, working the dryness out of my mouth. "What do you want? Didn't threaten me quite enough from the safety of my own kitchen?"

"I only have a few minutes," she says. "I'm a shit person. I get it. I don't need you to remind me."

That silences me for a moment.

"I know what you are," she tells me.

And then I remember—she's seen what I can do.

"Good and evil is black-and-white for you, Faith. You've always had that luxury. But none of this is that simple. A+ is more than just an upper."

"Yeah," I tell her. "You're hurting people with it. You're making animals and people your . . . experiments." The word leaves a bad taste in my mouth.

"It's not perfect, okay? Things like this don't just start out perfect, but what if I told you something like A+ could help us identify other psiots?" She whispers that last word.

"What do you even know about psiots?" I spit.

She doesn't answer me. "What if there was one tiny little pill that could have saved you all the pain and trauma of what happened to you last summer?"

"You don't know anything about what happened to me," I say through gritted teeth.

"We're so close, Faith. We're so close to perfecting this thing. Think of all the pain it could save people like us."

Like us? People like us? Is Dakota a psiot? I have too many questions and not enough brainpower to organize them. "At what cost?" I ask. "What about Gretchen and Colleen and the homeless people who went missing? And the animals, Dakota! Where are they? And Grant and Ches! They were arrested and now one of them is dead and the other is missing. I don't even know if my best friend is alive, Dakota!"

"Gretchen and Colleen were never part of the original plan," she assures me, like that's supposed to change something. "Besides, Colleen is safe for now. And I'm the one who planted Gretchen in the maze. I wanted her to be found . . . I can't explain it all right now. I have to go. Just . . . don't do anything rash, okay? Keep your head down."

"Was it real?" I manage to ask. "Us?"

There is silence for a long moment and I think maybe she's gone. "So real it stings," she finally says.

"It wasn't just my blog," I tell her. "You knew more than that."

"I did."

"Am I the whole reason why you're in Glenwood?" I feel foolish even asking her. Surely this entire operation and TV show didn't uproot itself just for me.

"One of the reasons," she tells me.

Tears threaten to spill. "You could just leave it all," I tell her. "We can save people. We can help people like . . . like you. Without hurting other people. Without making other people experiments. This doesn't have to be who you are."

"You have no idea who I have to be," she tells me, her voice clipped and unflinching. "You have no idea."

"Dakota—"

"Ches is alive. Now just stay out of it, Faith. Trust me."

And then the line cuts out.

Relief hits me like a gust of wind. Ches is alive. Somehow, I have more questions than I did before answering her call. I'm dizzy with possibilities and uncertainty. But Ches is alive! Before I even know what I'm doing, my fingers are fumbling to dial Matt.

The line only rings for half a second. "Faith? She's alive," he says. "I just talked to Ms. Palmer. She—"

I don't hear anything else, because both of us are crying so hard that words are useless.

"So where's Ches?" I finally ask.

"No one knows," he says. "Faith, I'm really freaked out."

"How does no one know?"

"I don't know," he says. "Ms. Palmer said it's like she was kidnapped."

Dakota knew Ches was alive, which could only mean that Margaret is behind this and she's going to great lengths to stop Ches and Grant from appearing in court. So great, in fact, that Grant is dead. He might have been awful, but that doesn't mean he deserved to die.

I don't know what exactly is going on, but I do know that whatever that drug does, it's already ruined Ches's life. And no matter what comes of this, Dakota had a part in that.

Colleen. I can't forget Colleen too, hooked up to all those monitors.

After I hang up with Matt, I almost call the police. That's the most obvious answer. But for very selfish reasons, I don't. If the police show up at the *Grove* headquarters, it's very likely that I'll never know what Dakota meant when she said there's something out there that could have saved me from the hell that was this summer. It's too late for me, but I know the Harbinger Foundation is out there trying to find other kids like me. Just because I'm safe doesn't mean others will be. And I can't count how many nights I've spent staring up at the ceiling, wondering what happened to all the other kids on my bus. When Peter broke me out, all the other dorms—no, cells—were empty. It's all too easy for my brain to rewrite history and for me to pretend that they all just happened to be in other parts of the compound, when the truth that eats away at me is that I was the only one to make it out.

At least I know Ches is alive. If they'd wanted her dead, they would have killed her on the scene. At least I think so.

I need a plan. I need a clear head and a good plan.

I reach for a blank pack of note cards on my bedroom floor and carefully remove every picture and article clipping from my corkboard. One note card at a time, I write down everything I know. I map every fact out just like Mrs. Raburn taught us.

The first card reads: *My name is Faith Herbert, and my psiot abilities were activated at the Harbinger Foundation by Peter Stanchek.*

28

All of Glenwood is buzzing with the news of Ches and Grant. A few hours after I found out Ches was alive, the local news breaks the story that she was the one taken in the unmarked armored vehicle. The next night, Grant's family's lawyer makes a statement, naming Grant as the deceased and asking for the media and citizens of Glenwood to give the Vincent family time and privacy to mourn.

Miss Ella sits on the couch with us and snarls as the lawyer takes questions. "That Francesca girl is all trouble. Faith, you're lucky. That could have been you in the morgue instead of that Vincent boy."

I unleash on her immediately without even trying to temper my response. "Don't you dare talk about Ches like you have a clue what's going on. Ches has more loyalty and character in her pinky than you have in your whole body. Maybe if you didn't spend all your time gossiping and speculating about other people, you'd have an actual life of your own to concern yourself with."

"Faith," Grandma Lou says gently.

Miss Ella stands, her lips pursed, and clears her throat. "I'll see myself out. Talk to you tomorrow, Lou."

The next morning, I leave a sticky note on Miss Ella's door with a short apology. Honestly, I'm not one for grudges, but that's the best she's getting out of me after what she said about Ches.

Over the weekend, I hang out at Matt's for a few hours, but nothing is the same. We awkwardly trip over each other's words and can't find anything on TV that doesn't remind us of Ches, so eventually I head home. I want to tell Matt what I'm working on and include him, but I've already got one friend in danger. I can't risk Matt getting hurt too.

The Wednesday before Thanksgiving, I drive Grandma Lou and Miss Ella to the grocery store. Miss Ella normally flies out to spend the holiday with her son's family in Arizona, but this year she said she's not up for having it out with her daughter-in-law over the correct way to make stuffing. Really, I think she just wants to spend the time with Grandma Lou while she still can, even if she's not willing to admit it.

That night, with her arm elbow deep up a turkey's ass while she looks out through her kitchen window into the dark backyard, Grandma Lou says in a matter-of-fact voice,

"I've put some thought to it. Faith, you turn eighteen in February. I don't feel right leaving you until after you're done with school in May. I've looked at a few assisted living places around town, and not all of them are that bad."

I look to Miss Ella, but she trains her eyes on the linoleum floor, and it's pretty clear that Grandma Lou didn't do this on her own.

"Starting in December, I'll hire a home care nurse, who will spend some time with me every day. I don't want you worrying at school or work. In fact, I'd like it if nothing about your life had to change."

Miss Ella grunts. "Well, if I'd known you were hiring someone, I would've taken the job."

Grandma Lou chuckles. "Ella, you couldn't pay me to hire you as my caretaker."

"Well, I'll remember that next time you need a ride to the grocery store," says Miss Ella, a smile curling her wrinkled lips.

Their banter does nothing to distract me. "Grandma Lou, we don't have to do all that. I'm happy to check on you. And I know Miss Ella is too."

Grandma Lou shakes her head firmly. "It's important that I make decisions while they're still mine to make. Don't you take that away from me." She looks over her shoulder. "But for now, let's just be thankful for what we've got, and what we've got is today."

I want to fight, but I've got no argument. I can't imagine how powerless she feels in all of this. I'll give her as many chances to make her own decisions as I can. That's the least I can do.

The next morning, I wake up later than I'd hoped for, and already Grandma Lou and Miss Ella are clamoring around in the kitchen, getting a start on our Thanksgiving feast. Miss Ella has made it perfectly clear that she expects to eat around noon, because she hopes to have an appetite for a turkey sandwich nightcap, and the only way that will happen is if she starts early.

After a quick shower, I let my hair air-dry and as I'm pulling a sweatshirt over my head, my phone rings.

"Hello," I answer, using speakerphone while I shimmy into a pair of leggings.

"Faith," says Matt, and he almost sounds like his normal self. "I was thinking we could go over and see Ches's mom tonight."

I plop down and take the phone off speaker. "Tonight?"

"Yeah. Sounds like the cops haven't made any headway on her whereabouts, and my mom wants me to bring a pie over, like this will all be fixed somehow with a sweet potato pie."

If only it were that simple. "What time?" I ask.

"Maybe like five?"

"Oh, um, I'm really not sure. Can I call you later this afternoon?"

He groans. "I guess so."

I have to remind myself that there are so many things he doesn't know. Heck, I haven't even found the time to tell him about Grandma Lou. "I really want to go," I tell him. "I've got to find out what Grandma Lou has planned for Thanksgiving dinner first." I swallow. That last part wasn't entirely true, and I'm finding myself lying enough that it's hard for even me to remember what's real and what's not.

"Whatever," he says. "I guess just text me when you figure out if you have time to visit our missing best friend's mom."

"Matt, you know I—" But he hangs up before I can finish, and at this rate, that's probably for the best.

I'm probably definitely the worst friend ever.

For a moment, I close my eyes and remind myself of all the facts I know to be true and how sometimes being the good guy doesn't leave much room for being the best person. At least, that's what I tell myself in an attempt to feel better. When I open my eyes, I find that I'm floating a few feet off the floor and that my hair is dangerously close to my ceiling fan. Talk about a hazard of the job. I haven't really figured out the exact rules of my abilities, but I'm starting to think that maybe the state I'm most comfortable in is not quite flying and not quite firmly planted on the ground, like the way it's so simple to let your body just float in a pool.

Downstairs, Miss Ella is quick to put me to work and has me peeling potatoes. She fusses at Grandma Lou, because Miss Ella has an actual formal dining room with fancier china and silverware. Grandma Lou takes it all in stride with smiles and chuckles, and I try not to concentrate on the fact that Grandma Lou is letting Miss Ella verbally trample her, because her lucid days are numbered and even Miss Ella's tiresome grumbling is something to be treasured. At least she's not trash-talking Ches.

It's a little ridiculous how much effort we're all putting into this one single meal. Grandma Lou and I don't normally go all out like this, but when we sit down at the kitchen table, cloaked in an orange plastic tablecloth and lit with candlesticks Miss Ella insisted on bringing over, there is something incredibly satisfying about it all. (If you can bring yourself to ignore the piles of dishes on the counters and in the sink and even the splash of mashed potatoes I managed to get on the wall—too high for me to clean without a step stool.)

Miss Ella holds her hands out for us both to take, and in a way, it reminds me of the time I played light as a feather, stiff as a board with Matt and Ches. There's something almost ceremonial about this meal and this moment.

"Lou, would you like to say grace?" Miss Ella asks.

Grandma Lou nods, even though I've never even heard the woman utter a word about her religious preferences. (Mom always said that was a result of Grandma Lou having a Catholic mother and a Jewish father, neither of whom were committed enough to either for anything to stick.)

"Dear God or Goddess in heaven—"

Miss Ella grunts.

I open one eye to catch Grandma Lou raise her brows and smirk.

"Like I was saying, thank you for this meal and these people who came together to make it happen. Today we're thankful for what we have and what we've had. Good things don't last forever, but that just makes every moment sweeter. We pray for our Ches on this day as well as her safe return." Grandma Lou squeezes my hand. "Amen."

"In *Jesus's* name, amen," says Miss Ella.

In between our quiet chewing as we enjoy the delicious fruits of our labor and throwing a few jokes and quips back and forth, I can't help but imagine the Friendsgiving I'd dreamed up with Dakota.

After the meal, we all sit around in the living room for a bit. Grandma Lou in her recliner, me sprawled on the floor, and Miss Ella spread out on the couch.

"Should I turn on football?" I ask.

"No," the two of them say in unison.

Once they're both snoring, I push myself up off the ground and start the first round of dishes. After that, in my room, I open my closet and reach for the outfit I set aside. Once I put it all on and lace up my black high-top Converses,

I can see very clearly that the whole ensemble doesn't really match the drawings of what I'd had in mind.

I dig into my underwear drawer for the notebook housing my sketches. I'm no artist, but the girl on the paper is sleeker and she's definitely not wearing sneakers, but I did what I could with the resources and time that I had. I'd sketched an elaborate jumpsuit with a billowing cape and knee-high boots. I look from the paper to the girl in the mirror, blond hair framing my face. Faded high-waisted skinny jeans and a white T-shirt with a homemade white cape with blue trim tied around my neck. I'd stitched a bright blue felt *Z* to my T-shirt, just like Laverne from *Laverne & Shirley*, Grandma Lou's favorite show. Except in my case the *Z* stands for Zephyr, the Greek god of the west wind. Bringer of light. And now 100 percent more badass. (The cape helps.) I don't look like your average superhero. I'm not perfectly sculpted with bulging muscles and ginormous gravity-defying boobs, but that doesn't matter. This body can fly. And I have to admit: I look pretty great in my makeshift costume.

Over the summer, when I asked Peter if he was a hero, he laughed in a way that made me feel silly for even asking. "Capes and good guys versus bad guys are comic-book bullshit, Faith."

Maybe that's true for Peter. Maybe he's stronger than I am. But I need a fresh skin to go out there and face the world. I need that extra layer of protection so that I can preserve who

I am deep down, so that I have something worth fighting for. Over this last week, while I hashed through every detail and connected as many dots as I could, I knew I couldn't do this on my own and that Peter wasn't calling me back anytime soon. I can't count on anyone else to save me, but maybe I can count on Zephyr. At least I hope I can. For Ches's sake. And Colleen's too.

I sit down in front of my desk and take one last look at the web of note cards and yarn on my corkboard. I couldn't connect all the dots. I couldn't make sense of it all. But what I do know is that Ches and Colleen need me, and if I'm going to save them and find out what it is exactly that Margaret is up to, today is the day to strike. Dakota herself said that almost everyone would be away seeing family. Here's hoping she didn't lie about that too.

With Grandma Lou and Miss Ella still snoozing, I leave a note on the pumpkin pie.

Be back soon. Save me a slice of pie. xo Faith

 **29**

My plan is simple:

- Find out what the heck is going on!
- Find Ches!
- Save Ches!
- Save Colleen!
- Save as many puppies and kitties as possible!
- Call 911!

Hopefully in that order. Okay. Maybe it's not so simple. But either way, I've got one window to strike and that's today.

Since almost all of Glenwood is either eating or passed out in food comas, I fly the whole way to the production offices. The only person who even notices me is a little girl playing on a tricycle in her backyard.

"That's a pretty bird," she shouts.

I've got nothing to lose at this point, so I do a quick figure eight for her—something I didn't even know I could do—and soar on to my destination, letting out a shriek of delight.

At the warehouse, I circle the perimeter, looking for an entrance. The place is locked down, and there's not a soul in sight. I decide to try something I've only seen on TV and take the scarf from around my neck and wrap it around my fist.

Walking up to one of the side doors with a window, I punch once and then twice, the glass shattering into the warehouse.

"Whoa," I mutter. Is this what it feels like to be a badass? I just punched my fist through a window. My fist! A window! Smugly, I reach through the frame to open the door, as I think of every gym teacher who ever told me to turn my fat into muscle. I bet those jerks weren't punching through windows. Hello, my name is Faith Herbert and I'm a badass fat girl.

As the door swings open, I force myself to concentrate as I plunge into darkness. *Check your ego, girl.* Small patches of light bleed in from tiny windows near the rafters, but not enough to make it any easier for my eyes to adjust.

The room where I last saw Colleen is dark, windows shaded, but that doesn't stop me from levitating over the set pieces and prop tables, past the stairs and to the door. My feet touch the ground, and suddenly I'm reminded of Nigel floating in the air before he crashed to the ground. Did I do that to him? Is that even possible? I've barely got a handle on flying solo; surely I can't take other things or people along with me for the ride unless I'm actually carrying them.

I try the door, but it's stuck, so I try again and this time I throw some muscle behind it. Finally, the door gives way and I tumble into an even darker room. My fingers fumble for the light switch, but when the fluorescents flicker to life, I find the room empty. No hospital bed. No fluid drip. No monitors. No Colleen.

I could kick myself for leaving her here. Across the room is another door, but this one is keypad protected. "Well, crud."

I tap the one, two, three, and four. A long beep lets me know I was wrong. Couldn't hurt to try.

Racking my brain, I try every significant number related to *The Grove* I can think of. First episode airdate. First episode directed by Margaret Toliver. Margaret's birthday. Dakota's birthday. Every address I can think of from the show.

I gasp. Margaret's favorite episode. Margaret went on record, citing Claire's abortion episode in 2006 as her favorite episode. Even though the network made the controversial decision never to air the episode, Margaret leaked it herself online. Episode 923.

I tap nine, two, and three into the keypad and hold my breath. The keypad chimes and the door clicks as it unlocks.

The moment I open the door, noise floods out. Raucous,

familiar noises. I step into a padded, seemingly soundproof room, the heavy door swinging shut behind me. Every inch, every wall from floor to ceiling is lined with kennels, and occupying every single one is a barking dog or a meowing cat.

"Oh. My. God." I'm immediately overwhelmed. I want to help them all. I want to save them all. But I have no way of doing this without it devolving into pure chaos. And besides, the minute I call the police, they'll all be freed. Colleen too. But I need to find Ches. And some answers too. I just need a little more time.

At least this place is immaculately clean. I've seen dogs come in from breeders gone bad that are in much worse shape. But still . . . who knows what kind of awful science experiment these sweet babies have been turned into?

Hanging on each kennel is a tiny clipboard with a subject number and other information.

A small black-and-white mutt cowers in the back of his kennel, and I stick my finger through the grate.

"Hey, sweetie," I coo. "It's okay. We're going to get you out of here."

He approaches me, tiptoeing closer. When his wet little nose is close enough to touch, I hold my finger out for him to sniff.

His jaw snaps as he snarls and nearly takes off my left pointer finger. "Okay," I say. "Maybe not so sweet."

I pick up his clipboard to read.

SUBJECT #0032

TEST GROUP: Generation B-2

ACTIVATION: Failed

STATUS: Infected; not contagious

NOTES: Subject is no longer necessary. To be euthanized at earliest convenience.

Activation? How? I know so little about the process of being activated. From what I gathered during my time at the Harbinger Foundation last summer, every living human carries the gene that could potentially activate their psiot powers, but for most people that gene is dormant. Inaccessible, Peter said. How could animals be activated?

I circle the whole room, looking for answers on each card. Some of the notes vary, mentioning mutations. None of the activations have been successful, but not all the animals are as snappy as the first puppy. Some are lethargic. Others catatonic. Like the dog I first saw at the clinic. Like Gretchen.

I gasp as it dawns on me. This is every science-fiction book or movie I've ever read. How is this even possible? I can barely figure out how to use the printer in the journalism room, while Margaret is trying to isolate the gene. The one Peter says we all have. The one that makes me fly.

But why? And how does that even relate to A+?

Hesitant to leave the room full of animals, I walk through the door on the other side of the room. Colleen has to be here somewhere, and maybe if I can get to her, I can find more answers.

I find myself in a partially constructed hallway. One side is covered in tarps and sheets of plastic, while the other side is a row of glass windows, partitioned into a dozen or so small hospital rooms. The first few beds are full, barely breathing people tucked inside. Before I can explore more, heels clack down the hallway and a woman in a lab coat with headphones on, studying a clipboard, is walking straight toward me. I duck into the first room and take cover behind a curtain.

The man in the bed beside me lies with his eyes wide open, staring at the ceiling. His breathing is steady, but he doesn't even notice me. Like Gretchen, he's catatonic. His long hair is wiry and brushed back neatly, and his beard appears to be recently trimmed. There's no hiding the sun damage apparent in his leathery reddish skin, almost like he's permanently sunburned. It takes a careful look, but I remember him. The homeless man who went missing—the one from the news. Horace Freemont. His family was all over the news, searching for him. He was here all along.

The woman's heels clack past the door, and the sound echoes before trailing off completely.

I peek out from behind the curtain to see if the hallway is clear and breathe a sigh of relief when I find that it is.

I check each room one by one. Nearly every bed is full, and there are anywhere from one to three people in every room. Some are catatonic, and others appear to be in a coma.

And then there she is. In a room all by herself. Colleen. Somehow her skin feels even more ashen and paperlike than I remember it being last week. She's tucked securely into the bed and several restraints are strapped over her body. Why would they even do that? She's obviously not going anywhere.

"Oh, Colleen. I'm so, so sorry." It was too easy for her to go missing. Too easy for no one to notice. I'm just as guilty as everyone else who didn't notice when she went missing. She coughs a little, but her mouth is covered with some kind of breathing mask, except I think the mask might be doing more harm than good.

I want to touch her. I want to let her know she's not alone. I need to find Ches before I can get Colleen out of here, but I need to comfort her in some way, even if it's more for my sake than hers.

"Colleen," I say again, but this time my voice comes out watery. "Colleen, I'm so sorry." She looks like a corpse. If it weren't for the beeping on the monitors, I'd think she was dead.

My hands touch her forearm again, and even though

I expect her skin to be cold and clammy, it's warm. Too warm. She's burning up. I touch the back of my hand to her forehead. She sputters again, coughing into her mask and wheezing. She can barely breathe. This is ridiculous. If I'm going to have to leave her here for a few more moments, the least I can do is remove this mask. "Hang on a second," I tell her as I reach behind her head to remove the strap. "I'll get you—"

The moment the mask falls from her mouth, Colleen Bristow's eyes shoot open and she screams. It's a scream like nothing I've ever heard before. The pitch of it knocks me off my feet, and I cup my hands over my ears.

People in scrubs and lab coats swarm the room with headphones over their ears—the kind people wear at the shooting range.

I skitter out of the way and into the corner. Glass shatters up and down the hallway. Colleen's supersonic scream is a tsunami of sound. I don't think I'll ever hear again.

A few men in navy blue scrubs and lab coats act with assured precision as they restrain Colleen and fit her with the mask she had on before I took it off, stifling her screams. Our eyes meet, and the only way I can describe the hurt in her eyes is betrayal.

No less than three seconds of silence pass before everyone turns to me and immediately sees that I don't belong.

Run! I have to run.

I make it two steps into the hallway before jolts of electricity shock my body and my head hits the floor. Is this what it feels like to be tased? Maybe I jumped the shark on the whole badass thing.

 **30**

When I open my eyes, I find myself in a damp, dark room, nothing like the sterile-looking hospital lab where I found Colleen, and I get the sense that I'm in an underground basement.

My body jerks, but I can't move, and it takes a moment for me to understand that I'm tied to a chair.

I try to fly. Who says I can't fly strapped to a chair? But it only takes a few seconds for me to realize that my captor has very wisely tied my chair to a metal pole.

"She's awake!" a voice calls. Not just any voice. Dakota's voice.

Dakota steps into the pool of light emanating from the very small light above me. Her spotlight. Her time to shine.

I shake my head and growl. "You're a monster."

Behind her, Margaret steps forward. "Well, well, Faith. Happy Thanksgiving. Gobble, gobble, et cetera, et cetera."

I flex against the ropes, but it makes no difference.

"You know," says Margaret, "you really ruined the holiday for some of us." She shrugs. "I guess the leftovers are the best part, anyway. Right, Dakota?"

"You just couldn't stay under the radar, could you?" asks Dakota.

"Oh, no," Margaret scoffs. "This one thinks she's going to save the world. No one's told her what a dirty job that is."

Out of the shadows, Margaret grabs a chair, the legs scraping against the floor.

She sits down in front of me so that our knees are only mere inches away. "Faith, you're a cog. You're a very small cog in a very big machine. What's one flying fat girl going to do for a world that's burning?"

I sneer and say nothing, but really, I think she might be right. Big whoop. I can fly. Grandma Lou's dementia will still get the best of her. Ches has a criminal record and her shot at getting scholarships is basically nonexistent and I don't even know where she is. Colleen still went missing. Gretchen is still comatose. Some silly little flying isn't enough to save any of them. Maybe all I am is a fandom blogger with a neat party trick.

Behind Margaret, Dakota folds her arms over her chest. "But you could be a part of something so much more."

Margaret's expression darkens. "Faith, my sister, Morgan, was special."

Special. The way she says it reminds me of that first time I met Peter.

She continues, "If you think what I've created with *The Grove* is incredible, you wouldn't believe what she could have been capable of. She was always smarter and funnier and quicker. I guess it shouldn't surprise me that the Harbinger Foundation plucked her from my life too soon. A girl as special as she was? Surely there was something there beneath the surface. Just waiting to be activated."

Memories of the Harbinger Foundation crash over me. Did I meet Margaret's sister? Was she one of the adults in charge? "Wh-what happened to her?"

"She died," she says in a sharp, matter-of-fact way. "She died as a normal teenage girl. No superhuman abilities. Just a normal girl whose body was destroyed by the activation process. Didn't you ever wonder what happened to all the other people who were brought to the Harbinger Foundation with you, Faith? Did you think about them when you returned home to your sweet little grandmother while their families looked far and wide for them, hoping for just a clue? Just a hint that their loved one was alive and well."

I'm speechless. Of course I thought of them, but sitting here with Margaret, the reality of their fates seems so much more real. I'd assumed something awful happened to them, but some part of my brain tried to protect me by never connecting the dots.

"There's nothing special about us, Faith," Margaret continues. "Me, Dakota, everyone who works for me. All of this. It's just normal, everyday people looking for solutions to really big problems."

"I don't understand," I say. "How is it all linked? The A+. The disappearances. Why?"

Margaret chuckles, shaking her head. "The A+ is just paving the way for the real solution. A+ is just a harmless street drug, but we needed something like A+ to get us into towns, communities, and neighborhoods. The future is Honor Roll, and with just a little more time, we'll be able to use it to safely identify young people like you, Faith. Imagine it. You could take a tiny little pill—harmless to most people—but with just a few symptoms, we could find more like you and your friend Peter. Then you could make a decision for yourself whether or not you want to be activated. The power would be in your hands."

It all sounds good, especially when I consider what Harada was trying to accomplish with Peter by manipulating him into making an army of psiots to do his bidding. But the reality of what she's saying . . . "What about people like Colleen? She wasn't given a choice. Can she even open her mouth without—without wreaking havoc? All those animals! The town's homeless population! What about them? They don't deserve a choice? What about their families? And if this stupid drug is such a miracle, why not do things the right way?"

Behind Margaret, Dakota trains her eyes on the floor, refusing to make eye contact with me.

"The right way?" Margaret scoffs. "You think Big Pharma is the right way? Or better yet, how about all these anti-vaxxers? You think they're going to get on board with this? Doing the right thing doesn't always look pretty, Faith. Wake up."

A door creaks open in one of the dark shadows of the room, and one of the security beefcakes—Remi, I think—who showed up at my house with Dakota says, "Ma'am, we've got a situation."

Margaret stands and the man whispers in her ear.

I stare long and hard at Dakota until she's forced to face me, but she quickly looks away. She joins Margaret and Remi.

After a moment, Margaret says, "Make sure she's not going anywhere and then meet me outside, Dakota." She points to Remi. "You, do one quick sweep. Be fast."

"What about . . ." Dakota tilts her head in my direction.

"Leave her."

"But—"

"You heard me," Margaret says, no room for interpretation in her voice.

Whatever's happening on the other side of that wall isn't good, and Margaret has no interest in letting me go.

Margaret and Remi leave quickly, and I'm alone with Dakota.

"You heard her," I say. "Leave me. That shouldn't be too hard for you. Leaving people. Abandoning them. Betraying them."

Dakota grits her teeth, pacing back and forth for a minute before spinning toward me. "Listen very carefully. I swear to God, if I ever see you again, I will kill you, and if I don't, Margaret will. If you make it out of here alive, say nothing. It's that simple, Faith. You want to enjoy the rest of the time you have with Grandma Lou? Keep your mouth shut. That's it."

She squats down in front of me so that we're practically nose to nose.

She exhales.

I inhale.

"We could've been really happy," I say.

She runs a hand through her hair. "I guess we'll never know."

A crash rattles the entire building, and I nearly lose my balance.

She reaches behind me and presses a cold piece of metal into my palm.

And then she's gone.

I fidget for a moment with whatever she left me, before my thumb runs over it and—"Ow!" I hiss. My palm immediately pools with blood, but that doesn't matter because Dakota left me her pocketknife.

There's no easy way to do this, and my wrist feels like it could snap, but I begin to saw into the ropes.

Something outside the door crashes, small building fragments and dust rain down on me, and I begin to saw faster until one arm is free.

The moment I have one arm free, I instinctively hold it to my chest before trying to shake the ache out of my wrist. I don't have any time to waste, though, so I swivel around and free my other hand.

I cradle my other wrist for a moment while I examine the pocketknife Dakota left me and then wipe the blood in my palm on my jeans. The knife is heavy with a wood handle and Dakota's name carved into the side. I race to the door just in time for another vibration to rock the whole building.

I whip the door open and quickly realize that the building wasn't just shaking. It was collapsing. Flames lick the walls and black smoke escapes through whatever gaps and windows it can find. I cough into my cape after inhaling a lungful of smoke.

"Faith! Go!" Dakota shouts as she races up the steps to where the labs were.

"I need to find Ches!" I yell back. "I know she's here!"

I begin to run over to the part of the building where all the offices are.

"Wait!" Dakota shouts. "You're going— She's this way."

I double back as I duck through clouds of smoke, still using my cape to shield me from the smoke. (I knew my cape would come in handy!)

Dakota races down the stairs and leads me deeper into the factory, through a door I didn't even realize existed and into a large room of perfectly preserved assembly lines and hulking metal vats. The fire hasn't reached this part of the warehouse yet, but small puffs of smoke are beginning to linger above us. "I'm just showing you where she is and leaving. I don't have time to get caught up in your little crusade to save your BFF. This way." Dakota waves me through a door and points down a dark staircase into another basement. "She's down there."

I push past her and nearly fly down the steps.

It takes my eyes a minute to adjust, but when they do, I see Ches—my sweet Ches—in the dress her mother must have brought for her to wear in court, chained to a pipe and slumped against a crumbling brick wall.

I rush to her and squat down beside her. "Ches, Ches, wake up, Ches!" I grip her shoulders and do my best to shake her awake.

"I'm . . . not now," she manages to say.

"What did they do to you?" I ask, yanking Dakota by the wrist down to us.

"Nothing," Dakota says. "Just a light sedative. She kicked a guard in the jaw last night. It's wearing off."

"You drugged her?" I'm incredulous. "And besides, I thought you didn't have time for my little crusade."

"Well, I didn't drug her," Dakota clarifies as she reaches behind the pipe to unlock the handcuffs Ches is chained with. "But someone did, yes."

"How am I supposed to get her out of here?"

She stands and takes one of Ches's ankles in each hand. "As fast as we can, preferably."

I stand up, determined not to let Dakota see how relieved I am that she's helping me, and reach under Ches's arms. "One, two, three," I grunt.

The two of us hoist Ches up, and I feel bad she's wearing a dress, but there's no nice way to do this, honestly.

The stairs are a slow and painful process, and I'm ashamed to admit that we accidentally knock Ches's head more than once, but we finally burst through the door and simultaneously drop Ches to the ground. She's not heavy, but she's lanky and all deadweight. I'm pretty strong, but carrying a grown person up a set of stairs is no easy task for anyone. And it's not like I had enough headspace to fly. *Wait! Fly!*

I look to Dakota. "Wait here."

"What?"

"Give me just a second," I say. "All I need is a second. Promise me you won't leave her."

Dakota studies the hard lines set into my forehead. "Just hurry."

The ceiling of the warehouse stretches up at least four stories and the very tops of the walls are lined with old, dirty windows. Harnessing all my optimism, I push off from the concrete floor with as much force as I can. I concentrate on one single window and cross my arms over my head, close my eyes, and say a prayer.

Glass shatters all around me as I burst through a window, shards dragging along my knuckles and arms, bracing against the cold November air. I hiss against the pain, but not until I inhale a fresh gulp of air do I realize how singed my throat and lungs are, like I've just swallowed a lit cigarette.

From up here, I can see flames beginning to lick the roof of the opposite side of the warehouse, so I waste no time looping back inside and landing on my feet beside Dakota and Ches.

"You waited," I say through a cough as my body readjusts to the smoky atmosphere.

She pauses for a beat. "We don't have much time." Dakota reaches down for Ches's ankles again. "There's no way you can fly with her on your back."

"Let me try something." I levitate off the ground a few feet and focus all my thoughts and energy on Ches and the weight of her body. This feels like sitting behind the wheel of the car for the first time. I have all the tools I need, but no idea how to use them.

I try channeling every movie I've seen and every comic I've ever read, but none of them help me harness the power I need to lift Ches.

Dropping back down to the ground, I resign myself to the fact that I'm going to have to do this the old-fashioned way.

"Come on," says Dakota. "There's no way you're getting her through that window."

"Oh yes, I am." I squat down to Ches and throw her over my shoulder. "I'll carry her on my back if I have to."

With a grunt, I stand up. "Get out of here," I tell Dakota. "Save as many people and animals as you can. And don't forget Colleen."

Dakota's brow furrows, and I'm sure there's something she's not telling me, but there's no time.

"Go," I tell her again.

Pressing deeply through my legs, I push off with as much force as I can. I'm slower than normal, and there's much more grunting and sweating involved, but I take off and up through the window. Outside, Ches chokes on the fresh air, and my body is all too ready to land. I try to be as gentle as I can, but we still tumble to the ground, which is part gravel and part dead grass.

Ches's legs are a little cut up, but she's still not completely awake. She's at least safe here, I think.

"Ches," I say. "I have to go back inside." I kiss her

forehead, so thankful that she's alive and okay, even if I don't know what the future holds.

"Faith," she says, her eyes fluttering, but never fully opening.

"You're okay. You're safe."

I stand up and look at her once more, lying there, her breathing shallow, before I walk back into a burning building.

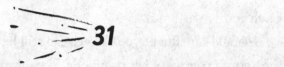 **31**

Sirens blare behind me as I race back inside through the loading dock. Inside is total chaos.

Colleen stands in a hospital gown, ragged and heaving. A man in a flame-retardant suit approaches her and she screams, his mask shattering. All it takes is one touch of her hand on his forearm and the man bursts into flames. His suit stands no chance against her. The man howls until the flames consume him.

Colleen's hands. Oh my God. Her hands. I remember the gloves on her hands at school. I didn't even think twice about it.

This girl has fire hands *and* a glass-shattering scream, and I can . . . fly? Really? That's it? Come on.

"Colleen!" I yell, but she barely even flinches at the sound of her name. Oh, Colleen, what did they do to you? "Colleen!" I shout again.

She turns and begins walking slowly to me. If I've learned anything from TV and movies, it's that if someone is walking slowly to you in a situation when they should be running, it's because you're the prey and not the predator. They could run or walk. It wouldn't make a difference. They're going to catch you.

I should run. But maybe Colleen can still be saved. Maybe she's not in control of her own body. I cough into my elbow, my lungs burning amid the flames and smoke. Did Colleen set this fire all on her own? "Colleen, I can get you out of here. This isn't your fault. They did this to you." She reminds me of the dogs that are rescued from dog-fighting rings.

She opens her mouth, and instinctively, I cover my ears, preparing for her splintering scream. But after a moment, I realize that the only thing coming out of her mouth is her normal voice, so I let my hands drop to my side.

"Of course," she says, her voice coming out more like a shriek. "When I speak, you never listen. You never have. You don't see me. You don't hear me. None of you do."

"I'm so sorry, Colleen. I never meant to ignore you in journalism—"

She laughs, but nothing about it sounds funny. "You think this is about journalism? You think this is about you and that spineless little shit, Johnny? Or Mrs. Raburn, who never let me do anything other than check for goddamn comma splices and proper nouns?"

"I don't understand . . ."

"6-968. That was my number."

"Your number?"

"Oh, you think you're the only special one?" she asks. "The only psiot in Glenwood? I was there over the summer, Faith. I was at the Harbinger Foundation, except no one cared to remember me when Peter rebelled. The two of you ran right past me. No, instead I escaped all on my own in the madness. I ran after you and Peter, but the two of you got into that car and left me in the dust. No matter how many times I screamed your name, you never heard me."

"You . . . but . . ." And then I remember seeing Colleen in journalism. Gloves on her hands.

"I hitchhiked the whole way back to Glenwood. Even accidentally caught some stranger's car on fire with him inside. Finally, I got home, and you wanna know what the worst part was? My sister didn't even notice I was gone. She thought I was at my aunt's." She holds up her hands. "And then there are these. I can't even touch my nephew without lighting him on fire."

She steps forward and I instinctively jump back.

"At least now you have a real reason to avoid me. My hands might be eternally burning torches, but I can control my vocal cords." She lets out a delighted sigh. "There's some sort of satisfaction that comes with the quietest girl in school discovering she has the gift of a siren's scream."

Behind Colleen, a woman in scrubs appears, terror written on her face. I need to keep Colleen distracted. "But how did you end up here?" I ask.

"I decided to investigate the story Mrs. Raburn tried assigning to you, and got stuck in the wrong place at the wrong time. You would've thought these people hit the lottery when they realized they could run their experiments on a real live psiot. Took a tranquilizer to take me down."

I pivot, hoping Colleen will follow. Trying my best to be discreet, I make a small waving motion to the woman, willing her to sneak off now before Colleen notices her. "I know what it feels like to be an experiment."

Colleen shifts, watching me quizzically. "You have no idea what—" In a brief, flashing moment, Colleen whirls on her heels, and all it takes is her bare fingers on the woman's shoulder before she's screaming, her whole body slowly catching on fire as she drops to the ground.

Spinning back to me, Colleen lets out a howling scream, bursting a handful of large windows, flames shooting out through them.

I'm already in the air, flying toward the landing where the lab is with all the animals and people. Even with my hands over my ears, I can feel the echo of Colleen's scream crawling up my spine, leaving goose bumps on my skin.

Below me, I can hear firefighters entering the building, and I just hope that Colleen leaves them and attempts to escape, because none of them stand a chance against her.

The door on the landing is wide open and so is the soundproof door to the room of kennels. I find Dakota fumbling with the keypad on the wall as she tries to get into the lab, dogs and cats frantically barking and meowing.

"Let them loose!" I tell her.

"But they're infected. We have to transport them all out of here. Or leave them." She throws her arms up. "Of course you couldn't just listen! For fuck's sake, Faith! You were supposed to get Ches and leave."

I march right over to her and slam her against the wall. "Let. Them. Out. Your little experiment is over." My voice softens slightly. "Show me you're more than this. Show me the person who carried Ches up a flight of stairs with me. I know you don't want to see all these animals and people die for no reason."

She sighs. "You want to let me go then?"

Quickly, she punches a six-digit code into a different keypad closer to the kennels and presses her thumb against a scanner. One section at a time, the kennel doors open. Both of us run around the room, helping whatever animals we can out of their kennels. I take a crate from below the counter in the middle of the room and squeeze in every animal who is catatonic or unable to move.

The crate is heavy. Maybe the heaviest thing I've ever carried, but if I could carry Ches out, I can carry these animals. When that one's full, I fill another until every kennel is cleared. Dakota helps me drag the crates out to the staircase as dogs and cats race past us, their instincts guiding them to safety.

There's no good way to do this. I have to get back and help the people. They should've been the first priority, but I can't second-guess myself now.

I take a deep breath and pick up each crate, before forcing my body into the air and over the railing.

Dakota runs down the stairs to meet me as I land much harder than I was expecting.

"I could have carried that," she says, yanking a crate from me and running off toward the exit as she covers her mouth with the collar of her shirt.

I do my best not to inhale and follow her, searching for any sign of Colleen, but she's gone.

I feel so lost. In the short moments I spent upstairs, the lower level has become nearly impossible to navigate. My eyes burn too much to open them, and just when I think we're done for and that we're going to suffocate, we burst through the smoke, blue skies hanging above us.

Immediately, we're swarmed with firefighters, and I don't think my lungs will ever be clean again.

"Dakota! Dakota!" I shout, but all I see is her disappearing back into the smoke. Firefighters pin me back. "Dakota!" I shriek.

Frantically, I try to string words together. "People! The missing people! They're all upstairs. All of them. You have to save them."

"We're on it," says a women in a full fire suit as she passes me off to an EMT.

"And the animals!" I shout. "Those are people's pets. We need to catch them! And Ches! My friend! She's on the other side of the building in the grass. She's been drugged!"

The EMT forces me to sit, clapping an oxygen mask over my mouth. "Dakota," I say again, but her name comes out muffled. "Dakota."

 **32**

I'm not surprised by how quickly the building is in flames, but I am surprised by how long it takes for it to burn out. In fact, when the ambulance takes me to the hospital, the fire is still burning. After preliminary questioning by Detective Wallace, who is surprised to see me again so soon after sneaking me in to see Ches, Grandma Lou and Miss Ella pick me up. The two of them fuss over me, and Miss Ella holds her tongue when I know she really just wants to shake the daylights out of me and ask me what the hell I was even doing at that warehouse.

I was visiting my friend Dakota Ash. I was visiting my friend Dakota Ash. I was visiting my friend Dakota Ash. I say it over and over again to Detective Wallace. We were exploring the parts of the warehouse she'd never seen when we stumbled upon Colleen Bristow, who was being held captive. Before I knew it, there was a fire and animals running everywhere. It was chaos.

I pretend to be in shock. It doesn't take much pretending.

Detective Wallace tells me that she believes everyone except for Margaret, Colleen, and Dakota are accounted for. It seems they were manufacturing A+ and testing other drugs for future use.

I cover for Dakota. It's probably stupid to even try. And who knows what the cops will find when they investigate the charred remains of the fire? But I cover for her anyway, because somehow I have even more questions now than I did yesterday, and the biggest among them is Dakota Ash.

I hope she survived. Colleen and Margaret, too. Even Remi.

The moment I have access to a phone, I call Dr. Bryner to let her know animals were being held captive at the warehouse and that as far as I know they all made it out of the fire. I told her I couldn't say much else, but that there were a whole lot of lost pets out there waiting to be found. Thinking of the snarling dog, I tell her to be careful before hanging up.

Ches is in the hospital, but Detective Wallace tells me off the record that it's pretty obvious she was an unknowing accomplice in the original shooting and that she'd been kidnapped out of police custody against her will. She wagers that Ches will be released after her hospital stay as long as she promises to stay in town while all this gets sorted out. I've got my fingers crossed that Detective Wallace's intuition is right.

When we get home late that night, Miss Ella heads back

to her place with a plate of leftovers, and Grandma Lou and I sit at the kitchen table with the rest of the pie, two forks, and a can of whipped cream.

Grandma Lou turns on the TV in the corner of the kitchen and we both watch, chipping away at our pie, as the evening news reruns.

The on-scene reporter stands in front of a fire truck, the remains of the building in the distance cordoned off by police tape. "Investigators say the source of the fire is as yet undetermined. Among the missing are Margaret Toliver, the much talked-about showrunner and creator of *The Grove*, who has been in local news lately for relocating the show to Glenwood. Thankfully, most of the cast and crew were gone for the holiday, but Dakota Ash, a fan favorite who was well known for her goodwill efforts, is still unaccounted for. Sources say Colleen Bristow, the missing Glenwood student, was seen in the building prior to the fire, but as of yet, we have no confirmations. Speculations are circulating that Ms. Toliver potentially used the show as a cover-up for a drug ring, but police are not prepared to comment."

"Not the way you expected to spend Thanksgiving evening, I'm sure, Valerie," says the studio reporter, his image taking over half the screen.

"Wade, you can say that again. A far cry from the early Black Friday sales I'd planned on covering. Now, rumors are already swirling about the fate of the much-loved show. If my sources are correct and Colleen Bristow was indeed in this warehouse, there's no telling what else or who else was being held inside these walls."

"Valerie, it appears there really is no business like show business."

Grandma Lou groans and hits the power button on the remote. "What a cheeseball."

I offer her a faint smile. Grandma Lou is good in times of crisis. She doesn't ask too many questions or try to get in my head. She's a one-foot-in-front-of-the-other kind of woman. Pie and sleep. Those are good first steps to her.

After today, I'm completely numb. I want to cry, just to remember I can feel something, but the tears won't come no matter how hard I try, and I think this is torture, this feeling of being so full and not having any sense of relief.

"Oh," says Grandma Lou. "I almost forgot. Some boy came here looking for you this afternoon. Real handsome."

"Did he give you a name?" I ask.

"Paul," she says. "Or maybe it was Phillip."

"Peter?" I ask. "Was it Peter?"

She snaps her fingers. "Oh, that must have been it. He said he'd see you online. Whatever that means."

I drop my fork and give her a kiss on the cheek. "I've got to get to bed. I'm beat."

"Good night!" she calls after me, and then quieter, she adds, "Don't mind me. I'll just finish this pie myself."

Breathless, I turn on my computer and quickly navigate to *Kingdom Keeper*, the three crowns on the screen lighting up as the game loads. I swore I'd never play this stupid game again.

"Come on, Peter," I mumble. "Don't ghost me now."

I draw on my last bit of hope and a dash of faith, because I've got nothing left to lose.

I sit at my desk, waiting for hours, dipping in and out of sleep. The sun is beginning to creep along the horizon when my in-game messenger chirps.

390209384: Sounds like a real shitshow in Glenwood right now.

YOUGOTTAHAVEFAITH: very creative username

390209384: I'm not trying to be found.

390209384: Speaking of, I had to ditch my phone. Sorry about that.

YOUGOTTAHAVEFAITH: I called because I had an emergency.

390209384: Are you okay?

YOUGOTTAHAVEFAITH: For now, I think.

390209384: I'm sorry I let you down. Things . . . are kind of a mess right now.

YOUGOTTAHAVEFAITH: Are YOU okay?

390209384: For now.

390209384: I think.

I breathe a short sigh. I'm careful not to ask any questions that Peter can't answer or anything that would identify him, but I do fill him in on Margaret and the drug she was trying to create in very nonspecific terms.

> **YOUGOTTAHAVEFAITH:** Is that even possible? To create a drug that could identify people . . . like us?
>
> **390209384:** Nope. God, I wish it were. I just don't think the science checks out.
>
> **YOUGOTTAHAVEFAITH:** Wow. All those people and animals.
>
> **390209384:** Sometimes people think they have good reasons to do bad things. At the end of the day, they're still bad things.
>
> **390209384:** I gotta run.
>
> **YOUGOTTAHAVEFAITH:** Is there any way I can contact you?
>
> **390209384:** I'll contact you as soon as there is.

The little green circle beside his username turns red and he's gone, but this time I don't feel alone. I don't feel helpless. Sure, I'm confused. I'm exhausted. But one thing I know for sure is that I have a gift and I'm ready to use it.

The dress I wore yesterday is torn and stained, but the Z I stitched across the chest survived the chaos. "Zephyr," I whisper to myself. "Reporting for duty and ready to take flight." A full-body yawn overtakes me. "Right after I take a nap."

# EPILOGUE

"I don't know," says Ches. "I feel weird about taking the money."

"I have never—not once in my life!—felt weird about taking money," says Matt while the three of us sit piled up on the couch, Ches's head in my lap and her feet in Matt's.

Ches shrugs and looks up to me. "Honestly, Faith, you should be the one who decides. Dakota is your baggage."

I throw my head back against the couch as *Rare Exports*, Ches's favorite Christmas movie, about a very scary Finnish Christmas legend, plays in the background. Tomorrow is Christmas Eve, so today, on Christmas Eve-Eve, we got together for our annual Christmas cookie decorating and movie marathon slumber party. I've barely been able to think about Christmas, though, and that only got worse when three days ago, Ches came home to find a package in the mail full of stacks of hundred-dollar bills and a note that read:

don't spend it all in one place

The only person either of us could think of with that kind of cash had to be Dakota. It's been nearly four weeks since the warehouse, and I honestly still don't know how I feel about her. She did some awful things, but she did some good things too when it really counted.

I look back down to Ches. "It's a no-brainer. Take the money. You need a good lawyer, and heck, there's probably enough to pay for school too."

I don't want to be in debt to Dakota, but the money isn't for me, and Ches needs it. Her legal fees shouldn't be too extensive. The more the police uncover, the more obvious it is that Ches made a few stupid decisions, but ultimately had no part in the bigger picture. Physically, she's mostly okay. The school assigned her a counselor, and she had a gash in her leg from our crash landing, but the stitches have since been removed.

Speaking of our landing, Ches is still fuzzy on the details of how she escaped the fire, which has given me time to think.

I hit mute on the TV, listening very carefully. "Does that sound like snoring to you?"

Matt chuckles. "Honestly, it sounds like *The Price Is Right*."

I check the time on my phone. Surely she's asleep by now. I don't like keeping secrets from Grandma Lou, but I also don't want to confuse her right now. "Okay, I gotta show you guys something outside."

"Seriously?" Ches groans. "It's freezing out there."

Matt stands and then reaches for her arms to pull her up. "This better be good, Faith."

"It'll be something. That's for sure."

After the three of us put on our boots and scarves, we shuffle out to the backyard in our pajamas where snowflakes are still slowly drifting down. A fresh dusting has just settled over the grass, and I catch a flake or two on my tongue while Ches jumps and shimmies to keep warm.

Matt pulls her close to him for body heat. "I don't get it," he says. "It's just your backyard."

"P-p-plus snow!" Ches says through chattering teeth.

"You two stay here," I say as I take a few steps off the patio and into the yard, snow crunching beneath my boots.

I turn back around to see my two best friends, huddled together as the snow slowly drifts down around them.

"I've been keeping a secret, but instead of telling you . . . I thought it might be easier to show you."

Ches and Matt share a confused look as I spread my arms out and take a deep breath, the crisp air filling my lungs. Like the earth is my own personal trampoline, I push off from Grandma Lou's backyard and into the sky, through the drifting snow, and I begin to fly. Unable to help myself, I let out a gleeful squeal.

Sometimes secret superhero identities are too good not to share.

ACKNOWLEDGMENTS

I didn't grow up thinking fat girls could be superheroes. But today, in the year of our Goddess 2020 when Lizzo reigns supreme, plus-size models are strutting down runways across the globe, and fat athletes are doing things like taking on the Olympics, we have been blessed with Faith Herbert. Longtime Faith fans know that Faith first appeared in 1992, but her most recent incarnation in *Faith Volume 1: Hollywood and Vine* is a Faith for right now. She's a shining example of the truth that any of us can be anything and that our greatness is not at the expense of our supposed weaknesses or differences, but because of them. Faith is fearless, warm, loyal, bubbly, smart, and fat too. All of those things make her great. Super, in fact.

Many people have been instrumental in the creation of Faith, and I owe them all a debt of gratitude, but especially the following people.

I would like to thank Jim Shooter and David Lapham (the original creators of Faith), as well as Joshua Dysart and Khari Evans (the creators behind her reboot). Of course, I owe so much gratitude to Jody Houser, Francis Portela, and Marguerite Sauvage for their work on Faith and the great inspiration they provided me with.

The team at Valiant has been incredibly collaborative in this process, and this process has been a delight as a result. I would especially like to thank Charlotte Greenbaum, Robert Meyers, Gregg Katzman, Walter Black, Fred Pierce, and Russ Brown. I would also like to thank Jen Marshall, Jennifer Gates, Erica Bauman, and the rest of the team at Aevitas Creative Management for all their time spent forging this relationship and growing Faith's story.

To my editor, Alessandra Balzer, thank you for going on this fantastic ride with me and investing in Faith's journey and for always nudging me in the right directions, which usually results in better makeout scenes and more animal rescuing.

Thank you to John Cusick, my agent, who is always ten full steps ahead of me. I live in anticipation of the day when you finally reveal your own superhuman abilities. Thank you as well to the entire team at Folio Literary Management. And of course, thank you to Dana Spector, my film agent.

This cover and iteration of Faith is such an inspiration to me. Thank you so much to Jenna Stempel-Lobell for this design, Kat Goodies for bringing teenage Faith to life, and Alison Donalty for your guidance.

I have an incredible team at HarperCollins, who are always championing me and my work and fixing my constant grammatical errors. In no specific order, thank you to Jackie Burke, Suzanne Murphy, Donna Bray, Andrea Pappenheimer, Kerry Moynagh, Kathy Faber, Nellie Kurtzman, Ebony LaDelle, Valerie Wong, Shannon Cox, Lindsey Karl, Kathryn Silsand, Patty Rosati, Caitlin Johnson, Caitlin Garing, Almeda Beynon, the Epic Reads team, the Harper360 team, and the Harper Frenzy team.

Thank you to Joy Nash for bringing the audiobook version of Faith to life with your heavenly voice.

Kristin Treviño, Bethany Hagen, Ashley Meredith, Natalie C. Parker, Tessa Gratton, Ashley Lindemann, Justina Ireland, Molly Cusick, Sarah MacLean, Louisa Edwards, Corey Whaley, Katie Cotugno, Dhonielle Clayton, Zoraida Córdova, Siobhan Vivian, Emma Treviño, Luke and Lauren Brewer, and my cohorts at Union Worx: whether you spoke with me in great detail about story and plot points, commiserated with me, or just offered a much-needed distraction from all things publishing, thank you for being my friend and keeping me afloat.

Thank you also the fat positive community for being a constant source of education and encouragement. Thank you especially to Corissa Enneking (and also for letting me steal your name), J Aprileo, and Sophia Carter-Kahn.

I would be nothing without my family, from nieces to in-laws to cousins to aunts and uncles. Mom and Dad, thank you for all the ways you've shown me that ordinary people can do extraordinary things.

Ian, my love and my BFF, you're always the first to believe in me and I'll never be able to say thank you enough. So instead, I'll just do the dishes without you asking. (It's definitely my turn, anyway.)

Lastly, I must thank my readers. It's because of you that I get to take on incredible opportunities like this one. I never in a million years thought anyone would ask me to write a superhero book, but if writing this book has taught me anything, it's that no matter your shape or size or background, the world is full of infinite possibilities. You just gotta have Faith.

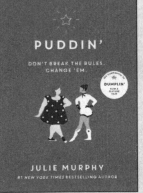

Meet FAITH,
the fan-favorite superhero
from Valiant Comics

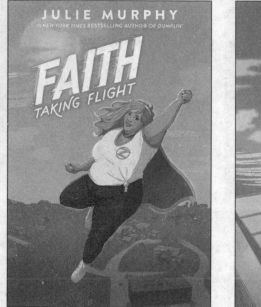

An origin story like you've never read before!